Lives of Regret

Raylond Gee

DEDICATION

Many thanks to God, for without Him nothing is possible, and to my family and friends for their help regarding my novel. This is a work of fiction and everything in this novel is the product of this author's imagination.

Prologue

"We've done everything possible. Now it's in God's hands."

Rage flooded me to the bone. It wasn't directed towards the doctor for his well-meaning remark, but towards the animals responsible for Little's death. I felt pain from losing a special person and guilt from not being able to prevent what happened. Little's death was a cross to be borne and a debt to be paid. My emotions were controlled. No one could see the rage, fury and hatred boiling inside me and it had to stay that way.

Since few people knew about my true relationship to Little, the funeral had to be discreet and private, paid by me. Nothing else would be acceptable. I spent as much as possible to help Little. Nothing helped.

Before leaving, I wished peace on Little. Walking out into the corridor and down to the chapel, I was grateful that the staff left us alone together. I knew that the next reunion would be on the other side or at the Resurrection.

Entering the chapel, I saw a young woman in her middle twenties on her knees in front of the Cross. Poorly dressed and attractive, she silently prayed, tears streaming down her cheeks. The scene reminded me of Hannah in the Old

Testament desperately, tearfully praying in the temple for the Lord to relieve her of her barrenness. And He answered her prayer. I wondered what she was praying for. Was she praying for her child or another loved one? I felt a mixture of tenderness and pity but I didn't want to intrude in her grief and I didn't want to talk to anyone.

Not wanting to disturb the woman, I kneeled in another pew and began to pray. After a few minutes, I got up and walked outside to the corridor. Continuing to the elevator, memories so painful began to flood inside that I had to use a great deal of control to prevent a total breakdown. I knew early on that the world was neither nice nor fair and that the wicked overpowered the good and the strong exploited the weak. Only Christ saved me.

As I sat in my car, thinking about how to settle the debts owed to Little, the answer became clear to me as I recalled a list of names. Three little angels in a row my ass! Three little bitches would be more appropriate! The bitches had to die, I coldly thought. No pity or compassion on them. And if Hell awaited, then so be it. Once I went down this road, there would likely be only prison or death. My career, family, friends and freedom would be gone. But who would stand up for Little? I felt alone and scared for the first time in many years.

Tears began to stream down my face and I began to weep and moan. There were times when I desperately had to get away from everyone and everything, my emotions threatening to overwhelm me.

Recognizing the warning signs, I calmed myself through a breathing technique. Once my emotions were under control, I drove home. Before arriving, most of the plan had been thought out, with one or two areas needing to be fleshed out. The plan had to be executed perfectly with the pros and cons being calculated. I knew perfectly well that there was no such thing as a perfect crime, since most criminals were caught and in most cases, judges and juries had little sympathy for those who were in front of them. I was perfectly willing to spend the rest of my life in prison. Also, my finances had to be structured so my family wouldn't suffer. Their loss would be as painful as Little's. But it had to be done. As for bringing the police in this, what a joke, I snorted contemptuously. There wasn't any evidence and the incident occurred years ago. I couldn't perform miracles, and if I did, it would be to bring Little back from the dead, healthy and whole.

I decided to stop at the side of the road and stretch my legs. It was late afternoon and anyone passing by would see an expensively but conservatively tailored pillar of the community enjoying a brisk day for a few minutes. One car even stopped to see if I had a problem. After being assured, the driver sped off. The light was beginning to shine into my darkness, I pleasantly thought with a smile.

1

Barbara Davies focused on the things that she and her husband Ernie needed to do around the house as she drove home from Pioneer Square Mall. The cold didn't bother her since the warmth flooding from the car heater at full blast complimented the warm clothes she wore.

Thank God Ernie and I have jobs, Barbara mused thoughtfully. Michigan and St. Marys' unemployment rates were acceptable to those who worked. People who still had jobs worried about hour or wage cuts or losing their jobs altogether, bringing a little fear into some St. Marians. As a precautionary measure, Barbara and Ernie began to save as much money as possible, switching to Koditscheks or Meijer from the gourmet food shops so beloved by them. They also cut back on entertainment spending, playing more and more card and board games with themselves and their friends. Their DVD collection also came in handy, since the movie theater prices were outrageous.

Sometimes, Barbara thought about the incident. She never thought about it beyond a second or two. It happened when she was younger and it wasn't something that she cared to be reminded about. It was in the past and she preferred to keep it that way. After high school, she never returned back to her hometown except briefly for funerals or weddings. Others she knew had the same attitude and she couldn't blame them.

Barbara's car flowed smoothly on the familiar road home. She enjoyed night driving while Ernie hated it. When they drove out of town she drove at night while he drove by day. The only time she didn't like driving was when the roads were ice or snow covered. Fortunately, it was in the middle of October and the snow generally arrived two months later in December. She recalled St. Marians telling stories of the entire county being cut off from surrounding areas for days or weeks. Some of the outlying towns such as Klingsburg and Appleton fared even worse. Wise people in the county flooded local stores for food and supplies when WSTM AM and WSTM TV broadcast snowstorm warnings.

Barbara smiled at the snow horror stories she recalled. Almost home, she thought. As she continued to think about the comforts of home, she spotted someone running directly in front of her across the road.

"What the hell..." Barbara exclaimed as she frantically swerved her car to avoid hitting the person. She realized with shock that she was on the opposite side of the road with a truck coming straight into her path, honking frantically towards her. Screaming, Barbara turned the steering wheel rightwards and slipped on a damp patch on the road, losing control of her car and slamming headfirst into a tree. Her last thoughts before darkness ensued focused on Ernie and her loved ones.

Ollie Johnson, the truck driver, quickly stopped his truck and pulled out his cell phone. After reaching a 911 dispatcher he said, "Get someone out here now! There's a bad accident at County Highway 23 and Wind Crest Road."

The dispatcher, Tanya Smith, asked, "Is anyone injured?"

"Don't know. I'm going to see and I'll be here until an ambulance arrives. Do I need to call the police?"

"No, I'll take care of it. We'll get someone there asap."

"Thanks."

Johnson hung up and ran to Barbara's car with some blankets. He quickly unloosened her seat belt and pulled her out of her car. There was blood on her face and she was unconscious. He felt her pulse on her left wrist and neck. She's still alive, he thought with a sense of relief. Quickly wrapping her up, Johnson then called his boss at Hunnibell Dairy and made a quick report. Hanging up, he quickly waited until EMS and the police arrived. Looks like it's going to be a long night, Johnson wryly thought.

A splash after a rock is thrown in the water, sighs of relief, an unwritten agreement, weddings, funerals— Barbara awoke after a moan. "Where am I"

"You're at Rothmann Lutheran Hospital," replied Nurse Candace Rouse, a short stocky woman in her early fifties with salt and pepper hair.

"But why am I here?" Barbara asked again.

"You were in an auto accident. Dr. Parmentier examined you and apart from a concussion and some bruises along with a gash on your forehead you're perfectly fine. It was fortunate that you were wearing your seatbelt."

"I remember. Has Ernie been contacted?"

"Your husband has been contacted and he's on his way now."

"Thank you. How long will I be here?"

"No later than late tomorrow morning if there are no complications."

Barbara wanted to say something else when a dark-haired man of medium height and build stepped into her room. Concern and relief lined his face.

"Ernie! Thank God you're here!" said Barbara happily as they hugged each other.

Ernie asked, "Are you alright, Barbara?"

"I'm fine. The nurse said I would be going home no later than tomorrow morning if there's no complications. By the way, nurse, can I have some sleeping pills? I'll probably need them for the rest of the night."

Nurse Rouse replied briskly, "That won't be a problem. Dr. Parmentier said that you could have sleeping pills if needed." She gave a tablet to Barbara and handed over to her a glass of water. Then she said, "I'll let the two of you talk. If you need anything, just ring the nurse's bell. Oh, and one other thing, visitors' hours will be over in about twenty minutes."

After Nurse Rouse left, Ernie asked, "What happened?"

Barbara replied with a groan, "I'm not sure. I was driving home from the mall and someone ran right in front of me. I lost control of the car and I hit a tree trying to avoid a truck."

"Do you remember anything else?"

"No. I didn't remember anything else until I woke up here."

"I don't want to tire you out, so I'm going home. I'll ask the nurse to call me if anything happens."

"Don't worry, I just have a concussion and bruises according to the nurse."

Ernie smiled at Barbara's remark. He kissed her forehead and said goodnight. Still smiling after he left the room, Barbara thanked whatever god existed that she survived her accident. Maybe it was Divine Providence, maybe it was just dumb luck. She didn't care. She was just happy that she still had time with Ernie and her loved ones. Perhaps I'll take the rest of the week off, Barbara mused dreamily after she took the sleeping tablet with a chug of water. Looks like everything will be all right. Have to call work and explain. Fillner's going to love this, so will everyone else....

Glancing at her watch, Nurse Rouse saw that it was closing time at 12:30 am. She liked to do rounds before leaving. You never know what could happen, she always thought. Most of her patients she liked, since they weren't troublemakers. If they did, well that came with the territory. Nurse burnout easily happened if you lacked the mental toughness for it. Yawning, Nurse Rouse noted that she had one final room to check. Opening Barbara Davies' door, she saw that Mrs. Davies was fast asleep. Nurse Rouse smiled and walked back into the light.

Sunshine along with clouds and cold greeted another

Tuesday morning.   One of the day nurses, Linnea Palmquist, went into Mrs. Davies' room to check on her. According to her chart, Dr. Parmentier requested further tests later in the morning.   A few years out of nursing school and in her middle twenties, Linnea had a strong crush on said doctor.   The running joke in parts of Rothmann was that she would hop into Dr. Parmentier's bed if he snapped his fingers.

Linnea was perky and handsome, not pretty.   She was of medium height and stocky, with long blond hair.   She would have been at home in any of the Seventeenth Century portraits painted by Flemish painters. Unfortunately, Dr. Parmentier completely ignored her except for job purposes.   Even so, Ms. Palmquist sensed that he had some interest in her.   Probably too shy or too concerned about a sexual harassment lawsuit, she thought. After all, if a woman accuses a man of sexual harassment, nine times out of ten the man is considered guilty and the formal proceedings are merely for appearances sake.   But she brushed the thoughts aside.   She had patients to attend and other work to do.

Entering the room, Linnea saw that Mrs. Davies was laying on her back with eyes and mouth open.   In the nurse's language, she was a goner.   Linnea confirmed it by checking for a pulse.   She walked back to the nurses' station and informed the senior nurse, Karen Justice, that Mrs. Davies was dead.   Immediately, Nurse Justice called Dr. Parmentier at home and advised him to come in as soon as possible.   Surprised by the call, Dr. Parmentier quickly arrived at Rothmann with a half hour.   Quickly, yet thoroughly examining the body, Dr. Parmentier concluded that the Medical Examiner's office had to be notified.

From the body's condition, the cause of death appeared to be heart failure. With the exception of a concussion, a cut on her forehead and bruises, Mrs. Davies shouldn't have died.

Still, Dr. Parmentier wanted to cover himself along with Rothmann. Worries about negative news coverage and money hungry attorneys like Gerard Feigenson had to be taken into account. Calling the Medical Examiner's office, the dear doctor reached Medical Examiner Robert Merewether.

"You don't call me this early unless you have a problem case, Chad," replied Merewether wryly.

"You're right, Robert. A woman admitted yesterday died early this morning of cardiac arrest after being in a car accident."

"And she had no history of heart trouble?"

"No, and the accident didn't affect her heart—she only had a concussion, a forehead gash and bruises."

"So, what do you think?"

"I don't know, and I don't want to have any problems for myself or the hospital. With these money grubbing attorneys—"

"Calm down. I'll send the ambulance over in an hour."

"Thanks."

Dr. Parmentier hung up the phone and cleared his throat. The widower, Ernest Davies, would have to be notified.

He may have to wait a while for the release of his wife's body. Terrible tragedy. Well, Merewether will figure it out. Once this problem has been resolved I can think about Linnea, pretty little thing…

Performing autopsies is never pleasant, Merewether thought as he examined Barbara Davies' body. Healthy white female in her middle thirties, with no excessive alcohol usage. No tobacco or drug usage. So why did she die? Merewether found his answer after examining Mrs. Davies' heart.

"Come over here, Emily."

Immediately, Emily Stuckart, Merewether's assistant, rushed over to the autopsy table. Pointing to Mrs. Davies' heart he asked, "What is this?"

"Looks like an air embolism in the right ventricle," Emily a heavy set woman with gray hair replied.

"Correct. Now the funny thing is that I've only seen one other case like this and it was a foul play matter. Let's find the injection site. It should be in the lower calf region, the femoral vein in the groin region or the posterior tibial vein."

"There's an injection mark in the right posterior tibial vein," noted Emily.

"Good. I'll call the police and tell them they have a homicide on their hands." As Emily walked back into her office for a moment Merewether wondered as he called the police who would be assigned to the case. Not my problem, he thought, though Chad and the rest of the

Rothmann staff would have some questions to answer regarding this.

Worry and concern lined Judith Bruschetta's face over the news she just received about Barbara Davies death. She had only been the CEO of Rothmann for a short period of time. Murder in a hospital hurt the bottom line and the parties affected by it. The board's demand to her was to clean up this mess as soon as possible. Mrs. Bruschetta's action plan was to cooperate fully with the police and compensation to Barbara Davies' family if necessary.

If necessary in regards to compensation was the key. If Rothmann was liable, then reasonable compensation would be necessary to keep the Gerard Feigensons of the world at bay. Reasonable being in the eye of the beholder.

Mrs. Bruschetta wanted to make sure that the police handled the investigation in a competent and thorough manner. She would also make it clear to the mayor and police chief that it was a high priority case. They would grant her request simply because Rothmann's board had people on it who could dole out pleasure or pain on a whim. Oh yes, Mrs. Bruschetta sardonically mused, they could do the same thing to me if I screw up on this. Still, Bruschetta Jewelers is still doing well and I'm getting money on the side from it, she continued as she called the police chief.

2

Lt. Frank Tindall of the St. Marys Police Department's Investigative Division yawned and cracked his knuckles as he read a report regarding a Mrs. Barbara Davies. Some chucklehead ran in front of her car, leading to her crashing it into a tree. Since the injuries weren't serious the uniforms would take care of it. He was grateful that he had no major cases on his plate. He had scheduled some time off for Thanksgiving, Christmas and New Year's to be with Mrs. Tindall and their relatives.

Tindall and the former Kathleen Behnke had only been married for about a year when in rapid succession Grandpa and Grandma Tindall passed away. Old Peter Meldrim, Kathleen's uncle, quickly followed. Despite their differences, Tindall truly regretted Old Peter's passing. Most of the Tindalls and Litzmanns attended his grandparents' funerals, including Uncle Oliver and Aunt Rachael, their daughter Elaine and her husband Phil along with their kids Catherine and Collin. The latter's cries filled University Lutheran Church while Pastor Dingle preached what Tindall considered one of the finest eulogies he ever heard.

As for Old Peter's funeral at All Souls Episcopal Church in downtown St. Marys, Kathleen's parents attended along with her sister Amy and other Meldrim family members.

Except for Kathleen, the other Meldrims lived in other parts of the state if not the world. Other mourners included prominent local families such as the Ballietts and politicians on all levels. It would have been an insult, if not a dismissible offence, for any non-essential employee of The Evening News Company not to have been present.

While thinking over the previous events along with other things, Tindall received a call from Capt. Ed Carter, his boss. "Hello Frank, I need to have a chat with you—it's very important."

Tindall's curiosity flared. "I'm coming right now," he said.

As Tindall walked to his boss' office, he wondered what happened. Was he going to be praised or chewed out for something? Or was a special assignment waiting for him? Well, he would find out.

After entering Capt. Carter's office, the latter motioned for him to sit down as he chatted on the phone. From his boss' expression and the tone of his voice, Tindall knew that something big was going on. Hope I don't get burned by it, he glumly noted.

The conversation began after Capt. Carter's call. "That was the police chief," Capt. Carter coolly noted, "and he had a special request for us, particularly regarding you."

Tindall had enough brains to know that when a superior asks an inferior for a request it was an order. "What's the special request?"

"You've heard about Barbara Davies?"

"Yes. Some idiot ran in front of her car and she cracked into a tree."

"True, but she was found dead earlier this morning after she was taken to Rothmann. Merewether ruled that her death was a homicide. When the brass at Rothmann received the news, all hell broke loose. Their CEO called the mayor and police chief and insisted that the case be made high priority."

Surprise lit Tindall's face. "But why me, since there are other people here who are just as capable regarding a homicide case such as Balk…"

Irritably, Capt. Carter replied, "You're right. But you've forgotten that Rothmann's new CEO is a Mrs. Judith Bruschetta. Remember her?"

"I do," admitted Tindall sheepishly. "Since I was in charge of her husband's murder case the chief thinks that I would be perfect for this?"

"Correct. And the police chief advised me that whatever resources you needed you'll get. He also hopes that Davies' homicide would be solved asap."

"Agreed. I'll talk to Mike regarding this. I'm curious about the runner. Is or isn't there a connection?"

"Maybe, maybe not," Capt. Carter sighed. "Anyhow, keep me posted regularly regarding this. The police chief wants regular reports, unfortunately."

Relieved, Tindall walked out and then down to Sgt. Mike Perez' desk.

"Hello again, Mike," Tindall said with a grin. "Looks like I've been assigned to the Davies case."

Surprised, Perez asked, "You mean the lady who smashed her car into a tree after some jerk ran in front of her? Aren't the uniforms handling it?"

"Not anymore. She died either late last night or earlier this morning. And Merewether ruled it a homicide. After I find Jim we'll have a little meeting about the investigation."

Tindall then walked away. Perez was intrigued by the little that he knew about the case. He brushed those thoughts aside after Tindall returned with Detective Jim Parkins.

After greetings, the meeting began.

"The case was simple and straightforward originally," said Tindall as he passed copies of the police reports to Perez and Parkins. "A woman named Barbara Davies," continued Tindall, "was driving home from Pioneer Square Mall when she crashed into a tree while trying to avoid hitting someone who ran into the road. Other than a cut on the forehead, bruises and a concussion, she was perfectly fine.

"After being transferred to Rothmann she was admitted for overnight evaluation. Again, no problems. Then the following morning one of the nurses finds Mrs. Davies dead. After examining the body, Dr. Chad Parmentier, who originally examined Mrs. Davies when she was admitted, was so suspicious regarding her death that he contacted Merewether. After Merewether examines the body and rules it a homicide, the case ends up in our hands."

"But why is this considered to be, in your own words, a "special project?" queried Parkins.

"Because Judith Bruschetta, Rothmann's new CEO, requested to the police chief that it be handled as a high priority. Obviously, he liked how I handled her murdered husband's case."

Perez groaned. "High profile cases are soo lovely!"

"You got it. Which also means that we have to check and double check everything or we could end up being demoted or worse. Looking for a new job at this time doesn't appeal to me."

"So how are we going to divvy up the work?" asked Parkins.

"Simple. I'll talk to Merewether, while the two of you start with the Rothmann people. I'll meet you there once I'm done."

"Fine. We'll see you."

After the meeting ended, Tindall then bundled up and walked down the street to the Medical Examiner's office. He saw signs of the upcoming Thanksgiving holiday. Decorations hanging from lampposts. Statues of Pilgrims and turkeys on the courthouse lawn. Special sale signs in the shops on Main St. and the feeder side streets in the Central District. The only thing missing, Tindall mused, are the ACLU protestors, and they would possibly arrive by Christmas. Soon he would have to deal with clearing snow from the sidewalk and driveway. Probably hire someone to handle it out of sheer laziness.

The building itself was solid and unpretentious, built of brick and serving the county taxpayers since 1922. Along with the County Health Department, it also included an annex used for additional work and storage space. Tindall took the stairs and walked up to the third floor. Entering the Medical Examiner's office, he warmly greeted everyone and waited for Merewether's secretary to usher him in. After saying and asking a few pleasantries Tindall sat down and asked, "So you're ruling Mrs. Davies' death as a homicide?"

"Yes," Merewether replied while sipping pomegranate and cherry juice at his desk. "A mass of air in the right heart ventricle is suspicious to me, since one previous case like this was a homicide. Plus, I found an injection on the victim's right posterior tibial vein."

Tindall asked, "So how does the death occur?"

"When air's injected into that specific vein, it'll travel up the inferior vena cava to the heart. Once the air bubble's in the heart, the blood flow in the heart stops, causing cardiac arrest."

Curious, Tindall then asked, "How long does it take for the person to die?"

"About a minute or two."

Merewether then looked at him irritably. "It's possible for an air bubble to appear on its own, but if I or my staff see an injection mark in either the femoral or popliteal veins then I'm ruling it a homicide. You'll get the unofficial copy sometime today and the official copy in about a week or so."

Tindall thanked Merewether and began to walk out. As he did so, Merewether added, "I heard that you and the better half are considering adoption. I have some contacts if you're interested."

Tindall was surprised. How'd the hell did he know that? Kathleen still wasn't pregnant and neither of them were getting any younger. But childlessness wouldn't have affected their sleep.

"Thanks," Tindall replied with laugh. "We may or mayn't have any kids. It's in God's hands. I almost forgot, how long is your estimate regarding the time of death?"

"About six to seven hours."

"Thanks again."

Merewether nodded. Tindall then hurried back to Headquarters and then drove to Rothmann.

Tindall sardonically noted that he never saw Mrs. Bruschetta outside of criminal investigations. Yet he was alert as always, eager to hear and sense the nuances and unspoken assertions made consciously or unconsciously by persons of interest or not.

Tindall and Mrs. Bruschetta greeted each other warmly yet warily. We both have our own skins on the line, they each noted inwardly. Both knew, as the old saying went, that success had many parents and failure none. They briefly asked questions about each other's family and then the conversation shifted to the business at hand.

"I received the information regarding Mrs. Davies' death from my boss and the Medical Examiner's office," Tindall noted politely. "It's a homicide case at this point. Now the question is who and why."

Mrs. Bruschetta agreed. "I, along with the staff here, have never had a case in which a patient was murdered under our very noses! It's horrible to think about! Mrs. Davies' family is devastated by this. And it's not good for the hospital either. Wolves like Gerard Feigenson would love to sue us for millions."

Tindall nodded in sympathy. "I agree. But tell me, is there anyone at Rothmann, either current or former, who would have a motive for doing this? No offense to you or the hospital, but no one would be able to just walk in and commit a murder."

"I understand your point of view," replied Mrs. Bruschetta guardedly, "but there's no one here either current or former as you say, that would do something like this. No, it has to be an outsider."

"You may be right," murmured Tindall. "At any rate, we will hopefully catch the killer soon. Most criminals make some kind of mistake. And when they do, we'll be right behind them."

Mrs. Bruschetta agreed. After he walked out of her office, Tindall wondered what kind of information Parkins and Perez were able to find out. Sighing, he briskly walked down the corridor, looking attentively at his surroundings, when he was almost knocked over by a harried- looking man.

"My apologies! How stupid and clumsy of me! Are you alright?" the man said, worry lining his face.

Tindall agreed about the stupid and clumsy part silently but graciously accepted the man's apology. "Nothing to worry about. I'm in one piece. By the way, have you seen two plainclothes policemen around here?"

"I'm on my way to see one of them—he wants to question me regarding a woman I treated last night who passed away earlier this morning."

"You must be Dr. Chad Parmentier. I'm Lt. Tindall from the Police Department and I'm in charge of the investigation."

"I'm him," Parmentier replied with a frown as he shook Tindall's hand. Tindall looked him at him closely, noting that he had a strong resemblance to a regular on the Seventies children's show The Electric Company. The regular in question had blond hair, glasses and a peculiar sounding voice along with a nervy manner. Quickly Tindall recalled the regular's name: Skip Hinnant. Haven't seen the man in years, Tindall noted, the guy may even be a stiff by now, and yet I'm talking to a dead-on caricature of him. Tindall irritably brushed those thoughts aside and retuned to business at hand.

"My apologies for detaining you. If Detective Parkins gives you a hard time about being late, you can say it's my fault. It was a pleasure to talk to you and perhaps we will talk again."

With obvious relief, Parmentier walked away. Odd character, Tindall noted thoughtfully. I wondered if he saw the nurse watching the two of us. That nurse was more interested in the good doctor than him. Tindall rarely got those kinds of looks and didn't care. The nurse herself was handsome, neither pretty or ugly. Parmentier's the kind of guy the woman would have to be aggressive with, he concluded as he walked to a visitors' lounge.

Parmentier was delighted to arrive at the conference room a bit early. Before entering, he smoothed his hair, applied lip jelly on his lips and made sure that he had dry palms. Parmentier walked in calm, cool and collected and then introduced himself to Parkins in a professional yet friendly manner.

The two men sat down and Parkins began the interview. "Tell me exactly what happened in your own words."

"Well, earlier this morning I received a call from the senior duty nurse, Karen Justice, who requested that I come in asap. I thoroughly examined Mrs. Davies and I was concerned that it appeared that the cause of death was cardiac arrest. Other than a concussion, a cut on her forehead and some bruises, she was perfectly healthy. I then called the Medical Examiner's office and I requested that they perform an autopsy on Mrs. Davies. Once they advised me of their findings, I then notified my supervisor and it was taken from there."

"You didn't see anything unusual?"

"The fact that a perfectly healthy woman dies due to cardiac arrest after a frightening but not serious car accident struck me as very peculiar, and I wanted to cover myself and the hospital. These damned money grubbing—
"

"I get it. Did you or anyone else see anything suspicious on Mrs. Davies' floor or close to her room?"

"Not as far as I know, though if someone was skulking around here off hours no one would have noticed."

Parkins smiled. "Thanks for your time regarding this case."

Parmentier blushed. "All of us want to assist the police in any way we can. You don't think that it was one of us?"

"We can't say anything at this point regarding possible suspects."

Parmentier was irritated by Parkins' answer. Oh, what rubbish! The killer wasn't anyone on the staff since everyone's credentials and references were thoroughly checked. On the other hand, the police had to do a thorough job.

He decided to throw caution to the wind and ask Linnea if she wanted to have coffee on a weekend. Damn, he thought, it'll have to wait until after the police interviewed her. He hoped that she wouldn't be overwhelmed by this, the first murder occurring at Rothmann within anyone's memory. God knows who else they're interviewing, Parmentier silently concluded as he quickly walked back to his office, deep in his thoughts.

Linnea Palmquist was a recovering nail biter. She used to bite her nails to the quick during stress times in her early and late teens. Prior to that, she chewed on her pencils to the point that they looked like items given to pet mice or squirrels. By the time Perez entered the conference room she was composed and ready to answer any questions asked by the police.

Both parties quickly sized each other up and were impressed by what they saw. After sitting down and exchanging pleasantries Perez asked, "Tell me exactly what happened after you entered Mrs. Davies' room to check on her."

Linnea looked at him calmly and replied, "After I entered her room, I first thought that Mrs. Davies was still asleep. But when I saw how still she was, along with her open mouth and eyes, I checked her pulse. Since she had no pulse and her skin was cold, I then told the senior duty nurse, Karen Justice, regarding what happened."

"Whom did Ms. Justice contact regarding this?"

"She contacted Dr. Parmentier, who originally treated Mrs. Davies when she was brought in last night. From what I gather, Dr. Parmentier contacted the Medical Examiner's office and they contacted you."

"Did any other nurse look in on Mrs. Davies other than you?"

Linnea promptly answered, "Candace Rouse was the nurse who looked in on Mrs. Davies before my shift started. She may have seen more than I did. Considering the extent of Mrs. Davies' injuries and the fact that she was sedated, I didn't check on her too much, perhaps once or twice."

Perez stood up and thanked Linnea for her answers. She beamed in appreciation as he walked out into the hall. Not a bad looking woman, Perez noted with a wolfish grin. Nice voice, nice body, clear intelligence—if Sheila could read my mind, I would be without my dessert for some time, Perez finished with an inward laugh.

"Ding dong, ding dong, the bitch is dead," I silently said as news of Barbara Davies's death spread throughout St. Marys. I mocked and cursed the dead woman with no remorse or guilt. People like dear Barbara deserved to die, I thought. My plan worked well except that the ME diagnosed it as a homicide. And it was so easy to walk into her room and kill her. So quiet and peaceful. I felt sad for Barbara's husband. No one should lose their family. I knew that personally all too well. Too bad justice couldn't be served in another way. Still, you can't make an omelet without breaking eggs. I thought long and hard about how to punish the other names on my mental list. I had all the time in the world. After all, patience is a virtue.

"So," Tindall asked, "did you or Mike get any information from Palmquist or Parmentier regarding Mrs. Davies?"

"We didn't get anything from either of them," replied Parkins. He along with Perez, were back in Tindall's office at Police Headquarters. "They didn't see or notice anything unusual or out of place."

"Well, I'm not surprised," Tindall replied thoughtfully. "Still, we have to question Nurses Rouse and Justice along with the widower. I'll see Davies while the two of you take care of the nurses."

The three policemen went back to work.

3

Ernest Davies tried to watch TV in one of Rothmann's visitors' rooms. Normally, he didn't have time during the day to do so since he was either working or otherwise busy. I'm not missing anything, he glumly noted. Nothing held his interest and the old magazines cluttering the tables didn't ease the boredom or concern for Barbara. Not even the book he tried to read eased his mind.

This was the first time that Barbara had been in Rothmann for something as serious as this. He hoped that the piece of garbage who did this to Barbara paid for what happened. Memories of his and Barbara's life flooded his mind—their first meeting and date, a marriage proposal, their semi-serious wedding and honeymoon, a loving and stable marriage. He prayed to whomever that they would continue to have their time together.

Looking around, he saw no one with him. The room itself was drab and austere, painted in white and lightly decorated with chairs, couches and tables. It looked like the maintenance crew kept it neat and clean on a regular basis. His overview ceased when he noticed an ordinary looking man with short brown hair and mild yet watchful eyes walking towards him.

The stranger held out his hand. "My name is Lt. Frank Tindall of the St. Marys Police Dept. Are you Mr. Ernest

Davies?"

Davies shook his hand and said, "I'm he. What is it?" He knew what was coming.

Tindall looked at him sadly. "I have bad news. Mrs. Davies passed away early this morning."

Outrage lined Davies' face. "Barbara passed away early this morning and you're telling me now? I should've known this before and whoever here should have told me!"

"I agree with you, and in a normal situation you would have been notified before now. Before I go any further, would you care to sit down?"

Davies shook his head. "No, I want to stay standing. You're leaving out something and I insist that you tell me everything!"

"I will. Mrs. Davies was found dead earlier this morning by one of the day nurses. The doctor who examined Mrs. Davies—Parmentier—found something odd about the death, since the accident wasn't serious enough to lead to death by heart failure. Because of that, the Medical Examiner's office was contacted and they came to the conclusion that Mrs. Davies' death was due to homicide."

Davies looked crushed. "What did the Medical Examiner's office find that led to their conclusion?"

"Fraid I can't say since it's now a murder investigation. Unfortunately, I have to ask you where you were late last night and early this morning."

Shocked, Davies stammered, "You don't think that I--"

"We can never assume when it comes to a murder case," Tindall replied quietly.

"Alright. I was at home and I don't have an alibi. The only other thing I can say is that I would never hurt Barbara and I never—" Davies began to weep, heartbreaking and moving. Tindall never felt comfortable around tears and he searched his pants pocket for a clean piece of tissue. Failing at this, he spied a full tissue box and handed quite a few tissues to Davies.

The two of them sat down and after a minute or two Davies calmed down.

Tindall quietly said, "I will say, Mr. Davies, that I and my team will do our best to find Mrs. Davies' killer. I also have to ask some questions about Barbara right now."

Eyes hardening, Davies snarled, "What does that mean?"

"I'm merely asking if she had any enemies, someone who would want to hurt her," Tindall replied gently.

Davies' look softened. "Barbara didn't have any enemies. The people who knew her either liked her or didn't see her as an enemy."

"Are there any relatives that need to be notified/"

Davies shook his head. "All of her relatives died when she was young and she was on her own by the time we met. My family is rather ordinary sized and they loved Barbara and she loved them."

"Thank you for your time. I lost my grandparents a

short time ago and it takes time to deal with the grief."
Tindall then handed Davies his card. "If you have any
further information, please don't hesitate to call me."

As he walked away, wondering where he saw Davies
before, Tindall heard his cell phone ring. "Tindall
speaking."

A booming laugh pierced Tindall's ears. "Normally the
coppers make the first move regarding a murder!" It was
"Mac" McElroy, Rothmann's security chief.

"Point noted, but I was just on the verge of calling you.
By the way, have you heard anything?"

"Nothing. I'm in the dark just like you and your team.
Any info we get you'll get. Do you think it was an inside
job?" There was a trace of amusement in McElroy's voice.

"Can't say," replied Tindall mildly. "On the other hand,
how easy would it be for an outsider to slip in and cause
mischief?"

"Depends on the factors involved. Someone coming in
late, dressing and acting appropriately, would be able to
pull it off. My staff's checking all of our info and there's
nothing unusual or out of place."

Tindall frowned. "But what about ID? Wouldn't
someone be more careful at night?"

"Like I said, if the person dressed and acted like they
belonged here, no one would give the person a second
thought. As for ID, all the interloper would have to say
was that they were a newbie and they left their ID at home
or lost it. Personnel's at home and no one's going to

call'em at home regarding it."

Tindall's mood brightened. "Can you do me a favor, Mac?"

"What is it?"

"Can you ask around to see if there was anyone hanging around last night who were unfamiliar to the regular staff?"

"Will do. By the way, I hope the missus is doing well."

Tindall laughed. "She is and thanks again." After hanging up, Tindall noted the lack of leads so far in this case. Well, perhaps Perez and Parkins would end up with more information than what he had. Wistfully, he hoped that Katy's day was going well. Have to get her some flowers or something else that she likes. The joys of marriage brightened and enriched their lives. Also, he needed to talk to Chuck and Ann in the Crime Lab to see if they found anything in Mrs. Davies' room.

Idle thoughts swirled through Kathleen Tindall's mind as she looked out from her third-floor office window in the Evening News building. She saw people walking to and from lunch or looking through shop windows. Interestingly, a young boy and his pals saw her and waved. Surprised she smiled and waved back. Children are so beautiful, Kathleen mused, so uncorrupted. So why would they hurt each other or why would adults hurt them? For a long time, she subscribed to the poverty/environment argument, but with age and experience she leaned towards the simple conclusion that Frank reached years ago, that the world was sinful and man was corrupted by it.

I'm thinking of theology at a time like this, Kathleen frowned. Of her immediately family, she was the most religious. Her parents considered religion to be positive without quibbling over theological points. Progressive Christianity in other words. Her sister Amy was irreligious, not caring about God or the afterlife at all. Once she turned eighteen, Amy only went to church if a wedding or funeral was involved. Kathleen knew that Amy wasn't an atheist or agnostic, she just considered religion to be something to think about sooner or later, preferably later.

Kathleen enjoyed her office. She spent many times there when Old Peter was still alive since it was originally his office. He treated her like a granddaughter, which she basically was, since she was old enough to be her mother's father. It saddened her that Amy didn't have a closer relationship with Old Peter. She knew that Old Peter and Amy had a chalk and cheese relationship. They just didn't have any warm feelings towards each other. Both Kathleen and her mother Mrs. Adelheid Behnke were unable to fill in the breach, she because of the sourness between her and Amy, and Mrs. Behnke because Old Peter wouldn't tolerate any interference in his personal affairs.

The office was simple and elegant, decorated and furnished in an old money style that impressed but didn't overwhelm. Kathleen decided to keep the office as is. It suited her personality and she didn't think that it was worth the time or money to renovate it. However, she did add certain feminine touches to it, easily recognizable in a woman's office. Other additions were the all in one computer on her desk, not liking laptops, and the radio/CD player on a side table. She thought about getting an iPhone or Smartphone but considered it a waste of money since her cell phone still worked well.

As chairwoman of The Evening News Company and publisher of The Evening News, Kathleen had a great deal of power and responsibility in her hand. Although the editor handled the day to day activities at the newspapers and the general managers did the same for the newspaper's sister radio and TV stations, she had to make the major decisions regarding important items such as political campaign endorsements, top management changes and the like. When she first took on the task, she felt a sense of being in over her head. Thank God that Frank, Amelia and her parents gave her the support that she could do this.

In hindsight, she realized that Old Peter believed in her too. Kathleen recalled the special projects assigned to her, representing Old Peter in important meetings and participating in conference sessions. It also explained why Kathleen was left most of Old Peter's estate, except for a few personal bequests to family, friends and charities. Mrs. Behnke and Amy were already provided for by a family trust set up years ago. There were also separate trusts set up for other Meldrim family members.

Kathleen always though that Old Peter had enough shares to control the company, but she found out after he passed away that he owned the entire company, buying out the other heirs' shares years ago. She considered it a wise move since it avoided family feuds that led to the breakup of companies such as Field Communications. It also avoided The Evening News Company being sold by money hungry heirs such as the Times Mirror Company. Kathleen would also have to in the future plan for her successor whether or not she and Frank had children.

Money was never an issue between Kathleen and Frank. Each of them pledged in their prenuptial agreement that they would keep the assets they brought into the marriage separate from each other. Old Peter insisted on it and Frank agreed. Kathleen could vote Old Peter's shares in whatever way she chose as the trustee but they were owned by a special trust. They would be passed to her children and if she didn't have any children, then the shares would go to her sister Amy's children. Apart from his salary, Frank had assets of his own from inheritances and investments that he could comfortably live on. The Tindalls, while not wealthy like the Meldrims, Ballietts or the other old money families in St. Marys, weren't poor either. In short, either of them could live without working, but life would be more fulfilling if they did so.

Glancing at the calendar, Kathleen beamed that she didn't have many meetings to attend for the rest of the year. But there were Christmas and New Year parties to attend along with visiting her parents and Amy for Christmas. Neither Kathleen nor Frank were partiers or outgoing types but they understood that sociability was an important part of friendship. She also thoroughly enjoyed visiting Frank's relatives, including Elaine, Phil and the kids.

As for their children, Kathleen wondered if they would have any, either by birth or adoption. Both she and Frank were interested in having no more than one child since any more would be too much for both of them. Kathleen wasn't desperate about it. Adoption would be quite easy since the Meldrims and Tindalls were well respected local families. None of the adoption agencies in the county would raise any objections. Still, Kathleen asked inwardly if it would be good for her and Frank to have a child. Children needed quite a bit of love and attention, qualities that both of them had in abundance. But Kathleen was scared, scared that she didn't have what it took to be a successful parent. Frank had the same concern, since he had seen firsthand parents who didn't give a damn about their children and their children becoming wards of the state via the FIA or prison. True, they could get help and encouragement from their relatives and friends, but the responsibility would be theirs and theirs alone.

Sighing, Kathleen swirled her juice with a straw. Why am I so glum right now? The sun's shining, everything is going well, but I have the blues. Perhaps it's old age or experience.

Amelia interrupted her reverie. "Ma'am, do you want something from the cafeteria? I'm going down for some food."

With mock severity Kathleen replied, "Amelia! Can't you call me Kathleen? This is the 21st Century, you know."

Amelia laughed. "Sorry! You know it's soo easy to forget!" Kathleen had inherited Amelia from Old Peter, who made it clear in the office that he would be called either sir or Mr. Meldrim. Only Kathleen and a few old timers called him anything different.

"No Amelia, but thanks. I'll get something around lunch time."

"You're the boss, Kathleen!" Amelia merrily replied as she skippped out of the latter's office. Kathleen enjoyed having Amelia as her secretary, or in modern terms, administrative assistant. Old Peter never used the term, calling those who used it "jumped up secretaries". Amelia had worked for Old Peter for about fifteen years at the time of his passing and knew the ins and outs of the office along with the business. Indeed, Amelia had been the de facto office manager, since everyone knew that a request from her was an order from Old Peter.

Kathleen knew that Amelia was around Frank's age but knew very little about her personal life. One passion they shared revolved around cats. Amelia had two cats and Kathleen wanted to get two. Frank would hem and haw but in the end, he would give in. She did the same.

As for Old Peter, Kathleen smiled about the stories he told about the life he led. What few people knew was that Old Peter worked in radio as Peter Purlingbrook. After graduating from University High School, he worked as a radio actor until he enlisted in the Army in 1942. He actually began working in radio in his teens on WSTM AM. A local soap opera, The Andersons, needed someone to play Rusty Anderson, the teenage son. Ellery Meldrim, Old Peter's father, didn't want him to play the role, but was persuaded to let him try it. And Old Peter was very good at it and was even able to persuade University High to let him do it during school time.

One story Kathleen vividly recalled was watching an episode of Soap with Old Peter with the sisters Jessica and Mary interacting with their senile father, "The Major". Old Peter laughed and said, 'That's Arthur Peterson and I know him quite well!"

"You do?" Kathleen asked skeptically.

"I do," replied Old Peter matter of factly. "I worked with him and we're friends."

Katheen was too shocked to respond. Over the years, Old Peter talked about the people he knew from "the business." As Kathleen grew older she began to ask more and more questions. After Aunt Kerstin passed away, Old Peter was willing to answer them. Perhaps it was because he knew that his life was coming to a close.

One evening, after Kathleen and Old Peter finished dinner, Kathleen asked, "So how did your radio career end?"

Wryly, Old Peter replied, "It was the war, Kathleen. After Pearl Harbor, the atmosphere was like September 11. Everyone who wanted to enlist did so. After New Year's, Loren and I enlisted in the Army."

"Loren was your brother?"

"And your uncle. It's a pity you didn't know him. He was a gentleman, so kind and decent, one of the few people no one had anything bad to say about."

"Didn't he die in the war."

"He did, in France after D-Day to be precise. When we heard of what had happened, it killed us, it truly did. No parent should have to bury their child before them. It reminds me of when--"

Old Peter stopped himself and continued on. "You see, Loren as the eldest was going to take over the company. He already handled the day to day work at the time the war broke out. I, on the other hand, was interested in radio acting and it didn't bother me that Loren was ultimately going to be in charge."

"So after Uncle Loren died you took his place?"

"No. I went to college only long enough to get my degree and then I went back to radio. By the mid-1950s what people now call "old time radio" began to shift towards television. I could have moved into television like Karl Swenson and Jack Webb, but by that time your grandfather was ill and I needed to come back home."

"And you've been here ever since?"

"Correct, and it looks like I will die here," concluded Old Peter with a smile.

Kathleen noticed that it was noon and time for lunch. Frank's probably at lunch with the guys, she thought. I wonder what case or cases he's currently working on now. I may call him before he gets home.

Tindall's lunch rarely changed since he liked light breakfasts and lunches. The only time he ate more than a simple salad and a piece of fruit was if it was a special or social occasion. He also usually liked to be left alone while at lunch, though Perez and the others knew that if something serious occurred he could be disturbed. Sometimes he liked to read or sometimes he liked to listed to the radio. Tindall had a shortwave radio that could pick up different stations by day or by night. Grandpa Tindall was also a fan of shortwave radios. He could also pick up different stations via the Net. Sadly, the chain where he bought it from had recently closed after filing for bankruptcy. It was sad for the employees who lost their jobs, Tindall opined silently.

Tindall had a personal item to resolve in accordance with his grandparents' wishes. He was scheduled to meet the family attorney Joseph Tallichet sometime this week to discuss it, and it more than likely involved Uncle Matt. He wasn't discussed in the house and the topic changed to something else if his name came up. Tindall suspected that Kathleen may have had some information from her mother but he would never ask her about it since he thought that he would be out of line in doing so. He knew perfectly well that the coolness Old Peter initially displayed towards him was due to Uncle Matt. Rumors swirled around the county regarding his relationship with one of the Meldrim girls but it wasn't considered something to discuss either out of respect or fear.

If the rumors he heard were correct about Uncle Matt, Tindall thought, then Grandpa Tindall did what needed to be done and he would have done the same thing. Still, it was terrible to lose a child either through their fault or the results of life. Finishing his lunch along with that thought, Tindall put the remains of his lunch in a Koditscheks plastic bag and threw it in his trash can.

Walking out of his office, Tindall went down the hall to see Chuck Roberts and Ann Mullins in the Crime Lab, whistling all the way. As he walked in, Chuck and Ann were in their offices, finishing up some work before going to lunch.

"Hello Chuck and Ann! I hope that you and the kids are doing well?" Tindall purred as they walked outside to him.

"We and they are," replied both in unison. "Kids when

they get older, you have to worry about them even more," noted Ann, "getting involved in sex, drugs or alcohol."

"Like us?" Chuck replied with a grin.

Ann shook her head. "You know that's not funny, and besides, I didn't inhale."

Laughing, Tindall replied, "I hope that you're not doing this for my benefit! That was the best laugh I've gotten so far today."

"You want to know if we found anything about Barbara Davies?" Ann wryly replied. Unfortunately, there wasn't anything there in her room. Nothing unusual or out of place. There were also no fingerprints on scene. We do have to advise that when Chuck and I were on the scene, the room had only been cordoned off after Rothmann received the word from the ME's office that it was a homicide. The official report won't be ready until we go through her phone."

"Lovely. Whatever fingerprints or other possible evidence could have 'disappeared' or been destroyed," noted Tindall irritably. "Well, you and Chuck did everything that you could."

"Thanks for your understanding," Chuck said with relief.

Smiling, Tindall said goodbye and walked back to his office. Well, Jim and Mike should be back in a moment and hopefully they will have some information. He was going to do some further checking regarding Mrs. Davies. There may have been things going on in her life that Mr.

Davies knew nothing about. Husbands and wives didn't share everything about their lives and it was unrealistic to expect them to. After all, humans were the most complex creatures God ever made, since only humans would torture or kill each other just for the hell of it.

Before he returned back to his office, Tindall saw Perez and Parkins. "Did the two nurses have any information possibly relevant to the case?"

"No," Parkins replied. "Rouse didn't see or hear anything suspicious before she left her shift."

Perez agreed. "The only information Justice had regarding Davies' death was the information given to her by Palmquist. The next thing to do would be to talk to her friends, relatives and coworkers."

Tindall said, "I'll call Davies right now and see what further information he has about her relatives, friends and job. He told me that her parents were dead and she was on her own." He walked back to his office and was able to reach Davies at home. After getting the information, he walked back to his office and briefed Perez and Parkins.

Handing the information over to Perez and Parkins, Tindall said, "Jim, here's the information regarding Mrs. Davies' friends and Mike, here's the information regarding her job. I'm going over to Davies' house to go through her stuff. Chuck and Ann still have to go through her phone. If it's too late, we'll meet back here tomorrow morning. Let's earn our keep."

The three policemen went their separate ways.

4

Ernest Davies didn't have the energy to try to make any kind of plans regarding Barbara's funeral nor did he feel like calling back friends and acquaintances who left messages giving their condolences. People had to be contacted, such as his family, who lived in Indiana. He also had to contact Hay & Daughters Funeral Home regarding the funeral date and he had to find out from the police when Barbara's body would be released. Since neither of them were religious, either he or someone else would have to do the eulogy. It wouldn't be ethical to find a minister to do it when the two of them spent more time not thinking about God than thinking about Him. If necessary, he could ask one of his relatives to do the eulogy.

As he waited for the police to arrive, Davies walked back and forth in his and Barbara's house, reminiscing about their shared memories and their hopes and dreams. Even though they had been married for only about six years, they entered marriage with the expectation that they would grow old together for richer or poorer and in sickness and health for the days of their lives. Too tense to sit and wait, Davies wasn't interested in reading, listening to music or watching TV. It was irrelevant to what was going on and he didn't want to deal with it. The words in books were meaningless jumbles of words, and the sounds of voices on the radio or TV were gibberish in a language incomprehensible to him at this point as Chinese would be all the time in his world.

He didn't even want to see the police again unless they could tell him that Barbara's killer was in jail. That would bring him out of his mental haze. Of course, his bosses at his job said that they would give him as much as time as he needed. But Davies knew that their patience wasn't infinite and that after a certain period of time he would have to return to work or else. Realistically, he would probably go back to work the Monday after next week.

Looking at Barbara's different objects around the house from the living room to their bedroom, Davies wondered what he would do with them. He couldn't just leave them there, since after a while he would have to move on. He could store her things in the attic or basement, he could hire a storage bin and place them there, the items could be donated to Goodwill or the Salvation Army, or they could be donated to his family, since Barbara never discussed anything about her family except that her parents had passed away.

As he sat down in his easy chair in the living room, Davies saw a Fiat 500x stop in front of his house. That's probably the cop I saw earlier today, he thought. Good Lord, my brain's so fried I can't even think of his name. Well, he won't shoot me over it. Glumly, Davies slowly rose from his chair and walked over to the door. He opened the door and Tindall walked in with a crate.

"Thank you and hello again," Tindall said as he shook Davies' hand. "It's a pity that I can't give you any more information that what I did earlier today."

"I understand and please sit down, Detective—"

"It's Lt. Frank Tindall and please don't apologize," Tindall said as he sat down in the living room. "You have a lot of things on your mind and I won't keep you long. I want to thank you again for the information that you gave me regarding Mrs. Davies' friends and acquaintances along with giving us the authorization to go through her personal items without having to request a search warrant."

"I've nothing to hide and I want Barbara's killer to pay for what they did to her. She didn't deserve to die like that."

Tindall didn't like the look in Davies face and eyes right now. He looked dead in his soul and Tindall knew too many people like Davies who ended up killing themselves quickly through suicide or on the installment plan through junk or booze. He detected the sour smell of beer on his breath and also noted that Davies had a slight slurring in his voice, which he also didn't like.

Quietly he asked, "Do you need to talk to someone?"

"No, the hospital gave me some grief counseling information. I may or may not use it. And don't try to push religion on me. Barbara and I weren't religious and I'm not about to start that trick now."

"Well, if you need to speak to someone you can either use one of the counselors or call one of the ministers around here. I didn't need to speak to anyone when my grandparents passed away. The only other advice I'm giving is to not drive anywhere today since you've been drinking. I don't want you to have your license chopped up and have to see you in jail downtown."

Davies laughed, a hard, bitter laugh. "You smell beer around here? I should have used some air freshener and mints. I'm not angry with you, lieutenant, you're doing everything you can do."

"Thanks for the understanding." In a lighter tone, Tindall asked, "Did Mrs. Davies have an office here?"

"She does, it's on the other side of the room in the back." Davies rose from his chair and escorted Tindall to the back of the house. Nice looking house both inside and out, Tindall mused as the two of them walked to Mrs. Davies' office. Looks like there's three rooms downstairs, not including the living room, dining room, bathroom and kitchen. Nice pictures on the walls, the kind you find in flea markets or at the annual City/County Art Fair. Now Tindall knew where he saw Davies before. He was a Realtor at Shadwell Realty, and proof of it were recent Realtor of the Month Awards from Shadwell in the room across from Mrs. Davies' office. The top Realtors made the top money but had to work brutal hours, including late at night, weekends and even some holidays.

"This is Barbara's office," Davies noted to Tindall as they stepped into Mrs. Davies' office. The office itself was tasteful and well organized. Nothing was in disorder or out of place. "As you can see," Davies continued, "Barbara was a stickler for neatness. I, on the other hand, am the typical pack rat. If you need anything, please feel free to ask."

Thanking Davies, Tindall began to work after the latter walked out of the office. Mrs. Davies didn't have a lot of furniture in her office, just a desk, a few chairs, a bookcase and two file cabinets. He noted that she didn't have a desktop computer, just a laptop, and it was set up like a desktop with its own mouse, keyboard and monitor connected to a docking board. She wanted a desktop setup but a laptop in case she had to work somewhere else, Tindall noted. He also saw a copier/scanner/printer on top of a table close by. Tindall also noted that her and Davies' office doors had locks on them. Not surprising, since he was a Realtor and she was an accounting specialist at Hunnibell Dairy--the two of them were undoubtedly privy to confidential information that outsiders needed to know nothing about. Undoubtedly, they also probably did some if not a lot of work at home.

Davies also probably had a shredder in his office, Tindall mused as he examined Mrs. Davies' shredder. It was the expensive kind, costing around $200.00 and was worth every penny, since it reduced the paper, credit cards and CDs to confetti size. Tindall had the same one at home and his junk mail and old bills and confidential documents ended up as confetti. He saw that Davies left a ring of keys on the desk, probably for the desk and the file cabinets. Tindall also had the keys that Mrs. Davies had at the time of her passing.

Sitting down at the desk, Tindall began to examine its contents after putting on a pair of thin latex gloves. He noted that there were stacks of bills with "paid" written on them. Nothing was unusual about them, just some utility and credit card bills. He also noted bills for a storage place on County Highway 23. Will check the storage place out later, he thought, probably with Mike or Jim, and he made a copy of the bill from the scanner/copier/printer. He also found a little black notebook inside. Flipping through it, Tindall saw that Mrs. Davies used it to keep track of her user names and passwords. He pushed the notebook to the side and continued to look through the desk. Tindall saw nothing else of interest and seeing a laptop bag, he carefully removed the laptop from its docking board and put it in the bag. He also put the copy of the storage place bill and the notebook in his crate.

Rising from the desk, Tindall grabbed the keys from the top of the desk and walked over to the two file cabinets. After a minute or so, he opened both file cabinets and began to look through the first one. Tindall then carried all of the documents to the desk and went through them. Nothing of interest, just official paperwork, additional bills and copies of tax returns. Sighing, he put all of the items back into the file cabinet.

Tindall then went through the second file cabinet and saw the same items that were in the first one. He wasn't surprised since other than pictures of Kathleen and Grandpa and Grandma Tindall in his office he kept his personal things at home. Tindall was going to ask Davies if Mrs. Davies kept her personal items somewhere else in the house. If not, then more than likely she kept them in the storage place she rented out. He wasn't going to tell Davies anything about the storage place. Tindall didn't believe that Davies was involved in Mrs. Davies' murder, but he didn't like to tip his hands while the case was still being investigated.

Shrugging his shoulders, he put the laptop bag on his shoulder and walked out of the office along with his crate. Entering the living room, he asked Davies, "Mr. Davies, is there any other part of the house where Mrs. Davies kept her personal items such as Christmas cards or scrapbooks?"

"No," Davies replied, "Barbara was a very private person, and there were parts of her life that were closed off. That was one of the few non-negotiable parts of our marriage. Her office was another part and because of it she never tried to go into my office unless I was inside. I couldn't even tell you where she kept her really personal stuff."

"Sorry if this sounds offensive, but how much of Mrs. Davies' life prior to meeting her do you know about?"

"No offense taken since you're doing your job. Very little. Like I said when we first met, Lt. Tindall, the only thing I knew about Barbara's background is from what she told me and it wasn't much. Neither of us come from around here, she came from the Thumb area and I come from Metro Detroit. She didn't talk about any relatives other than her parents being dead and I didn't push."

"Thank you for your time. Hopefully we may have further information soon."

Davies grunted and walked Tindall to the door. Neither man said anything as Tindall walked to his car and drove off.

Looks like this case may be quite interesting, Tindall mused while he drove back to Headquarters. A very private woman who didn't want to discuss much about her personal life and who also didn't keep her personal items in her own house. It looked like she had something to hide. It didn't have to be criminal, it could be something too embarrassing or humiliating to be made public. He was quite sure that her personal items were in that storage place. Tindall doubted if there were any secrets in her laptop, since someone who was as secretive as Mrs. Davies wouldn't put intimate or confidential items in a computer since it could be hacked.

It was close to 4:00 pm on Tindall's car radio and he called All Star Storage on his cell phone in the parking lot at Headquarters. The office itself closed at 6:00 pm but the lot itself was open until 9:00 pm. He decided to go there tomorrow morning, since he didn't like to check anything unless there were witnesses to avoid anything being tossed out by the courts. Tindall also decided to call Perez and Parkins later before he went home to tell them that they would meet early tomorrow to discuss what they found out.

Once back in his office, Tindall typed up his report on his computer, checked it to make sure that there were no grammatical or written errors in it and sent it to Capt. Carter. He would only send a daily report regarding Mrs. Davies only if he or Perez or Parkins had any new information. Checking his desk phone, he saw that Kathleen and Joseph Tallichet left him messages. Tindall left a love and kisses message with Kathleen and a message with Tallichet telling him that Saturday at 9:00 am would be perfectly fine. He liked the fact that Tallichet would schedule Saturday appointments since during the week he didn't want to schedule anything during regular business hours.

Feeling his hair, he noted that he would have to get his haircut this week. Since the Olde Barber Shoppe in the Central District was open until 6:00 pm on weekdays

Tindall would need to go on Saturday as well. Normally, he and Kathleen went to the Farmers' Market on Saturday morning and then he would go to the library afterwards. Well, Tindall thought, Kathleen will have to go to the Farmers' Market on her own.

On Sunday, it would be his turn to go to church with Kathleen. He was Missouri Synod Lutheran and proud of it and she was Anglican and proud of it, since her church, All Souls, had pulled out of the Episcopal Church USA and was now part of the Anglican Church of North America. Kathleen wasn't unduly grieved over it, since the Episcopal Church had moved in a direction that she didn't support. She was progressive in some issues and not in other issues. When her parents found out about the separation, they were disappointed and Amy didn't care either way. Tindall mentally noted that Missouri had its own separation movement during the Seminex controversy in the 1970s when pastors, seminary professors, administrators and laymen either left or were kicked out of Missouri due to doctrinal issues. Grandpa and Grandma Tindall didn't support the people who left or were kicked out and told him that if what happened hadn't happened Missouri would have ended up a mess similar to the ELCA or the Episcopal Church.

I'm thinking of theology at a time like this, Tindall yawned. He was a bit tired but there were still things to do before he went home. He walked Mrs. Davies' laptop and her black notebook down to the Crime Lab. Only seeing Ann Mullens, Tindall brightly called out, "Hello again Ann! Where's your partner in crime?"

Laughing, Ann replied, "He stepped out for a moment.

Not for a smoke, since he doesn't smoke. I don't keep track of him since he sets his own hours."

"You're pulling my leg. You put a tether on him the last time we met."

"I may have, but he wouldn't dare. I see that you have a laptop and a black notebook for us to look at."

"Yes. The laptop belonged to Barbara Davies and she kept her usernames and passwords in the notebook. How long will it take for you to go through it?"

"Depends on how much stuff is in the laptop. We'll have to look at it and since it's close to closing time, we'll have an answer for you tomorrow. By the way, we're still going through Davies' Smartphone."

"Thanks, and good evening to you and Chuck. By the way," Tindall said with a smile, "why does it seem that I usually only see you two in the Crime Lab?"

"It's because all of the worker bees are in the back slaving away," Ann replied with a laugh. "You know perfectly well that rank has its privileges."

"Touché," noted Tindall as he walked back to his office. Police officers his rank and above had offices that weren't the best but were better than being stuck in a cube. Besides, St. Marys was his and Kathleen's home and they didn't want to leave. Yawning again, Tindall noted the work he had to finish before going home. He would get Perez's and Parkins' information in the meeting tomorrow. After wrapping everything up, Tindall drove home.

5

"Come in," Lillian Rogers said as Perez walked in to her office with a crate. As the accounts supervisor at Hunnibell Dairy she had a schedule that was frantic on some days and calm on other days. When her secretary informed her that a Sgt. Mike Perez of the Police Department wanted to see her she was surprised. Mrs. Rogers liked to say that the only times she was ever in a court room was for either speeding tickets or jury duty and she wanted to keep it that way.

"Would you care for something to drink, Sergeant?" Mrs. Rogers calmly asked as the two of them sat down.

"No thank you," replied Perez. "I'm here because we have questions regarding a Mrs. Barbara Davies due to the nature of her passing. Unfortunately, I wouldn't be able to say anything more than that. We were advised that she worked in your department as an accounts specialist."

"I heard about Barbara's passing and all of us are shocked by it. She is, I mean was a very good employee and nice on a personal level. It's also strange that one of our trucks was involved in the accident."

"Fortunately, the driver wasn't at fault. She didn't have any work issues?"

"Oh, not at all. Her work was very good and she was

very skilled in handling the accounting challenges of our department. She had been here for about twelve years and I had been her supervisor for the entire time. Barbara started with this department right after college. Our department is small since our organization isn't huge like some of our competitors such as Dean Foods, and because of that we're close knit."

"I've heard that close knit can sometimes translate into Peyton Place."

"Well, we're nothing at all like Peyton Place," Mrs. Rogers replied with a smile. "For one thing, we get along well with each other and for another thing, I won't tolerate any disruptions since the business comes first. I'm surprised that you know anything about Peyton Place due to your age."

Perez laughed. "My parents were Peyton Place fans ever since the first movie came out. They never read the original novel, but they've seen the TV show as well as the made-for-TV movies."

"I was never a fan of Peyton Place at all. The first movie was bad, the second movie was worse and the TV junk was the worst of the lot. I don't know if Barbara was a fan of Peyton Place at all."

"Did Barbara discuss much about her personal life?"

"Not really. She did talk about Mr. Davies but not a lot about herself. She was friendly but distant. You knew not to ask certain types of personal questions."

"Like family?"

"Correct," responded Mrs. Rogers as she sipped her tea. "All that I knew was that her parents were dead and she either had no other relatives or she wasn't close to them."

"Did she provide a contact person for emergency purposes?"

"Of course. The contact person that she gave was a friend from college and after she married Mr. Davies he became her contact person."

"Can I take a look at her desk?" Perez asked as he rose from his chair.

"By all means," said Mrs. Rogers as she rose from her chair in turn. "Follow me."

Mrs. Rogers and Perez walked out her office and he followed her down to an area filled with cubicles. Stopping at one Mrs. Rogers said, "This is Barbara's cube. We wanted to wait for a bit before calling Mr. Davies to see if he wanted to pick up her personal things or if he wanted us to ship them. You probably also want to ensure that we give our authorization for you to go through her things without a search warrant."

"You're right. We received Mr. Davies' consent to go through Mrs. Davies' personal items already."

"You have it." Before Mrs. Rogers left Perez asked, "Regarding the friend Mrs. Davies originally used as a contact person, do you still have their information available?"

"We do and I'll have it for you in a moment."

"Thanks."

As Mrs. Rogers walked back to her office Perez scanned Mrs. Davies' cubicle. There were a few pictures of her with Mr. Davies and other people, presumably friends and acquaintances. In most of them Mrs. Davies was smiling and enjoying herself. He looked through her desk, going through her files and paperwork wearing latex gloves. Nothing of interest, just business work and the usual pads, pens and other office supplies.

Perez noted that Mrs. Davies' computer was an all in one desktop. Unplugging it, he gently placed it in the crate. He also placed in it a black notebook that she used to keep track of her computer passwords. After he finished and waited for Mrs. Rogers to come back he received a call from his Smartphone. "Hello?"

"This is Frank. How's it going at the dairy?"

"I didn't find anything, but I'm bringing in Davies' computer and the black notebook that she used to keep track of her computer passwords."

"Well, Chuck and Ann will have some more work to do. Anything else?"

"Turns out that before Mrs. Davies gave Mr. Davies as her emergency contact she used a college friend. I'll phone it in to Jim once I get it from Mrs. Rogers."

"That's fine and since it's late in the day, Jim can follow it up tomorrow if he wants. We'll meet tomorrow morning and discuss what we found. See you tomorrow."

"Same here." As Perez hung up, he saw Mrs. Rogers

walking back to him. Handing him a slip of paper, she said, "Here is the contact information. It may be out of date since it has been a few years."

Thanking Mrs. Rogers, Perez then called Parkins. "Hello Jim, it's Mike."

"What happened?"

"I have another person that we have to interview. The only thing is that the information is probably out of date. She was Davies' original emergency contact for her job before she used her husband. Her name at the time was Gwendoline Nancarrow and her address was 222 S.5th St., Apt. 2 in St. Marys and her telephone number was (269)555-6817."

"I'll check her information out and I'll see her tomorrow."

"Thanks."

Perez hung up and walked out of Hunnibell Dairy with the open crate. Once he dropped the crate off at the Crime Lab, he had to jot down a brief report about what happened today for tomorrow's meeting. It wouldn't take long, just a few minutes. Then he would be done for the day and go back home to be with Sheila and the kids. Kevin and Angelica were twelve-year-old fraternal twins. Both he and Sheila were concerned about them getting mixed up in drugs, alcohol or sex. He, along with Tindall and Parkins, had seen too many young people ending up on the street, jail or a graveyard due to any or all of those three things.

Very shortly we'll have to think about high school for

the kids, Perez thought. Since he and Sheila were both Catholic, the local Catholic high school, St. Anselm's, was a no brainer; Sheila was also a school counselor at St. Anselm's. The cost was reasonable for a private high school, and the school itself had an excellent reputation both locally and statewide. There were also two Lutheran high schools and two public high schools in the county, along with Hamilton University's high school. Everything's going well, Perez thought as he drove into the parking lot at Headquarters.

As he stepped out of his car his Smartphone rang. "Hello darling!"

"Sheila! You just caught me walking into the building to finish up. What's up?"

"We just wanted to know if you'll be late."

"No, I'll be home in about an hour or so. Need for me to pick anything up from Koditscheks?"

"We're fine. Chao."

What a woman and kids, Perez smiled as he walked into Headquarters.

6

Another long day, Parkins mused as he drove back to Headquarters. He interviewed three of Barbara Davies' friends today and was going to interview tomorrow Gwendoline Nancarrow, the college friend that Davies used as an emergency contact prior to her marriage. He would find out tomorrow what Frank and Mike found out.

The interviews went well, and the information that the three women gave a glimpse of what kind of person they thought Davies to be. They were all the same age and roughly came from the same background as Davies. One of them, Melanie Hunter, graduated from college with undergraduate and graduate degrees and worked at different organizations while the third, Sierra Bassett, was the owner of a bookstore in downtown St. Marys.

Melanie Hunter was the first interviewee. An auto claims adjuster, she worked out of the local branch of a major insurance company. She, along with the others, was perfectly willing to give as much time as needed to answer Parkins' questions. Her statement is below:

I first met Barbara around the time I started out as a claims adjuster trainee about twelve years ago. It's long work with extended periods of time out on the road. Even with the new technologies available, you're still going to spend a lot of away time. That's probably why I'm still not married. My apologies for rambling. I'm very lively and outgoing, I love to roam around the downtown area on weekends when I'm not busy working. It was on a weekend when I was in Hedermans Bageri at the University Inn. I was looking as the pastries when someone accidently bumped into me. She apologized and we began to talk about the pastries and other nonsensical things. I liked her, I truly did. She said that she was Barbara Davies and she was starting out as an accounting specialist at Hunnibell Dairy. We were two working girls starting out of college.

Barbara was a kind and decent person to me as well to those who dealt with her, but she was closed in terms of letting other people in emotionally or personally. You sensed that she would only let you in so far. Ernie, her husband, is far different. He's far more outgoing, the kind of person who will make friends within a few seconds. Barbara never talked about her family and the one and only time that I asked, she simply said with a forced laugh, "Ask me no questions and I'll tell you no lies."

I don't want you or anyone else to think that Barbara was an oddball. She wasn't. She was a person who had her special place in the world. I don't know if you know this, but neither she nor Ernie are religious people. I'm a Christian and all three of us enjoyed each other's company. In fact, I encouraged Barbara to ask Ernie out on a date. She hated parties and when she would go, she was the proverbial wallflower. We were at a party and I noticed that Ernie was trying not to stare at her. I whispered, "Look, Barbara! That guy over there is trying not to look at you!" She said, "He looks interesting." I then said, "Well if he looks 'interesting,' then you need to go grab him!" After some hemming and hawing she did and the rest is history.

I called Ernie and left a message giving my condolences. Barbara's the first friend I had who has passed away. I'm more concerned for him than I am for myself. When a friend passed away it's terrible, but it's even worse when it's a spouse or family member. I'm saying prayers for the two of them and I hope that Barbara is at peace.

Sam Carroll, the second interviewee, was a paralegal. Her interview took place in her office in downtown St. Marys:

My name is Sam Carroll. My actual name is Samantha but everyone calls me Sam. I'm a paralegal with my own practice in downtown St. Marys, a proud Steinhardt College of Law grad. I decided to become a paralegal because I was interested in the law field but I didn't want to stand up in courtroom filled with strangers and people I barely knew to defend cases. I'm shy and introverted. Oh, I'm also engaged and the wedding will be in early spring. I didn't think that it would happen!

How I met Barbara? Well, one summer Saturday about ten years ago I was walking in Southerne Park when a jogger ahead of me slipped and fell. Concerned, I rushed over to her to see if she was ok. Thankfully, she wasn't hurt and we began to talk. Her name was Barbara Davies and she was a very good conversationalist, able to move with the conversation, never boring. There was similarities and differences. It's a cliché, but variety is the spice of life.

Even though Barbara was somewhat reserved and

withdrawn, I sensed that she wasn't always like that. I sensed that she was more lively and outgoing previously that she currently was. Introverts can generally sense if someone is like us or if they're an extrovert. We can also be very lively and outgoing to those who know us well or if we are in situations that aren't challenging to our sense of space.

As for Barbara's past, she never discussed her family or when she was younger, except for the period from her college time and up. Anything from that period onwards she would discuss, sometimes with laughter and sometimes with groans. She loved talking about her husband Ernie. He was truly her world and it was obvious to me that they loved each other very much. He's a good guy and it's terrible that he has to go through this. It's even more terrible what happened to Barbara.

On Saturdays, Barbara, Melanie, Sierra and I would go out and about. We would generally do breakfast or lunch. My apologies, Melanie is Melanie Hunter and Sierra is Sierra Bassett. Melanie's an auto claim adjuster and Sierra's a bookstore owner. There was also a fifth person who came along a few times, let's see, her name was Gwen or Gwennie Nankin? I don't know much about her except that she was a friend of Barbara's from college. She lives in the area, I know that, since I've seen her around once or twice. St. Marys is an odd place since it's big enough that you can lose yourself but small enough that you can see different people from time to time.

One story about Barbara that sticks in my mind involves me telling her one day early in our relationship not to do a Linda Severinsen. It was in regards to something I can't recall. It's a saying my mother used to say and it was a nonsense name, much like you'll tell someone not to be a Debbie Downer; my mother's family is Swedish, by the way. Well, once I said that, Barbara's mood began to change. Her face hardened and there was an odd glint in her eyes and she began to hyperventilate. After a minute or so she returned back to her normal self and we didn't discuss it further. I wasn't scared for my personal safety since it looked like she didn't even know that I was there. She never explained what happened and I never asked. You know, detective, that sometimes in relationships it's best to let sleeping dogs lie.

If you need any more information about Barbara, you need to speak to Melanie and Sierra. Oh, so you already have their contact information? The only other person that I know of who may have more information than we have would be Gwen or Gwennie. I don't even know if Nankin is her last name or something else. She knew Barbara longer than we did and since she was her friend from college, Barbara may have been more comfortable talking about her past with her than with us. I respected Barbara's privacy. Don't hesitate to come back if you have any further questions.

Sierra Bassett, the third interviewee, was interviewed at the Ivy Book Shoppe in downtown St. Marys:

I'm Sierra Bassett, and I'm the owner of the Ivy Book Shoppe. I've worked in bookstores ever since high school. In the summer I worked fulltime at Goransson's, and fulltime round the clock after high school. Not interested in going to college. I always wanted to run and own my own bookstore, and I was able to take over Ivy a year ago after the owner, Sally Hansen, retired. Sally's the only person offhand who I can't think anything bad about. Before taking over, I had worked at Ivy for fifteen years. Prior to that, I worked at the University bookstore for four years.

I've done everything at a bookstore, from stocking the shelves and cleaning the store to manning the cash register. Since I knew from high school that I wanted to own my own bookstore, that meant that I had to learn every part of the business. College wasn't part of the deal in my book.

I first met Barbara right in this store. It was the late part of the year about ten years ago and she came in to get some calendars. The reason why Ivy, along with Goransson's is still open is because we provide services that the big box bookstores can't or won't provide. We along with the University Bookstore do special orders to find books around the world. The big box stores don't do that. She was trying to find a special calendar and none of the other stores had it. Even Goransson's didn't have it. It turned that we had one left. After that, Barbara became a regular customer. We chatted and shot the breeze and after a while we became good friends.

As for Barbara's personality, she was even tempered and lively. Very funny and intelligent. Even though she knew that I wasn't college bred like her she respected me and didn't try to talk down to me. Some people look at you like dirt if you don't go to college. My father before he died always said that he wanted me to be a doctor.

Though Barbara was also kind and decent, there was also a side to her that you couldn't reach. You could only go so far and she would politely yet firmly warn you about pushing further. It was about her family and her early life. I was very comfortable about talking about when I was younger and my family. She was never interested in doing so. I don't know if they were all dead or if she had a falling out with them. All I knew about her past was that she wasn't a St. Marys native and she didn't go to school here. She said that she was a Michiganian or Michigander, I never know which one is correct, but she was cagey in terms of what part of Michigan she came from.

The one person who may know something more about her past may be Gwen, Gail? I can't think of her first name and I can't remember her last name. She came along with Barbara, Melanie, Sam and I sometimes for Saturday breakfast or lunch. Very prim and proper even when slumming but not stuck up, someone who drank champagne at a bar while you drank malt liquor. Even though she was the same age as us, she was an "old soul," someone who was middle aged in a twenty -or thirtysomething body. We weren't happy that she wasn't able to spend more time with us. She had a quiet humor and listened more than she talked. If anyone knew Barbara's secrets it would be Gwen or Gail.

One final thing. Even though Barbara and I were irreligious and I'm agnostic, if He exists then I hope that Barbara is at peace. I may even go to the Catholic Church downtown and light a candle for her. My family's Catholic, you know. Sometimes I even pray.

Parkins typed up his interview notes and saved them on his computer at Headquarters. After doing so, he called his wife Millie. "I'm coming home at last!"

"Took you long enough!" Millie laughed.

"I'll see you in a few minutes."

"Yeah, and don't stay at Koditscheks too long."

Chucking, Parkins hung up and went home.

7

"This is delicious," purred Tindall as he ate some leftover timpani cooked by Kathleen a few days ago. Both he and Kathleen were eating dinner in the dining room, finishing off the timpani and drinking cherry juice. Tindall loved good food and would have been seriously overweight had he not been strict about his diet. A bowl of high fiber hot cereal and two glasses of milk for breakfast, fruit and either nuts, popcorn or salad for lunch and a heavy meal for dinner. He also liked to cook when he had the time and he rotated the cooking with Kathleen.

Kathleen also liked good food and like Tindall she didn't enjoy heavy or rich food. She was also careful about her eating habits since she didn't want to go to an early grave due to poor food. She roughly ate the same way as Tindall did so they complimented each other regarding food. She loved to cook from scratch when she had the time, which usually restricted her from all out cooking until Sundays and holidays. Old Peter knew how to cook well since he noted that particular skill kept him from having to eat out of cans and later frozen food.

After dinner, Kathleen asked as Tindall cleaned up, "Who's assigned to the Davies case? It's going to be on the Evening News's front page tomorrow and it's already on the stations. Even though I know some of the board members of Rothmann very well, that kind of news has to be on the front page."

Tindall flashed a smile. "You're looking at him. The police chief decided to assign the case to me. Mike and Jim Parkins are working on it with me."

"And the police chief probably assigned you to the case due to your connections to the new CEO at Rothmann?"

"Bingo. This is a high-profile case since this is the first time that anyone can recall that someone has been murdered at Rothmann," Tindall concluded as he finished up the dishes. After he was done, he walked back into the dining room and sat down next to her. "I've talked enough about my day. How was your day?"

"The same old same old," Kathleen replied in a bored tone. "I didn't have to rescue cats from trees nor ticket people spitting on the sidewalk. I just had to run a media empire."

"And I didn't have to interview Madonna nor did I have to talk about the best way to raise people from the dead from best-selling author Kevin Trudeau. I just had to work a murder case." Hilarious laughter then roared from both of them.

"On a more serious note," Kathleen inquired, "can you say anything about the Davies case?"

"Nope. We still investigating and I'll give a report to Capt. Carter tomorrow after our meeting. It'll be interesting to see what Mike and Jim found out."

"Journalism and police work are similar in a few ways. You do an investigation, spend hours, days, weeks and months on it, and then you have to present it to your higher authority to sign off of it. Did you ever think, Frank, that you would have married a journalist?"

Smiling, Tindall replied, "I didn't know who I would marry and I didn't even know if I would get married at all. Marriage is a lot of work and you have to put sweat equity into it. There are times when I get home I just want to relax and nothing else. But I can't do that, Katy, because you're my kinnikin and I don't want to hurt you."

Kathleen agreed as she sat in one of the dining room chairs. "I feel the same way. Sometimes, you're so tired mentally or physically you just want to shut other people out. But you can't shut people on and off at your convenience. That's using people and God will hold you accountable for that."

"You're right." In a light tone, Tindall asked, "So what do you want to do the rest of the evening? Music, TV or reading?"

"Oh, I prefer just some quiet time reading a good book."

"No problem." Tindall and Kathleen went to their separate book cases and took out a book to read. Afterwards, they sat down in their recliners and began to read. Tindall favored foreign writers such as Henning Mankell and Leif G.W. Persson and also loved ghost, horror and mystery stories. He also liked family biographies, political science and current affairs, and theological books. Kathleen liked classic literature and also shared a love of political science and current affairs along with theological books. Tindall was interested in purchasing some of Missouri theologian C.F.W. Walther's theological writings off of Amazon. He also looked forward in the future of purchasing the entire collection of Martin Luther's works from the Concordia Publishing website.

Kathleen was reading Gary Taubes' The Case Against Sugar, which pointed out the danger of sugar in society due to its damaging effects on people's health. It was an interesting book and the writer was making a good argument, but she subscribed to the idea that eating too much of any food, vitamin or mineral could be damaging or even dangerous to your health. Kathleen's attitude towards food, which was also shared by Tindall, was that you could eat anything you wanted as long as it was in moderation.

She loved reading since she was a kid and also loved reading books written about people who had ideas differing from hers. Kathleen considered it important to be able to defend your point of view based on logic and fact instead of emotion, which she learned from her parents along with Old Peter. Tindall agreed with her and had no patience with people who were either unwilling or unable to defend their points of view. Grandpa and Grandma Tindall always taught him to be able to defend his point of view with logic and facts.

Tindall was reading "Manhole 69" from The Complete Stories of J.G. Ballard. He loved short stories and enjoyed collecting short story collections. Some short story collections that he didn't want to keep after reading them, such as the Everyman's Library version of Leo Tolstoy's short fiction, were donated to the St. Marys Public Library. To him, a short story collection was like a box of chocolates: one or two at a time was perfect but more than that would be too much. Tindall, like Kathleen, loved collecting books and their bookshelves revealed loved and cherished books.

Tindall's favorite book was the Bible and it was the only book that he had read for years from cover to cover that never bored him. This was why he waited for a certain period of time before reading a book again to avoid the boredom factor. It was the second time reading Ballard and Tindall didn't like science fiction, but he liked Ballard because his science fiction was more in the category of weird than science fiction. Indeed, some of Ballard's short stories were more in the area of fantastic fiction then in science fiction.

Both Tindall and Kathleen looked and the clock and saw that it was 9:00 pm. Time for bed, both noted to themselves, for they were both early risers needing to get to their jobs no later than 8:00 am.

"It's the end of another day, Frank," Kathleen noted with a yawn. "We'll both have to go back to work and make some money."

"You're right, Katy," replied Tindall with a similar yawn. "We'll have some more work to do regarding the Davies case and we'll be meeting regarding the case before we go back on the road."

"I'll see you upstairs. Don't make me wait too long, sweetie pie," said Kathleen with a grin as she went upstairs. Tindall went into the kitchen and drank some water straight from the tap. As he did so, Kathleen did a quick shower and teeth brushing, finishing it off with dressing in her pajamas. She found it odd that she liked pajamas and

Frank liked nightshirts. He loved the flannel nightshirts from L.L. Bean and the lighter fabric ones from Penney's. She loved quick showers and Frank liked baths. Both of them liked fragrance free soaps such as Dr. Bronner's and Kirk's.

Waiting for Frank, Kathleen enjoyed laying in the bed that they shared together. Their marriage was going well and both of them were prepared and willing to make the necessary compromises to make it work. They also viewed marriage as a covenant and not as a contract, a commitment or a convenience that could be disposed of at any time. They lived in the house that Frank grew up in with his grandparents and Kathleen enjoyed sharing a part of his life prior to them meeting together. She inherited Old Peter's house and sometimes on vacations she and Frank would spend intimate times together there.

Kathleen would never sell Old Peter's house since Meldrims had lived and died there ever since The Founder, Peter Heil Meldrim, built it in the 1880s. She considered writing a history of the Meldrims but something or other led her to not sitting down and doing it. Perhaps I'll commission someone from Hamilton's History Department to write it or a free-lance local writer like Bruna Vanden Boeynants. Unlimited access to the family papers and the Evening News's archives in return for my approval of the manuscript before publication. Since I'm on the Board of Trustees at Hamilton it wouldn't be an issue and I'll get what I want.

Kathleen's musings ended once Tindall entered their bedroom. He changed into his nightshirt and slid into bed with Kathleen after brushing his teeth. They kissed each other and said "Nighty-Night" to each other before falling asleep.

8

The streets of St. Marys on Wednesday morning by 8:00 am were filled with those either trying to get to work on time of those already fretting about being late. Downtown St. Marys didn't begin to show signs of a bustling and hustling nature until after 9:00 am when most of the offices began to open and even more so when the shops began to open at 10:00 am. Even Police Headquarters didn't begin to show signs of life until after 8:00 am. During the late-night shift, there were usually few people at Headquarters and the people there mostly manned the jail section area. The Crime Lab only had two or three people on staff to handle the usual tasks and the same was true for the Records Department.

There were also skeleton late-night shifts at the Fire Department and the Sheriff's Office and there were no one at the county courthouse or the Medical Examiner's Office late at night except for security guards keeping watch. Weeknights in the city and county tended to be quiet and peaceful and there were very few issues even on the weekends. The partiers and bingers tended to be more restrained unlike those in Kalamazoo or Grand Rapids. And for those few who stepped out of line, well, the police and the Sheriff's Office would deal with them and the county prosecutor's office wouldn't hesitate to prosecute them to the fullest.

But Perez wasn't thinking of any of this, he was just thinking about leaving Sheila and the kids for another few hours for another day. Driving to Headquarters, he noted that it was close to 8:00 am. He would arrive in about five minutes with some time to spare. Perez hoped that he and Sheila would be able to have some time together on the weekend but it all depended on the status of the case. If more work needed to be done, then it would have to wait until the next available weekend. Weekends were the best time since Kevin was busy with Trail Life USA meetings and Angelica was busy hanging out with her friends. Changes in the Boy Scouts led to the troop that Kevin was in at St. Anselm's Catholic Church changing over to Trail Life USA. Both Perez and Sheila approved of the change and were active supporters in raising money and assisting on weekends when they could.

Perez arrived at his desk at 7:55 am and turned on his computer. He scanned his e-mails, answering those that needed a response, and reviewed his interview regarding Lillian Rogers. The top brass said that at some time in the future the detectives and some other departments would have laptops but he would believe it when he saw it. He also said hello to the new arrivals that he saw and waited for Tindall and Parkins to arrive. Both arrived at 8:00 am and their meeting began at 8:15 am.

Tindall began the meeting with a question, "What information did you get from Mrs. Davies' job and friends?"

Parkins answered, "The people that I spoke to—Melanie Hunter, Sam Carroll and Sierra Bassett—all stated that Davies didn't like to talk about her past prior to arriving in

St. Marys. Nor did she like to talk about her family."

Perez agreed. "Her boss Mrs. Rogers said the same thing. Polite and friendly but guarded."

"I got the same vibes from Mr. Davies," Tindall noted thoughtfully. "Are there any other people that you or Jim need to interview?"

"There's no one else for me to interview. The other people at Hunnibell Dairy gave me the same information that Mrs. Rogers gave me. By the way, Jim, were you able to interview Ms. Nancarrow yesterday?"

"No," replied Parkins, but I'll interview her after our meeting."

"Who's Ms. Nancarrow?" Tindall asked with surprise.

"She's Gwendoline Nancarrow, a friend of Mrs. Davies from college. Davies used her as an emergency contact at Hunnibell Dairy before she got married. I got her new address."

"That's fine, and after our meeting, I'll brief Capt. Carter of what's occurring and we'll have to take a look at some of Mrs. Davies' stuff at a storage place she rented. Mike, I want you to come with me since it may take two people to bring her stuff back."

"Ok, and while you're briefing Capt. Carter, I'll ask Ann and Chuck about the status of the stuff they're working on for us regarding Davies."

"I'll see you again in a few minutes and Jim, I'll see you later this morning." The three men moved on.

9

Pen in her mouth, focused on her work, Gwendoline Nancarrow worked busily in her office reviewing which hymns she would play in the Sunday services at St. John's United Methodist Church in south St. Marys when she was interrupted by the church secretary. "Gwen, there's a cop that needs to speak to you."

"You can send him in, Maddie." After a minute or two Maddie returned with a tall dark-skinned policeman in civilian clothes and then quickly left. "Ms. Nancarrow, my name is Detective Jim Parkins from the St. Marys Police Department and I have some questions regarding Mrs. Barbara Davies."

Sadness lined her face. "You can call me Gwennie, Detective. Please sit down," Gwennie said as she moved her hand over to an empty chair. Parkins noted that the office was cheery but it was obvious that serious and thoughtful work was done here.

"I knew you would come," Gwennie unhappily noted. "After I heard what happened, I called Ernie and gave him my condolences. I also wanted to know when the family hour and service would be so I could pay my respects. I also put in a request for a prayer to be said for Barbara and her family at the upcoming services. What do you want to know?"

"I'm interested about finding out about Barbara's life, particularly if anyone had any grievances towards her, or if she had anything that she was worried about."

Gwennie wrinkled her face and thought for a minute or two. Then she replied, "Barbara wasn't worried about anything as far as I knew. If she did and didn't tell me, then she may have told Ernie about it. Or she may have told her other friends such as Sam, Sierra or Melanie. People may talk about private things to you and not to others and vice versa. It is their right to do so."

"So how did you and Barbara meet each other?"

"We met in college. We both went to Marygrove College in Detroit. I was a music major and she was a business major focusing on accounting. We met in a history class and before the class began we would chat about different things and we decided after the class ended to keep in touch; shortly thereafter we became very good friends. I come from Metro Detroit, Mt. Clemens to be precise, and I still have friends there."

"Did she talk about her life before college or family and friends prior to it?"

"Oh no, she never did," Gwennie asserted with a serious look on her face. "I tried once and she politely but firmly refused. She didn't have a problem with me talking about my life prior to Marygrove. My parents are still living and they and I both immigrated from England when I was still an infant. We are Methodists and that is why I am the organist at St. John's. I always wanted to serve in the Church and since I love listening, playing and composing music, being a church organist would be an excellent way for me to do so. In fact, the organist at Historic Trinity Lutheran Church in Detroit, Karl Osterland, a fine gentleman whom I know, is also a composer and some of his pieces have been published and performed. I am also a member of the American Guild of Organists," Gwennie concluded with pride shining from her face.

"When was the last time you saw or heard from Barbara?"

"I called her a few days prior to her passing and we spoke for a few minutes. We talked about the gang getting together. Since all of us are busy and we all have things to do, particularly with Sam since she is engaged and Melanie is sometimes out of town for extended periods of time, it can be difficult for us to find a Saturday to meet. I am happy that I had a chance to hear her voice one last time." Gwennie then began to sob. Parkins moved over to her out of concern but was stopped by Gwennie's raised hand. "Thank you, but I am fine. I should not be worrying about myself but about Ernie."

"No one wins when someone loses their life," Parkins thoughtfully noted. "You seem so reserved and Barbara was so lively. How did the two of you end up becoming best friends?"

"Well," Gwennie answered with a gentle smile, "chalk and cheese sometimes attract each other as my mother likes to say. Also, I was an only child and my closest relatives other than my parents were back in England, so I had to rely on myself and Barbara was in the same position. Also, I saved her life at Marygrove via the Heimlich maneuver when she almost choked to death on a piece of food."

"My final question. Did Barbara say anything about where she came from?"

"All she said was that she was from the Mid-Michigan area near Lansing."

Rising from his chair, Parkins said, "Thank you for your time, Gwennie. We'll be in touch if we have any additional questions." They shook hands and Parkins walked out of Gwennie's office.

Nice woman, Parkins noted as he drove back to Headquarters. Very prim and proper but not off putting. Honest too, just like Davies' other friends. Parkins had been a policeman for enough years to know if someone was lying to him or was a bad guy or worse. It was clear from all the conversations that he had that Davies had a past that she didn't want to discuss. It may or mayn't have been criminal, but something happened.

Parkins decided that when he got back to Headquarters, he would do a search regarding Davies to see if anything came up. Even if he didn't find anything criminal it could just mean that she wasn't caught and prosecuted for the crime. And if he found anything, he would call Frank and give him the information. Shouldn't take more than a few minutes, Parkins thought as he arrived at Headquarters.

After walking in and coming to his desk, Parkins began to search various databases for any information regarding Barbara Davies after checking his voice and e-mails. What he found was quite interesting but not surprising. Shaking his head, he called Tindall to give him the information. .

10

"I'm sorry, Mike," Ann Mullins said wryly, but we're still working on the Davies' stuff. From the way it looks, we should be done with everything by tomorrow. I'll tell Chuck and the kids that you said hello and say hello to Sheila and the kids from us."

"Same here," replied Perez as he walked out the door and down the corridor to Tindall's office. Tindall was getting ready to walk out with some crates and latex gloves when Perez arrived. "So the Crime Lab is still working on Davies' stuff?" he asked Perez.

"Yeah, but Ann said that everything should be done by tomorrow."

"Well, they're doing it as quickly as they can. They also probably have some other things that they're working on. Anyway, we got to stop by Davies' storage place to see what she stored there."

"Agreed." Tindall and Perez each took a crate and a pair of latex gloves and walked out to Tindall's car, a new Fiat 500x. They then drove to Brown's Storage Place on County Highway 23. The place looked clean and spotless, Tindall noted as he drove through the open gate. Seeing the office on Perez' side, Tindall parked next to it and the two of them came out and walked inside. A middle-aged woman was quickly typing at the front desk as Tindall and Perez walked in, Tindall hearing the clack, clack, clack on the keyboard. He cleared his throat and the woman immediately jumped to attention.

Embarrassed, the woman said, "My apologies! I hope that you haven't been waiting long? I was just working on some accounts when you came in. My name's Angeline Brown and I'm one of the owners. And who are you, may I ask?"

"I'm Lt. Frank Tindall from the St. Marys Police Department and this is my partner Sgt. Mike Perez," Tindall said as he and Perez showed their badges. "We're here to ask some questions regarding Mrs. Barbara Davies and to check her storage bin."

"I heard about what happened to Mrs. Davies and it was a shock. I do have to say that after Mrs. Davies did the paperwork to rent her storage bin, I only saw her a few times and the times that I did see her she was always very polite and nice. She mailed in her monthly payments to us. No airs at all. I'll ask Willie and the crew if they ever talked to her."

"Who's Willie?"

Ms. Brown blushed. "Oh, Willie's my husband, the worst half. He's mainly out and about, making sure that nothing's falling off and that the area's well kept. We can't have sloppiness or dirt around. It's bad for business."

Perez laughed. "Since you're by yourself, can you tell us where Mrs. Davies' storage area is located?"

"Never you mind that, as my mother used to say, I'll just close up for a few minutes to show you. This is one of the nice things about being a business owner, you sometimes get to set your own hours." Ms. Brown then closed the office and escorted Tindall and Perez to Mrs. Davies' storage bin. Tindall noticed that it was close to the office but those in the office couldn't see what Mrs. Davies was doing in her storage bin. Neat, Tindall thought. She would be able to come in and out quickly and without Ms. Brown nor the rest of the staff knowing what was going on.

"Well, if you need anything just call me. I'll be in the office and I'll ask the crew if Mrs. Davies said anything to them. I didn't ask you, lieutenant, if you or your partner had search warrants since we got nothing to hide here and we don't want any police problems. Say goodbye once you're done," Ms. Brown concluded before handing a set of keys to Tindall and walking back to the office.

"Let's see what Mrs. Davies put in here," Perez said as Tindall opened up the storage bin door. He noted that there wasn't a lot of things in the bin, just two portable plastic storage containers. Neither of the bins were clear, so the only way to see what was in them was to open up the top covers. "Frank, I'll go through this one here."

"Ok," Tindall replied as he opened up the second storage container. He first went through two scrapbooks that had no information under Mrs. Davies, but had information regarding celebrities and different movies and TV shows. From the items put in the scrapbook Tindall saw that both were completed around the time Mrs. Davies was in high school. He also saw that the name Linda Severinsen was written on the front page of both scrapbooks.

Tindall figured that Ms. Severinsen was a friend or relative of Mrs. Davies and the latter may have been given the scrapbooks as a gift or present. Setting the scrapbooks aside, he then turned to the four high school yearbooks. Mrs. Davies wasn't listed in any of the yearbooks but Linda Severinsen was in all of them. The high school was small, so the freshman through senior classes weren't large. Tindall noted that Ms. Severinsen looked remarkably like Mrs. Davies based on the pictures at Mrs. Davies' home and the autopsy photos.

Intrigued, Tindall then went through a file at the bottom of the storage container. Here he found letters, progress reports, report cards, reports and school work all in Linda Severinsen's name. Tindall wondered if Ms. Severinsen and Mrs. Davies were the same person or just relatives. He received his answer when he found an order issued by the Honorable Jamie Heliste from the Family Division of the Oakland County Circuit Court on October 28, 1998 granting approval for Linda Severinsen's new name to be Barbara Russell. There was also a letter from the State of Michigan Vital Records Office dated December 7, 1998 confirming the new name along with a certified copy of the amended birth certificate. Confirmations from the Secretary of State office and the Social Security Adminstration regarding the name change were also in the file.

"Mike, can you come over here and take a look at this?" Tindall asked. "You'll probably find what I found to be very interesting." Perez walked over to Tindall and looked at the documents in the file. After reading them for a few minutes, Perez replied, "Looks like Davies was hiding or running from something."

"Exactly. What did you find in your storage container?"

"School records, letters and docs under Barbara Davies' name. From the docs, she started at Marygrove College about two years after graduating from high school. So, between graduating from high school to entering college she changed her name along with her birth certificate."

Tindall smiled. "Obviously, she wanted to disappear without a trace. Other than Jim, the only other person who's going to know about this is Capt. Carter. We need to keep this under our hats. It also means that we're going to have to investigate Ms. Linda Severinsen."

"From what you went through, where did Davies come from?"

"She looks like a native Michigander, but we're going to have to look through all of the Severinsen paperwork to see from which part of Michigan she came from. It's more than likely that no one else knows about her past considering how well she kept it a secret. She was also smart in not trying to reveal too much info to Mr. Davies and her friends. You tend to forget your lies."

"You're right about that!" Perez laughingly said. "We've caught quite a number of criminals who forgot about their lies. You ready to get out of here?"

"As my great grand pappy used to say, 'Let's went.'"

Tindall and Perez carried out the two storage containers and locked the storage bin. After returning the key to Ms.

Brown and putting the containers in the trunk, they drove back to Headquarters. On their way to Headquarters Tindall received a call from Parkins. "What's happening, Jim?"

"I just found out that Barbara Davies changed her name from Linda Severinsen."

"Mike and I found out the same thing. We're bringing back two storage containers Davies kept at a storage place. We'll go through all of the containers once we get back. See you in a minute or so."

"Ok."

Tindall hung up and put his cell phone back into his pocket. "That was Jim telling me that he found out the same thing that we also found out."

"It'll be interesting to see if all of this is connected to Davies' death."

"Maybe, maybe not. She could have been running from abuse, a bad relationship, a crappy hometown. We may never know."

Tindall and Perez lapsed into silence until they arrived at Headquarters. After arriving, they removed the containers out of the car trunk and carried them into Headquarters. Meeting with Parkins, they decided that Tindall would go through the Severinsen container and Perez and Parkins would go through the Davies container. Perez and Parkins commandeered an empty table close to their cubicles and began to go through the container's contents. Once the contents had been reviewed, the containers would be sent to the Records Department to be logged in as evidence.

Tindall read through the paperwork chronicling Linda Severinsen's life with interest. She was a member of the Drama and French Clubs in high school, a good student from Norrie Elementary School through Luther L. Wright High School, and a sociable person with a lot of friends. Ms. Severinsen, he noted, was a Yooper based on both schools being located in Ironwood. We'll have to call the police up there, Tindall thought, and see if she still had any relatives there. He didn't have any contacts in Ironwood but he knew that there wouldn't be any issues in getting the information needed from the local police there. Nothing scandalous or objectionable Tindall saw in the paperwork he read.

Glancing at his watch, Tindall noticed that it was noon and it was time for lunch. Calling Kathleen, he said, "How's your day going, Katy?"

"It's fine, and yours?"

"Nothing to complain about. We're still working on the Davies case. I'll be at home around 5:00 or such."

"I'll be waiting, snookums!"

"Ha, Ha!"

Tindall then hung up and then opened up one of his desk drawers. He took out some dates and salt and pepper cashews, and enjoyed his lunch. As he did so, he thought about the Christmas/New Years' party that he and Kathleen were already planning. His side of the family and friends would be invited along with Perez, Parkins, Capt. Carter and the rest of the police gang. Kathleen would invite her relatives and friends along with members of the Evening News family. They've done it ever since they had been married, which was only a few years, and everyone had thoroughly enjoyed the fun and friendship. Kathleen and Sheila were friends and they both got along well with Parkins' wife Millie. Tindall and Kathleen planned on mailing out the invitations to everyone by the middle of November.

At 12:30 Tindall resumed his work and finished going through all of Ms. Severinsen's paperwork in about an hour, jotting down notes as he read. He then reviewed the scrapbooks, finding them amusing but uninformative. The only other items needing to be reviewed were the yearbooks and photos. The yearbooks showed that Ms. Severinsen was a popular and outgoing woman based on the numerous photos that she was in along with the fact that there were numerous notes and signatures from her fellow student along with teachers and administrators.

Rubbing his chin thoughtfully, Tindall mused that this was a young woman who seemed to have good relations with both sides of the fence without antagonizing neither. A far different person from Barbara Davies. Brushing those thoughts aside, Tindall began to look through Ms. Severinsen's pictures. Some showed her as an infant, others as a child and still others as a teenager. The pictures varied, from group pictures, to family and friend pictures and solo pictures. There were also prom pictures either solo or with her prom date.

One picture drew Tindall's attention. It showed Ms.

Severinsen with three other girls her age and they all appeared to be high school juniors or seniors. It reminded Tindall of a picture, also in color, that he saw in one of the yearbooks. He found the same picture in Ms. Severinsen's 1996-1997 junior year book. There, the picture was captioned <u>Best Friends Forever</u>, just like on Ms. Severinsen's photo. Unfortunately, there were no other captions regarding the identities of the persons in either photo. A picture of happy and carefree young women, Tindall pondered. How long did they continue to be happy and carefree? Adulthood tended to reduce happiness and free schedules in a variety of ways.

Tindall took the picture and yearbook and walked out of his office to where Perez and Parkins were going through the second storage container. He asked, "Have you found anything?"

"Nothing yet," replied Parkins. There's nothing odd or out of place in this stuff, just letters from different people, old catalogs and pictures of Davies with Mr. Davies and other people."

"I second it," answered Perez with a shrug. "You found far more than we did. After I told Jim about Linda Severinsen, he told me about the almost violent reaction when her name was brought up by one of Davies' friends."

"Yes," Parkins continued, "the impression that I got was that something odd went on, and the fact that Davies and Severinsen were one and the same makes it more understandable. Mrs. Davies was running from something or someone. Maybe the someone found her?"

"Possibly." Tindall then handed the photo and yearbook

over to Perez and Parkins and asked, "What do you think?"

After looking at both Perez replied, "It looks like the same picture and it also looks like Davies were in both. So Davies had the same picture away from the yearbook?"

"Correct, and based on the records under Severinsen's name, it looks like Ms. Davies was a Yooper from Ironwood. Do either of you have any contacts in Ironwood or Gogebic County where it's located at?"

"I don't," answered Parkins.

"The same here," replied Perez.

"Tis a pity," said Tindall with a frown. "That means we'll have to go through official channels, and it may take days or longer to get the info. If it's not the feds or the State Police, there may be some foot dragging if they feel like it. I'll just have to use my persuasive charms."

Perez and Parkins laughed and went back through the container as Tindall walked to Capt. Carter's office. They just came back from lunch at Grissom's and enjoyed the food. Sometimes Tindall joined them if it was for a special occasion such as someone's birthday or anniversary. Grissom and his crew were excellent cooks, Parkins thought, though not as good as Millie's. He liked to say privately and jokingly that his wife's cooking was like smoking crack, addictive and hard to put down.

Perez had the same attitude towards Sheila's cooking, though he would phrase it more elegantly. Cooking wasn't his thing. Other than boiling water, it had to be instant cooking or he would end up eating out of cans or boxes.

That garbage is terrible, Perez would say to his family and friends, and I don't want to end up dead at an early age. Sheila agreed with him, and both of them vigilantly tried to prevent their kids from stuffing themselves with junk food. They allowed the kids to have certain kinds of junk food and soda from time to time but they had to eat healthy for the most part. Kevin and Angelique didn't mind because they saw their parents eating healthy and the healthy food was cooked in a way that looked and tasted good.

By 2:00 pm Perez and Parkins finished going through the storage container with no results. Davies had noting scandalous or unsavory in the container. "Well, I'll send it over to Pete in Records to catalogue in," said Parkins. "Frank'll probably send his over after his chat with Capt. Carter."

"He hasn't come back here yet," Perez replied, "he's probably still talking to Capt. Carter or lugging the container down to Records."

"Barbara Davies was originally named Linda Severinsen?" Capt. Carter asked Tindall quizzically as they sat in the former's office.

"Yes," replied Tindall. "She went to elementary school in Ironwood and graduated from the high school there. She then legally changed her name and the name on her birth certificate after she turned eighteen. None of her friends here knew about her past."

"Have you contacted the Ironwood police yet regarding this?"

"Not yet. "I'm going to call them after I drop my

container off at Records and talk to Mike and Jim."

"Do you think that the Severinsen part may be connected to Davies' murder?"

"I don't know at this time, but it's clear that Davies was hiding from someone or something. I would be speculating if I said that the two items were linked at this time."

"You're right and keep me posted. I'll brief the chief regarding this."

"Thanks." Tindall then left Capt. Carter's office, went back to his office, and walked down to Records. After greeting Pete Messinger, he handed over the container and asked Pete, "Can you please document this yearbook and photo now? I need to hold on to these two items for a bit longer. I'll bring them back once I'm done."

"Allright, Frank." After Pete documented the two items Tindall walked back to his office, dropped the items on his desk, and walked out of his office over to Parkins and Perez. He asked, "Did you find anything?"

"We found nothing," replied Perez as he typed on his computer.

"I thought so," Tindall noted, "but we had to go through all of it. I'm going to call the police up in Ironwood and ask if they can find out who the other three girls are in those photos. I don't know how long it'll take them to find out. Once we find out who they are we can contact them if they live around here and if not, then we'll ask the local cops to interview them."

"So there's nothing else that we can do at this point?"

concluded Parkins.

"That's right," said Tindall, "and after I call Ironwood I'll type up the report after you send me your information."

"I just sent our information over to you," replied Perez after clicking some keys on his computer, "and you should have it right now."

"Thanks, and if we don't see each other later, I'll see the two of you tomorrow morning."

"Same here," replied Perez and Parkins.

Tindall walked back to his office and saw after he entered his office that it was close to 4:00 pm. He quickly called the Ironwood Public Safety Department and spoke to the administrative secretary there, explaining the nature of the case and advising that he would be faxing the photos over to them. After concluding the call, Tindall then faxed the photos over and typed up the report. He then sent a copy of the report over to Capt. Carter and remembered that he needed to ask Ann and Chuck regarding the status of Mrs. Davies' items. Tindall then walked down to the Crime Lab.

He was delighted that Chuck was still there and asked him about the status of the items.

"Well, there wasn't anything unusual or out of place in the computers or the iPhone."

Frowning, Tindall asked, "Did you or the rest of the team see anything regarding a Linda Severinsen or Ironwood."

"Nope, the info we found only pertained to St. Marys, Mrs. Davies, her husband and his relatives and their friends. There was of course info regarding her job on her work computer only."

"Thanks. So that means now you or Ann'll have to lug all of that stuff down to Records?"

"I'll be the one responsible for lugging all of it down to Records via a cart," Chuck replied dejectedly. It's not like Ann can't do it after I put the stuff on it."

Tindall laughed. "Well, that's how it works when you married. I now have first-hand experience regarding it. Take care and say hello to Ann from me.

"Will do."

Walking back to his office, Tindall noted that 5:00 pm was coming very quickly. After then, it would be relaxation time with Kathleen. Everything was going well for both of them personally and professionally. He sat down at his computer and checked his e-mail box for anything recent and he didn't see anything. All of his paperwork had been completed and there was nothing left to do. He didn't know how long it would take for Ironwood to get back to him. Probably a few days at the most. Since one of the pictures came from the local high school yearbook, the Ironwood police would contact the local high school there. Undoubtedly, they would have records about the girls in the picture.

Yawning, Tindall turned off his computer and lights, put his hat, coat and gloves on, locked his office door, and went home.

11

Perez left Headquarters a few minutes after Tindall and arrived at home shortly thereafter. When he arrived, Sheila was busy preparing dinner in the kitchen. After kissing her, he asked, "So what's cookin' today?"

Sheila laughed. "It's a quick Hamburger Helper that I stuck in the oven. It should be done in a few minutes. We're having salad with it. The kids are behaving as usual and I'll call'em down in a minute after we chat."

They both sat down in the kitchen and Perez then asked, "How did it go at school today?"

"It went well. When you're dealing with high schoolers, they can change from day to day due to hormones, breakups, problems with parents, yadda yadda yadda. And how did it go for you?"

"Well, we're still working on the Davies case and of course mum's the word regarding it. I can say that it's an interesting case."

"I understand completely, since there are some things at school regarding students that I can't discuss."

"Are you enjoying being a school counselor now?"

Sheila smiled. "It's going well. Moving from the classroom to the school counselor office is a big step. I enjoy it and I really want to make a difference. Since St. Anselm's is a private school, we can get rid of problem cases with no muss or fuss unlike the public school district."

Perez understood, since he knew that some public school districts were basically dumping grounds for kids who had serious problems. He was glad that since Sheila worked at St. Anselm's, they received a steep discount. Ironically, for the first few years of her career, she worked in the public school system in a nice school with parents, teachers and administrators who cared and did their jobs. Teaching ran in Sheila's family since her parents were high school teachers in the Grand Rapids area. Perez' response was interrupted by the tramp of feet rushing down the stairs. Two separate pairs of feet from the sound of it.

Walking towards the stairs, Perez was rushed by Kevin and Angelica, crying "Dad!" He hugged them and asked, "How did your day go today?"

"Fine," Angelica said, "but Ms. Finnerty makes us work soo hard! We have to do so many different things."

"Right," responded Kevin. "Mr. Olszak wants me to work harder."

"Well, Kev and Angel, your teachers want you to be prepared so that you can take care of yourselves when you get older. Your mother and I would agree on it. Plus, you do have to admit that it's a bit fun to do more stuff than what you're used to."

Twisting her hair on her finger, Angelica sighed, "Well, you're right Dad, some of the new stuff that Ms. Finnerty wants us to do is fun."

"Oh, I don't know," retorted Kevin, "it's still just stuff."

Laughing, Perez concluded by saying, "We can't talk all night, dinner's getting cold and you guys will be getting off to bed soon."

"Okay!" Kevin and Angelica yelled together as they walked with Perez to the kitchen. After everyone filled their plates and sat down to dinner in the dining room, drinking water or juice, both Perez and Sheila were amazed at how their children were beginning to look more and more like them, Angelica with her red hair and ruddy, freckled complexion and Kevin, with his dark brown hair and olive-colored skin. Like Kathleen, Angelica quickly reddened in the sun and became even more freckled while Kevin quickly bronzed in the sun. They were also proud of them for their manners and respect for others.

After dinner, Perez cleared the table and Kevin and Angelica washed the dishes. Perez also put the leftovers in the refrigerator. He and Sheila made sure that the kids did household chores to teach them the importance of giving back to the community. They didn't want their kids to end up being parasites and they also made sure that they walked the walk and talked the talk in their own daily lives. Sheila liked to say that "your actions are so loud that I can't hear what you're talking."

Later, when the kids went to their rooms, Perez asked Sheila what she wanted to do. She replied, "Why don't we listen to some NPR for an hour or so?"

"That's fine for me, and then afterwards we can see if there's anything worth watching on TV."

Perez agreed, and they listened to WHAU FM, the local NPR affiliate. For years, the station played classical music interrupted by NPR news on the hour, but beginning a few years ago, the format changed to news/talk during the day and classical at night and during most of the weekend. Perez and Sheila were sad about it but they understood that classical music wasn't as popular as it used to be. They loved classical music and enjoyed the Saturday Met Opera broadcasts. Kevin and Angelica were never interested in classical music since they preferred the music that most pre-teens and teenagers liked. Live and let live regarding music was the rule provided that the music wasn't the obscene garbage that some stations broadcast.

At 8:00 pm Sheila turned the radio off and turned the TV on. They were able to pull in quite a few stations due to their roof antenna. Neither of them were willing to pay for cable or satellite and Kevin and Angelica could watch up to an hour of TV per day with the only exception being holidays such as Christmas, New Year's Day or Thanksgiving. She and Perez also monitored what they watched and they themselves could go for weeks without watching TV. Flipping through the channels, Sheila concluded, "There's nothing to watch tonight. So what will we do?"

"How about us reading?" answered Perez with a smile.

"Ok, we'll read until we have to tuck ourselves and the kids in at 9:00."

Perez read the <u>Evening News</u> while Sheila read Hans

Olav Lahlum's <u>Satellite People</u>. Despite the fact of, or perhaps because she was the wife of a policeman, Sheila enjoyed crime fiction, particularly foreign crime novels. Perez demurred regarding crime novels, wryly saying that to read one after a long day's work would be the equivalent of a chef talking about food after hours. He liked non-gory ghost and horror stories and historical novels. Kevin and Angelica were voracious readers like their parents, with Angelica beginning to read adult books in the 4th Grade.

The grandfather clock next to the stairs chimed 9:00 pm. Yawning, Sheila said to Perez as she walked upstairs, "Mike, I'm going up to make sure the kids are in bed. See you in a minute or two."

"I'll be there in a few minutes."

Sheila climbed the stairs and called out after reaching the top floor, "Kevin, Angelica, are you in bed?"

"We're in bed, Mom!"

"We love you!"

"We know that!"

Sheila smiled as she walked from their rooms to her and Perez' room. She undressed, changed into her nightshirt and brushed her teeth and hair. Perez came a few minutes later and also changed into his pajamas. Then they hopped into bed and fell asleep.

12

Edith Dowling tossed and turned as she sometimes did during her Wednesday night's sleep. It was only an issue when she was still married, and annoyed her ex to no end. But there were other reasons than the tossing and turning led to divorce. Ken Dowling, the ex, was a man of enormous patience and kindness, but the possibly of becoming disease ridden along with being a cuckold more than once led to his walkout. Even after all of this, Edith was set for life, since Ken was very rich and still loved her for all of her faults, including overfondness of liquor and shoplifting incidents.

It was annoying to Edith to have a full eight hours of sleep and then wake up still sleepy because of the tossing and turning. For some, it would be a sign of a guilty conscience, but she never suffered from that problem. Even in regards to what she silently called "The Accident". Edith enjoyed the benefits from her divorce settlement by stopping her shoplifting and restricting her drinking. Even when it was more than what it was, she never got out of control publicly or privately. She would just quietly drink on weekends and free time periods until she fell asleep.

Edith never considered herself to be an alcoholic, since she was always clean and presentable and didn't vomit on or soil herself. She also never disgraced herself or Ken in public. Ken couldn't understand that. He also couldn't understand that if she had her little flings, it didn't mean that he was an inadequate husband or lover. The sex was great between the two of them even though he was passive and didn't want to do anything that he considered to be perverted.

They still were friends and went to lunch and dinner from time to time, but Edith never tried to seduce him, being afraid of destroying the friendship that they still had. She also had too much respect for herself and Ken to try to get him involved in FWB. Nothing but whoring, she disgustedly thought. When the divorce occurred, most if not all of Ken's friends wanted nothing to do with her and they were shocked that he still wanted to keep a friendship with a woman who was so sluttish in their minds. Ken made it clear in a polite yet firm way that it wasn't open for discussion.

As for Edith's friends, they automatically took her side and tried to badmouth Ken, but she also made it clear that it wasn't open for discussion. Ironically enough, their relationship was stronger after the divorce. Another ironic thing was that she didn't want to have sex that much after the divorce. Some of friends cynically or seriously believed that it was due to guilt. Edith didn't feel guilty about that or anything else. She knew of guilt from Catholic church and school (not from her parents, though) and had left all of those items in the back alley of her younger days.

Edith woke up with a start. Something fell and shattered downstairs. That damned cat! She swore as she got up and walked out of her room to the stairs. She loved Mink but he could be a damned nuisance, jumping on different things. Since Edith never fed him people food she didn't have to worry about begging. Mink received the best food and medical care, far better than some adults got, she smugly noted. She also considered getting another cat for him to play with while she was out and about.

As Edith walked over the top step she lost her balance, crying "What the hell?" as she fell down the stairs, fracturing her neck and suffering a serious head injury. As she lay lifeless at the bottom of the stairs, a shadow detached itself from its darkness after a few minutes and moved over to her. The shadow then moved up the steps and removed a light but strong rope that straddled the stairs at the second from the top step. It then moved down the steps and disposed of the smashed vase, quickly tidying up the area and caressing the cat. Quietly, the shadow moved towards the door and the latter closed with a lock afterwards.

Poor Edith. No more booze or men, I sneered as I drove home. Like Barbara, she was so easy to kill. And so easy to watch as well in regards to her activities. I used electronic spyware on her, but it wasn't the kind that you used on a person's phone or computer; I didn't want the feds to spoil my fun. Because of my schedule, I had to watch her mainly on the weekends and at night. Plus, the cover of darkness aided me in not being seen. I needed to be patient and my patience was rewarded. Since she didn't live too far it wasn't a burden. She was easy to track down since she hadn't changed her identity like Barbara did. A little surf on the Internet and I was able to find about her new name, marriage and divorce.

I also had pictures and recordings of her coming and going and even of her in compromising situations with other men in various places. Amazing how many different sexual techniques Edith practiced! I knew her schedule even better than her former husband did when they were married. The rich lived differently from others---I believe that F. Scott Fitzgerald said something to that effect. Because of my skills, I was able to come in and out of her house without her knowing it. Poor Edith wasn't a stupid woman, just a soulless one. That poor devil married to her should have received a reward for what he had to deal with.

As for the women involved in Little's death, only one had a conscience and she suffered for it, and that's how it sometimes has to be. Conscience and a soul are really the only things that separates us from animals, and a person without a conscience or soul is nothing more than an animal or devil in human form, potentially as savage and brutal as the most vicious wild beast. People like that can only be caged or killed. Reform's impossible.

The police haven't released any further information about Barbara's death publicly, but I do know that they did find out that she was actually Linda Severinsen in her previous life. Some people looking at Barbara's case would think that she ran away from her previous life due to guilt. I highly doubt it. She ran away because she didn't want to face the consequences of her and her friends' actions, which was to turn a beautiful and intelligent person into a vegetable. That was truly unforgiveable. I truly prayed that the two little bitches received a nice welcome in Hell. Perhaps they'll have a meet and greet when the third little bitch arrives.

I'm home, safe and sound. It's early in the morning and I have a few hours to sleep before I have to go back to work. Since Thanksgiving, Christmas and New Year's is coming very quickly I will have to prepare for family from out of town. Hopefully the visit with another of Edith's friends will go well. I don't know how the visit will go. Should I surprise them or should I be up front? The possibilities are endless.

Sometimes alone in bed I think of the person who slept with me, who made love to me, and I weep. Why did God do this? There's nothing I can do regarding it. Hopefully, I will be reunited with all of them on the other side. Fortunately, I can sleep for only a few hours or I can do catnaps if I need time late at night to do something. It's a trick I knew how to do as a child and I strengthened it as I got older out of necessity. I look in the bathroom mirror and I see my own face as usual. I say "Goodnight" to my reflection as I go to bed.

13

"Have we received a fax yet from the Ironwood Public Safety Department yet, Ann-Marie?" Tindall asked Departmental Secretary Ann-Marie Simonini. It was late Thursday morning and Tindall knew that it could take time to get the information from Ironwood. Still he had to keep track of everything regarding the case for briefing purposes.

"We haven't received anything from them yet," Ann-Marie replied, a thin woman in her early fifties with shoulder length dark hair and glasses. Tindall thanked her and walked back to his office. All incoming faxes came through Ann-Marie's office and everyone had to come in and pick up their own faxes except for the police chief and his assistant. Their faxes Ann-Marie or her assistant delivered directly to them.

Tindall briefed Capt. Carter earlier and advised that he was still waiting to receive information from Ironwood about the photos and once the persons in the photos were identified, they could be tracked down and interviewed either by him and his team or by the local police in the jurisdiction that they were located it. Captain Carter agreed and noted that the police chief was satisfied with the progress of the investigation.

Tindall also had his daily meeting with Perez and Parkins in which they all agreed that nothing further could be done until the information from Ironwood arrived. After the meeting, each of them had calls to make regarding other cases and paperwork to do. Everyone was grateful that most of everything had been updated in terms of technology for the 21st Century. Badges were now used to get in and out of the main doors and almost everything had been loaded into a new database for easier retrieval. There was talk of laptops for everyone but the City Council and the mayor turned it down. On the other hand, detectives like Tindall and the higher ups had their own computers and didn't have to share theirs like the uniforms did. All in all, there was a ringing of the changes that were occurring, and Tindall was on the committee who recommended the upgrades.

He loved being a plainclothes officer since the hours were far easier and you didn't have to worry about having drunks vomiting in your squad car while driving them to Headquarters. You also didn't have to worry about ugly domestic disputes in which you had to pull some knuckle dragger off of a woman screaming to keep your hands off her man. The pay was better and the chances for advancement were far better than if you were in the uniforms. Almost all of the police chiefs in the police department came from the Investigative Division.

On the other hand, Tindall knew that the uniforms were on the frontline and they had to worry about the drunks and abusers and the few if any gangbangers in St. Marys. The plainclothes got to skim the cream off of the top and didn't have to do overnight unless it was a serious case such as the serial killer moonlighting as a football player at Hamilton.

That piece of garbage strangled four women before he was stopped. Hell later got a new permanent resident after the killer was shanked in Jackson.

Tindall wasn't involved in the case and Judge A.T. Carlile, whom he along with Perez and Parkins worked very closely with, was the district court judge who bound the serial killer over to the circuit court for trial. Judge Carlile was very delighted to be the center of media attention. Not too many serious crimes or murders in the St. Marys area received a lot of attention. Normally, the furthest attention received was from Grand Rapids or Kalamazoo, perhaps even Chicago if you were lucky. The judge even received a few offers from such places as Court TV. He turned them all down, though once he turned 75 he would have to step down from the bench and doing a Judge Wapner wouldn't be a bad idea. The money would be good and maybe he could tape the shows in Chicago, rather than go back and forth from Los Angeles or New York City.

Time for lunch, Tindall silently noted as the clock on his wall turned to noon. He called Kathleen and asked, "How's your day going so far?"

Kathleen laughed. "It's going and you?"

"Fine. I'll be back after five. See ya!"

"Same here!"

Tindall hung up and pulled out his pear and sesame sticks. He bought the sesame sticks from one of the local health food stores and they were delicious. Drinking some water as a chaser with the pear and sesame sticks, he was in seventh heaven. After he finished, he read through

Hawthorne's Tales and Sketches from the Library of America. The short stories were interesting, though the writing was archaic in most respects. Tindall tried reading the Library of America's edition of Charles Brockden Brown's novels and had to give it up due to the archaic thee and thou type of writing. It was 12:16 pm when he received a call from Ann-Marie Simonini:

"Hello, Ann-Marie, did you receive the info from Ironwood?"

"I have it right here, Frank. You can pick it up when you're ready."

"I'll be down there after lunch."

Tindall returned to his lunch. At 12:30 pm he walked down to Ann-Marie's office to pick up the information. After returning to his office, Tindall read through the information. Now he and the team needed to know what happened to those girls. Were they still living or did they pass away suspiciously like Barbara Davies?

Rising from his chair, Tindall walked out to Perez' and Parkins' cubicles, hoping that they hadn't gone to lunch yet. Seeing that they had, he decided to finish up on his other cases until they came back. He also made copies of the Ironwood docs.

Perez and Parkins returned from Grissom's around 1:00 pm and returned to their cubicles. While there were finishing up old cases, Tindall walked over to them and said, "I received the docs from Ironwood and we can discuss what they sent," as he handed copies over to Perez and Parkins and sat down at a table next to them.

"Based on the information we just received," Tindall continued, "the three other girls in the pictures other than Davies are Edith Albanese, Cecelia Killian and Heather Rowlands. The public safety officer who sent the docs, a Sgt. Clement, also wrote that the three girls in question moved out of Ironwood once they graduated from high school. We need to track them down to see if they kept in touch with each other and particularly if they kept in touch with Davies. I'll track down Albanese and you can choose which of the others you want to track down."

"I'll take Killian," replied Parkins.

"That leaves me with Rowlands," chuckled Perez.

"If I find anything interesting, I'll be back," answered Tindall as he walked back to his office.

"We'll do the same," said Parkins.

Tindall figured that he would be able to find out everything that he needed to know about Ms. Albanese in a few minutes to about an hour. Within an hour he found out that she was now Edith Dowling and she lived right in Klingsburg, which was about twenty miles northeast of St. Marys. She was also divorced from a Kenneth Dowling with no children.

Tindall called Red Friman, Klingsburg's constable and asked, "Red, what info do you have regarding an Edith Dowling? My team and I are working on a case and she may have some information that we need."

Friman sighed. "That's going to be impossible unless you're interested in seances, Frank. Ms. Dowling's dead."

"How did it happen?"

"She was found dead at the bottom of the stairs in her house earlier today by one of those rent a maids. Looks like it was an accident. We had no previous run ins with her."

"Was alcohol or drugs involved?"

"Not as far as we know, though the ME will examine her."

"From the info I have, she had an ex, a Kenneth Dowling. Does he live around here?"

"Nope, he lives in the Detroit area. We contacted him and he'll be here by tomorrow morning. He'll be in by about 11:00."

"Do you mind if I or one of my team members watch while you question him?"

Friman laughed. "Of course! And you'll get a transcript afterwards."

"Thanks. Say hello to Lizbeth from me."

"And the same to Kathleen."

Tindall hung up and went through the notes that he jotted down while speaking to Friman. So Ms. Dowling has recently passed away, he noted with a frown. He walked out of his office and back over to Perez and Parkins. "Have you guys found anything out about the two girls?"

Wryly, Perez answered, "Rowlands was found drowned in the Detroit River about three years ago; it was ruled an accident. She had a drug problem at one time but was clean and sober when she died."

"Where was she living at when she died?"

Flipping through his notes, Perez replied, "She was living in Detroit and was working at the Fr. Casey Soup Kitchen in Detroit. I requested the information regarding the case from the Detroit Police Department. We should have it within a few days."

"Cecelia Killian is still living and she lives in Appleton, right in our county," said Parkins.

"I don't like this," Tindall noticed glumly. "Three of the four girls in that picture are dead, one murdered and two others passed away in accidents. Mike, Jim, see if you can get any further information regarding Killian and Rowlands. We have to find out if they had any contact with each other after high school. I'm going to Klingsburg late tomorrow morning to watch while Constable Friman questions Dowling's ex."

"I'll contact the Appleton police regarding Killian."

"Fine. Let me get back to my office. If I don't see you guys later, I'll see you tomorrow."

"Same here."

After Tindall returned to his office, he decided to call the Ironwood Public Safety Department to see if they had any information regarding the four women's families and if the four women ever came back for any high school reunions held there. He then walked down to the Crime Lab to ask Ann and Chuck if they saw any e-mails or phone messages from the women on Davies' computer or iPhone. Ann was sitting at her desk and going through paperwork when Tindall greeted her.

"Hello again, stranger!" Ann yelled. "And what do you need from us now?"

"Regarding Barbara Davies's computers and iPhone, can you go through them again and see if there were any messages given or received by an Ethel Albanese or Ethel Dowling, Cecelia Killian and Heather Rowlands?"

"Sure, we'll go through the stuff again. It may take a few more days, though."

"Where's the significant other? I haven't seen him all day."

"He's here, he's just been in the back all day doing the tech work while I'm doing the paperwork."

"Ok, just tell'im that I said hello."

"We'll do and see ya!"

Laughing, Tindall walked back to his office. Once he returned, he noted that he would be on his way home in about three hours. We probably won't hear anything from Ironwood at the earliest, he thought. It was interesting that except for Rowlands, all of the other women were living or had lived in St. Marys. Were they in contact with each other or did they even know if they lived in the same area? Even though St. Marys County wasn't as large in terms of population as some of the counties in the southeast part of the state, it was possible to lose yourself among the small towns and villages in the county or even in St. Marys city itself. Well, at least some progress was being made, Tindall mused as he returned back to his work.

"Hello, Jim! How you and the family been doing?" asked Sgt. Steve Gould from the Appleton Police Department.

"We're fine, Steve. And you and yours?" replied Parkins.

"We're doing well and what do you need? This doesn't sound like a social call."

"Unfortunately, you're right. We're working on a case here and I just wanted to know if a Cecelia Killian has had any issues or run ins with your department."

"She doesn't sound like any of our regulars. Let me put you on hold while I do a quick check." After a few minutes, Gould came back and said, "We don't have anything regarding her officially or not."

"Ok and thanks for the help, Steve,"

"You bet. Talk to you later."

Parkins hung up and then sent an e-mail note to Tindall stating that Appleton had no information official or otherwise regarding Ms. Killian. Almost time to go, Parkins said to himself as he looked at the wall clock. Checking out Ms. Killian further, he saw that the only brush with the law that she had was regarding a few parking and speeding tickets. Nothing that would lead to prison time. An hour later, Parkins said good evening to

Perez and the rest of the department and went home to Millie.

14

As you drive into Klingsburg along Main Street, you see neat, well-kept houses and stores, and depending on the time of day, you can see people walking back and forth between different stores throughout the week. On the weekends during Spring and Summer there are different concerts in the village square right on Main Street. The Public Safety Department is located in the Village Hall along with the village trustees and village employees and the Fire Department is right across the street.

Tindall was no stranger to all of this since he occasionally travelled to Klingsburg either for work or for play. After parking his car, he walked into the Hall's main entrance and greeted the receptionist at her desk. It was 10:55 am Friday morning. Once he informed her that he had an appointment with Constable Friman she called the latter and was advised to let him through.

Friman's office was on the main floor and there were cubicles for four assistant constables, with one always being on duty. Tindall stepped inside while Friman was on a call. After motioning Tindall to sit down, Friman finished the call. "Nice to see you again, Frank! How's you and Kathleen doing?"

"We're fine and you and the missus?"

"We're fine as well. Anyhow, Dowling's in the interrogation room and you'll be able to watch outside."

"Let's go then."

Tindall followed Friman, a thin, wiry man with dark hair and beard to the interrogation room. Tindall watched as the latter stepped into the interrogation room. He also saw a stenographer along with Kenneth Dowling, who looked pale and subdued. Sitting down, Tindall proceeded to watch and listen.

Transcript of Kenneth Dowling's statement:

My name is Kenneth Dowling and I'm Edith Dowling's ex-husband. We were married about seven years ago, I was 35 and Edie was 29. It was the first marriage for both of us. We were surprised that we decided to get married. Neither of us was the marrying kind, I because I never found anyone interesting enough to marry and Edie for reasons that I found out later.

We met in all places in Eastern Market in Detroit, a kitty corner from the downtown area. Our relationship began over the sole remaining loaf of rye artisanal bread that both of us wanted but only one of us could have. Being the gentleman, I offered Edie the bread but she, being the gentlewoman, said I could have it. After a few minutes of going back and forth, she decided to take it home. From then on we met on a regular basis, going to the movies, dining out with each other and friends and other things.

There were differences, my family being Grosse Pointers who made very big money by selling some foundries down in Detroit to Billy Durant, the founder of

GM. We wisely decided to cash out of the auto industry years before it collapsed in the Great Recession. I, along with other family members, don't have to work unless I want to. Edie told me that her family came from up north but she didn't say where they lived or even if anyone was left. The impression that I got was that she came from an ordinary background and she didn't want to discuss her past. I didn't push. Some of my relatives live throughout the world and only a few still live in Metro Detroit.

Well, the marriage fell apart basically because Edie, to put it mildly, was sexually uninhibited. I had limits on what I was interested in but she wanted to do anything as long as it didn't include children, teenagers, animals or inanimate objects. This was prior to our marriage. She also would sometimes drink too much. I wouldn't call her an alcoholic due to the fact that she kept her liquor well and she never embarrassed herself or me. I can't stand drunks or drug addicts.

Well, I decided to leave after I found evidence of someone other than myself in our bed. I moved out and began divorce proceedings. I didn't want to hurt Edie, I just wanted to be out of an adulterous marriage. I still loved her and I still do. She still loved me until she died. I also respected her because she didn't try to beg or grovel when I left, she simply said that I had to do what I needed to do. The divorce settlement was very generous since I didn't want to see her on the street and I didn't want to spend years on paying alimony.

I also respected her since she didn't try to sleep with me after the divorce. Both of us despised the "friends with benefits" crowd. You don't respect yourself or you so-called "friend" in that kind of situation. What drew me to Edie? She was funny, sexy and uninhibited. She loved to read just like me and books were all over our house. Because we really liked and respected each other we stayed friends even after the divorce.

Edie didn't tell me why she decided to move here. I asked her once, but she didn't want to talk about it. That was fine with me. She moved to Klingsburg about three years ago and I remember when she moved, because it was in the Fall and most people want to move in the Summer before the kiddies have to go back to school. I also remember about it that her move was rather abrupt and that she was in a hurry to go.

I live in Birmingham, a suburb north of Detroit. It's a lovely place and I live in one of the town houses very close to the downtown area. I invited Edie numerous times to come and visit but she always made excuses not to come. It wasn't that she didn't want to be bothered with me, since she always had an open house for me and I would spend weekends or up to a week here in one of her guest bedrooms. Something about travelling must have soured her. Edie could be very secretive and if she didn't want you to know something, you didn't know it. I hope that I was able to assist you regarding this. I also hope that you tell her family about this and if there's no one, then I'll handle her funeral.

"What do you think?" Friman asked Tindall after Dowling left the Village Hall.

Shifting in his seat, Tindall replied, "Why do you ask? Did you find anything suspicious in Ms. Dowling's house?"

116

"We did. It looks like someone picked the lock on her back door. We can't say if it was done recently or not. Whoever did it knew what they were doing."

Tindall frowned. "Do you think that it was connected to Ms. Dowling's accident?"

"Can't say," Friman replied with a shrug. "It didn't look like foul play to us. Sometimes people just accidently fall down the stairs. You'll get the statement in a few minutes."

"Have you examined Ms. Dowling's computer and cell phone yet?"

"No need to since it looks like an accident. If you think it's something different, we can get someone from the Sheriff's Department to take a look at it. As you know, we don't have people trained here to do that kind of thing or crime lab stuff."

"I hear you, Red," Tindall noted with sympathy. He received Dowling's statement within a few minutes and gave his goodbyes to Friman and his team. Odd that Ms. Dowling should have a picked door right around the time of her passing, Tindall thought. It could have been simply someone trying to case the house out for a burglary. Klingsburg wasn't the place where you had a high crime rate or alarm systems. Most of the thefts and burglaries were cases of people just walking into an unlocked garage or house or smash and grabs from cars where people left their purses or laptops in full view of passersby. A murder hadn't occurred in Klingsburg for quite some time.

Tindall arrived back at Headquarters at 12:30 pm and

checked for any e-mails or messages before he went to lunch. Ann-Marie Simonini and Mac McElroy left him voice messages and there were no e-mails that needed to be responded to. He would handle those two after lunch. Today Tindall decided to have salad, and to cut down the calories, he didn't use croutons, meat, cheese or bacon bits. He also tended not to add salad dressing on it and if he did, it was only Italian dressing since he didn't like cream dressings.

At 1:00 pm Tindall called McElroy back. "Hello and I just listened to your message, Mac. What happened?"

McElroy laughed. "I just wanted to tell you that me and my team checked the video from the time that Mrs. Davies was at Rothmann and there was nothing suspicious on it."

"No one stood out on it?"

"That's right. Since I'm not a cop anymore I'm not offering any theories. That's you and your team's responsibility."

"Point taken and thanks."

"You bet."

Tindall hung up and let the words swirl in the mental air. What McElroy didn't want to say, but which Tindall heard between the lines, was that whoever murdered Mrs. Davies was either an insider who knew how to blend in or someone who knew the operations of the hospital. He and his team may have to check on that angle later after they further reviewed Mrs. Davies and her friends.

Seeing Perez and Parkins walking back to their cubicles,

Tindall decided to talk to them after he went down to Ann-Marie's office. While he did so, he said hello to those he hadn't see earlier in the day. Nice day, Tindall though, even though it was a bit cool. He hated high temperatures and preferred cool weather. He picked up the fax from Ann-Marie and went back to his office after making separate copies for Perez and Parkins.

After reading his copy, Tindall walked over to Perez' and Parkins' cubicles and asked, "Do you the two of you have a moment?"

"What do you have, Frank?" asked Parkins.

"It's information that I just received from Ironwood. I've made copies of it for you to read." Tindall then handed copies of the fax to Parkins and Perez and then sat down next to their cubicles. After a few minutes, Perez mused, "This is quite interesting about our dear girls."

"It sure is," replied Tindall. "None of the girls involved in this case—Dowling, Davies, Killian, Rowlands—has ever come back to Ironwood after their high school graduation. Their relatives still live there mostly along with their childhood friends."

"From the information in the fax it seems that Killian's car was involved in a hit and run seriously injuring another local girl named Lesley Blandick. Ms. Blandick was jogging on the road at night when the incident happened."

"According to the records," Parkins added, "the hit and run occurred when all of them had graduated from high school and were on their way to college. Ms. Blandick was in their graduating class."

"Now according to the police report," Tindall continued, "Killian and company stated that the car was stolen while they stopped in the woods to drink some beer. The car was later found in the woods torched and it was so badly charred that the police couldn't get any forensics regarding it. They insisted that the car was stolen at the time of the hit and run."

"Sounds fishy to me."

"I second that," said Perez soberly. "Didn't the Ironwood cops run Killian and her friends in?"

"They did and they all insisted that the car was stolen while they were drinking. Of course, they were fined for drinking and their licenses were suspended for a few months but the cops couldn't prove that they were behind the wheel at the time of the hit and run, though it's clear from the case and interview notes that they didn't believe them."

"Which is why they haven't haunted Ironwood since."

"Correct. People in small towns tend not to forget certain things or people."

"Particularly when someone ends up in a permanent coma like Ms. Blandick. She passed away earlier this year at a nursing home in Ironwood."

"I see here," Perkins jumped in, "that both of her parents have passed away. There's no information about any siblings or other relatives."

"We can track them down if necessary. I'm going to contact the Appleton police and tell them that I'm going to interview Ms. Killian. Mike, have you heard anything from the Detroit police?"

"Oh, I almost forgot," replied Perez with embarrassment, "I received a fax from them regarding Rowlands. Although her death was ruled an accident, the medical examiner noted that there was bruising on the back of her neck and body but they couldn't determine what it was caused by since she had been in the water for a few days and there's all kinds of stuff floating in the Detroit River."

"So the only one who's still breathing is Killian. Well, she'll have to do for now. I'll see you two later."

Tindall returned to his office and called Sgt. Steve Gould from the Appleton Police Department. "Hello, Steve. I'm calling because I need to interview Ms. Killian, and since she lives in your area, I wanted you to know about it."

"Thanks for the call," Gould replied. "Go right ahead."

"And thanks for your understanding. I'm going to try to interview her within the next few days."

"You still have her address and phone number?"

"I do and thanks."

"No problem."

Tindall hung up and then called Cecelia Killian. "Hello, Ms, Killian, this is Lt. Frank Tindall from the St. Marys Police Department. I need to talk to you regarding an old schoolmate of yours named Linda Severinsen."

Cecelia asked, "What happened to Linda? Is she ok?"

"It would be best it I discuss it with you when we meet here at the St. Marys Police Department." Glancing at his wall clock, Tindall continued, "Let's say at 1:00 tomorrow."

"Tomorrow at 1:00 will be fine, Lieutenant. I will be there."

"Thanks for your cooperation."

"You're welcome."

Tindall would have to make sure that his meeting with Joseph Tallichet went quickly tomorrow. It probably would, since Tallichet scheduled it for 8:30 am and he was known for his meetings being polite yet quick and to the point, an attitude that his clients appreciated since most of them didn't want to spend hours in their attorney's office on a Saturday or any other day if they could avoid it. That meant that Kathleen would have to go to the Farmers' Market on her own, since he would have to get ready for the 1:00 pm meeting with Ms. Killian. They could have lunch together at 11:45 am so he would have fifteen minutes to get to Headquarters. Seeing that it was 5:00 pm, Tindall went home.

15

Joseph Tallichet enjoyed the good life modestly. He made a nice living through handling wills, probate matters, trust setups and administration, conservatorships, and minor business and real estate work. His clients weren't the heavy hitters such as the Meldrims and Peppiatts, whose legal matters were handled by the Ballietts, but they were honest, law abiding and hard-working folk. No one ever had a bad thing to say about him and he preferred to keep it that way.

Sitting at his desk in a comfortable office on Main Street, working on some odds and ends on a chilly Saturday morning, sunlight streaming through his office, Tallichet was in his own little world when he heard the doorbell ring. Rising from his chair, he walked to the door and saw Frank Tindall. Opening the door, Tallichet said, "Good morning Frank and come in!"

Tindall replied, "Good morning, Mr. Tallichet! And how have you been doing?"

"I'm fine and you?"

"Nothing to complain about." Tallichet and Tindall walked to the former's office and they sat down. Tindall was always impressed by Tallichet's office and the obvious marks of success. The undergraduate and graduate degrees along with awards lining the walls, the solid but unpretentious furniture, the tastefulness of everything along with the discretion of Tallichet's secretary and receptionist when they were working all showed a well-developed prudence and caution.

After a few pleasantries Tallichet continued, "As you know, Frank, you have an uncle named Matt Tindall. Your grandparents preferred not to discuss him due to a past indiscretion that he was involved in. They thought that it would be best if everyone didn't keep in contact with each other. Your grandparents entrusted this letter to me to give to you after they passed away. They requested that you open this letter when you get home and that you follow their instructions to the best of your ability."

After he received the letter from Tallichet, Tindall asked, "So my grandparents wanted to make amends to my uncle after their passing?"

"That I wouldn't be able to say, Frank. It was a personal issue and I tend to steer clear of personal issues unless it involves legal issues."

"Perfectly understandable. Do you have anything else for me?"

"Not at this time. If you have any questions after reading the letter, don't hesitate to call me." Tindall and Tallichet shook hands and the latter left for home. Checking his watch as he drove home, he saw that it was only 9:15 am so he would have time to read the letter and think about the contents before Kathleen came back with the things from the Farmers' Market. After he arrived home, he went into his office, sat down on his desk chair and opened the envelope containing Grandpa and Grandma's letter and began to read it:

Dear Frank,

If you're reading this letter, we've passed away and we're requesting that you do something for us regarding your uncle our son Matthew Tindall. He wasn't someone that we wanted to discuss either privately or publicly. What he did was wrong and it couldn't be overlooked or forgiven. But we don't want him to suffer or to be alone. We also don't want him to be in need and not receive any help from us. Because of this, we're asking you to find Matthew and make sure that he doesn't need anything and if he does, you can you use a fund that Joseph Tallichet, our attorney, is the administrator of. He will do everything he can to assist you regarding this and he has our trust. Thank you, Frank for assisting us and God bless you and the family.

Albert Tindall & Lilliane Tindall, 12/6/14

Tindall saw that it was written by Grandma and that both she and Grandpa signed it. Now he needed to track Uncle Matt down. Unless he changed his name and identity, he would be easy to track down. Even if he was dead, he would still be easy to track down. Since this was a private issue, Tindall couldn't use official police resources regarding this. And because it was private, he wouldn't use unofficial police resources either. He had Uncle Matt's social security number and birthdate among his grandparents' paperwork so it would only take a few minutes at his computer to track Uncle Matt down. Far easier than in the old days before everything was centralized and computerized and before social security numbers and birthdates were used as identification.

It was 10:00 am and Tindall spent the next hour tracking down Uncle Matt on the Internet. It actually took less than an hour to find where Uncle Matt lived at. He lived in Bloomington, Indiana, the home of Indiana University. Tindall initially knew nothing about what kind of work Uncle Matt did or if he had a family. Doing a further search, he found out that Uncle Matt was an owner along with his wife Sally Tindall, of Waldron's True Value Hardware Store in Bloomington through an article in The Herald-Times, Bloomington's local paper. The article also noted that the Tindalls had two children.

Looks like I have two additional cousins, Tindall wryly noted. I wonder what Kathleen's response will be. He also wondered if Aunt Rachael and Uncle Oliver or Elaine and Phil knew anything about this. Well, he would have to pay a visit to Uncle Matt once he and the team were done with the Davies case.

Kathleen arrived from the Farmers' Market at 11:00 am and Tindall helped her carry the items that she bought into the fridge or pantry. On Fridays after work she shopped at Koditscheks for things that she couldn't get at the Farmers' Market. She loved shopping at the latter and bantering with the sellers there. It was always clean and you could also buy non-food items such as clothing. It was also open throughout the year. During the winter, there was a booth that sold alpaca products such as gloves, socks, hats, scarves and other items. Both she and Tindall bought the gloves and socks since they were stylish along with being comfortably warm.

The Farmers' Market sold other seasonal items based on

the time of the year. During Easter, they would sell Easter lilies and other Easter friendly plants and during Thanksgiving and Christmas they would sell wreaths and knickknacks. Tindall loved seeing Kathleen smile when she talked about the things that made her happy. And she also loved seeing Tindall happy as well.

After everything was settled Tindall asked, "Since it's 11:30 do you want to go to lunch early? I can stop by the office afterwards and then drive to Appleton for the interview."

"But of course," replied Kathleen with mock severity, "since you should never be late for an interview."

Tindall laughed. He and Kathleen made it a rule since their one and only knock -down and -drag out fight while they were dating that they would never behave like that again. It was over an issue that they both had very strong views over and it was so contentious that both of them refused to speak to each other for two weeks. Both ached for each other during that time, Kathleen suffering crying spells and Tindall quietly suffering in angry silence. Mutual friends arranged for them to meet each other at Blest Park, infuriating them both initially but grateful afterwards. From then on, and into their marriage, Kathleen and Tindall never let their arguments get out of control and they never went to bed angry with each other.

Kathleen liked to joke that she didn't fit the stereotype of redheads due to her gentle and warm personality while Tindall noted that he understood Johnny Carson since he had the same introverted and withdrawn personality as he had. Though Kathleen could be hard like Old Peter if she was provoked and Tindall could be sociable with close friends, associates and family or if he had to be. In short, they were the classic examples of opposites truly attracting each other.

This Saturday Kathleen and Tindall decided to go to the University Inn Restaurant on Main St. in downtown St. Marys and have a nice Swedish lunch. The University Inn itself was one of the finest hotels in St. Marys and most of the high society dinners and weddings were held there. It, along with its restaurant, had four to five stars in the travel books and magazines. As they entered the restaurant, they saw pictures of celebrities with Meghane Hederman, one of the Hedermans, the owners of the hotel along with Hedermans Bageri, which was right next to it. She was the star of the long-running soap <u>Remember Me</u> and had plenty of local and international fans. The show was unusual in it still being thirty minutes instead of a full hour. Grandma Tindall loved watching it as much as she loved watching <u>Love of Life</u>. Sometimes, during vacations, he would watch it with her. Before she passed away Tindall told her that there were clips of its final episodes on You Tube. Apparently one of the cast members, Chandler Harben, who played the second Ben Harper on it, posted the clips. Grandma Tindall enjoyed the clips and it brought back fond memories.

Tindall and Kathleen was shown their table by the waitress, a tall young woman with dark hair. After they sat down and received their drinks the waitress asked, "What would you like to order?"

"I'll have the fried cod with fried potatoes and the soup of the day, please," Kathleen said.

"And I'll have the meatballs with mashed potatoes and

salad, please," Tindall said.

The waitress nodded and walked away with their order. After a few minutes, she returned with their order. Tindall and Kathleen noticed the different people eating lunch, talking with family and friends, and in general, thoroughly enjoying themselves.

Swirling her iced tea with lemon and sugar, Kathleen asked, "How's your Sprite?"

"It's fine," replied Tindall with a smile as he sipped it. "It's not too sweet and it's not too watered down. Of course, Pripps Blue would have been better, but it's too early in the day and I have to do some driving."

"Touché. On the other hand, I'm not in the mood for anything stronger than ice tea at this point."

"Well, I have to finish my food so I won't be late for the 1:00 meeting."

Kathleen laughed. "I hope it's not to see another woman!"

With mock seriousness, Tindall answered, "It is, but I'm already spoken for."

"Better watch yourself, buddy!" Kathleen and Tindall then quietly laughed out loud. They both trusted each other completely. They both liked to say that you shouldn't marry someone if you didn't trust and respect them. Afterwards, they quietly ate and when they were done, Tindall paid the bill and dropped Kathleen off at home. It was 12:30 pm.

1:00 pm arrived and Cecelia Killian arrived at Tindall's office. She was an average looking woman in a warm winterproof jacket. "Come in and sit down, Ms. Killian," Tindall said. Cecelia sat down after saying "Thank you" and after taking off her coat, revealing a stylish turtleneck sweater and blue jean pants.

Tindall said sadly, "Thank you for coming down here at such short notice. It's tragic when you hear an old high school friend and hometowner pass away, particularly in a tragic way."

"What happened to Linda?"

"Well, she passed away here recently in St. Marys and her passing was ruled a homicide. Since they did, my team and I are in charge of the investigation. We're speaking to anyone who knew Ms. Severinsen to find out who want to kill her."

Concern lined Cecelia's face. "How was she killed?"

Soberly, Tindall replied, "It's not something that can be discussed publicly, unfortunately. We know that you and Ms. Severinsen were friends with two other young women, Edith Albanese and Heather Rowlands, who recently passed away. Did any of you keep in touch?"

"No, we didn't. Sadly, high school friends sometimes drift away from each other. You know how it is."

"That's true," Tindall mused. Then, changing the topic, he asked, "What kind of work do you do."

"I'm a teacher at Stephen Woodfin High School in Appleton. I teach the English and literature classes there."

"And how long have you taught there?"

"For about twelve years, a few years out of college. NMU grad and proud of it," Cecelia concluded with a smile, the only smile that Tindall had seen so far.

"So have you been back to Ironwood since high school?"

"Regretfully, I've been so busy that I literally haven't had the time. With my job, my husband and my daughter, I've so much to do and so little time."

"I see. Do you know someone named Barbara Davies?"

"Isn't she the woman who passed away recently?"

"Yes, but she was previously known as your friend Linda Severinsen. Where were you Monday night through Tuesday morning?"

Shifting in her chair, Cecelia said, "I didn't know that Linda changed her name. Like I said, I lost contact with her and the other girls years ago. During the time you're asking about, I was at home with my family."

Tindall noted the restrained anger and fear in her tone. "I understand completely and my apologies for the questions," he replied soothingly, "but we have to do a thorough investigation regarding homicides. Everyone who knew the victim has to be questioned."

Somewhat mollified, Cecelia said, "I also understand as well. I want to do everything possible to help you out so that whoever killed Linda is arrested. Do you have any other questions for me, Lieutenant?"

"Not at this time and thank you for coming in."

Tindall noted the controlled irritation in her face as she walked out of his office. She's a good liar, he silently thought after she left. She knows more than what she admitted. Already he requested Perez and Parkins to ask everyone who knew Davies and Dowling if they saw Killian with them or if Killian's name was brought up. Offhand, Tindall didn't believe that Killian was involved in Davies' murder since her shock at hearing the news wasn't staged, but he didn't believe that she was shocked at the name change. She had something to hide and it was likely connected to the hit and run that she and her former BFFs were involved in. Well, if they found anything out it would be sent up to the Ironwood police and they would deal with it. He also decided that they needed to speak to someone who was very close to Rowlands at the time of her death. We'll cross that bridge when we get to it, Tindall dryly noted after he locked his office and drove home.

Cecelia was impressed by Tindall's attitude and behavior as she drove home. She couldn't tell whether or not he believed her or not. It didn't matter since she had nothing to do with Linda's death and Edith apparently died of natural causes. She was at home in bed with her husband Jeff and their daughter Shawna was in her own bed. Even if it was different Jeff would provide her an alibi out of love. Though Cecelia was shocked at their deaths, she wouldn't suffer sleepless nights over it. No one was alive who knew the truth except for her.

Strangely enough, Cecelia sometimes sensed that someone was watching her outside of her home and school. She would turn around and no one would be there. She even thought that someone else other that herself and her family had been in their house without anyone knowing about it. Things would be in different areas than they would normally be and she even sensed that someone was actually in her house while she was there! To say anything about this to Jeff and her friends would be silly beyond belief. She would end up being labeled a crazy.

Sighing, she marveled at how far she had come. A far cry from backwards and primitive Ironwood with its backward and primitive people. The whole UP could be sunk in Lake Superior and she wouldn't give a damn. She didn't give a damn about her parents, whom she considered broken down losers. Drinking and fighting was what they did the best. As soon as she could, she got out of that shithole and never went back.

What attracted her to Linda, Heather and Edith was that they had dysfunctional families like her and wanted to get away from them as soon as possible. They loved and hated their families equally. All of them were somewhat popular but others kept their distance.

One of them was Lesley Blandick. Her father was the branch manager at the local Bank of Marquette and her mother was a cataloguer at the Ironwood Carnegie Library. Cecelia envied and resented her at the same time for her grades and the way she was respected by everyone inside and outside of school. Her parents were salt of the earth types who loved and cared for her and weren't lowlifes. Well-respected people they were. Lesley also had a much older sister, who lived somewhere due south. Cecelia never met the woman nor did she know her name.

The few times that Cecelia tried to befriend Lesley she

was politely yet firmly rebuffed. Clearly, the latter had heard enough from others not to be interested. From then on, Cecelia watched her from a distance, noticing that in competition with her she always came in second, such as the president of the French Club and the Student Council elections. Lesley even got the guy she wanted as her boyfriend, Sherman Hillstrom.

Frustrated by Lesley at every turn, Cecelia was looking forward to graduation and not having to deal with her again. She was even more delighted when she found out that Lesley was accepted by The University of Michigan. Cecelia was going to NMU due to the cheap tuition and would have to do the work-study and financial aid route, her parents being unconcerned about their daughter's education. For them, they couldn't understand why their daughter didn't want to stick around Ironwood. "Because I don't want to be like you!" she wanted to cry out in rage and frustration.

Not surprisingly after the incident, Cecelia and the rest of the gang were forced out of Ironwood permanently. Too many people made it obvious that they didn't believe their story and the Blandicks were highly respected members of the community; there were also other unspoken things involved. She never came back but she always sent her parents birthday and Christmas cards; really, it would have been too much to send Father's Day and Mother's Day cards. They told her that they found religion and started going to one of the Lutheran churches in Ironwood.

Because of her parents, Cecelia was determined that her husband would be far better than her father and she would be far better than her mother. When she walked into her daughter Shawna's bedroom while she was sleeping, she vowed that she would do anything to protect her daughter, even if she had to kill to do so.

She was perfectly willing to do the same thing for Jeff, her husband. They met when she was first hired at Woodfin as the new English and literature teacher. He was the history and civics teacher there and was ten years older than her. Cecelia was shocked that she was attracted to an old guy who was never married and had no kids. Jeff was also shocked that a much younger woman was attracted to him. He was also concerned about sexual harassment issues. Only after discussions with her and with their principal, Russell Finkbeiner, was he willing to proceed further. They married after a year of dating and Cecelia kept her maiden name instead of changing it to Jeff's last name, which was Stevenson.

Cecelia finally arrived home and Jeff greeted her. "How did the meeting go?" he asked.

"It went well. I was shocked that someone that I knew from high school had been killed! I didn't even know that she was Barbara Davies, the woman at Rothmann."

"She changed her name?"

"She did. When I knew her, she was Linda Severinsen. I don't know why she changed her name." Lie, Cecelia thought.

"It's shocking when someone is murdered at a hospital. You end up not trusting the doctors or staff."

"Let's talk about something else," Cecelia said with a

smile. "Shawna's at her Girl Scout meeting?"

"I took her there myself," replied Jeff. "She loves the Saturday meetings and gets along well with the other girls from what I see and from what the scout leader, Mrs. Vasiledes has said."

Cecelia agreed. "Mrs. Vasiledes never has said a bad word about Shawna. It's good that she's involved in the Scouts, since 'idle hands and minds are the devil's workshop'".

Jeff laughed, "I didn't know that you were religious."

Dryly, Cecelia replied, "You know I'm not." Then she grinned. "But you married me anyway!"

"I did because I loved you and I still do," he said as he hugged and kissed her. "By the way, since Shawna won't be back for a few hours we'll have the house to ourselves."

"I know. Let's go upstairs!"

After about a half hour of sex, both Cecelia and Jeff were satiated. The former was lying in their bed, staring at the ceiling while the latter was on his side, asleep. One of the things about Jeff that amazed Cecelia was that he usually drifted off to sleep after sex. The sex was good and Jeff was a sensitive lover, which Cecelia appreciated. Not the spread your legs and quick thrust kind. She was inexperienced in that kind of sex and was frankly scared when she had to do it the first time. Now she was comfortable and loved it.

She wasn't a fearful person, but the deaths of Linda and Edith, coupled with the thoughts of being watched, scared her. She couldn't talk to Jeff regarding it since she would have to reveal things that she didn't want to disclose. Maybe she could even make peace with her parents. Jeff, her Baptist other half, gently suggested this. Once everything was okay she would seriously consider it. Not now, not now, she mused, tightly twisting the bed sheet in her hands.

16

Kathleen's probably going to have quite a few questions for me, Tindall silently thought as he entered the house. He heard music in the background, Phil Collins to be exact, along with Kathleen's voice singing in the background. What a beautiful voice, Tindall mused as he walked into the living room. "Hello stranger!" he called out to Katheen.

"And hello back!" she replied as she turned the Philips boombox off and sat down. "You probably won't be able to tell me anything about the interview since it's a police issue but what about Tallichet?"

"Well, he gave me a letter from Grandma and Grandpa regarding something that they wanted me to do for them concerning Uncle Matt."

Concerned, Kathleen replied, "If you don't want to discuss it with me, Frank, I won't push it."

"No, Kathleen, I do want to discuss it with you." After handing the letter over to her Tindall continued, "Here's the letter. After you read it we can discuss it further." She quickly read the letter and replied, "When will you begin to track your uncle down regarding this?"

"I already know where Uncle Matt lives and I'll contact him once I'm done with this case. He may spit in my face and I may not want to have anything to do with him, but I have to carry out Grandpa and Grandma's wishes. I know that he must have done something horrible but no one wants to tell me what."

"There may be someone who can give you the answer you're looking for," said Kathleen in a quiet voice, "but they have to get permission to discuss it. I'll be back in a few minutes." She then left the living room and went upstairs.

"Thanks." Tindall knew that Kathleen had the information but she couldn't disclose it until she had authorization to do so. He remembered hushed conversations regarding Uncle Matt that ended when he came into the room. It also initially affected the relationship between him and Old Peter and made the relationship between Grandpa and Old Peter even worse than what it already was.

While Tindall waited downstairs, Kathleen called her mother on her cellphone, Mrs. Adelheid Behnke. The phone rang twice before her mother answered, "Hi Kathleen! Are you okay? You normally don't call before Sunday unless it's something serious."

"It is Mom, but before that, how's Dad doing?"

"He's doing fine. He's here in the house watching CNN. What happened?"

"Frank received a letter regarding his Uncle Matt from his grandparents' attorney Tallichet. Basically, his grandparents requested that they find Uncle Matt and make sure that he's okay."

"And you're calling to get my permission to discuss what happened with Frank?"

"Yes."

"It would be better for me to talk to him regarding this. Is he there?"

"He is. I'll take the phone down to him."

"Thank you, Kathleen and I'll wait."

Kathleen went back downstairs to the living room where Tindall was quietly waiting. She silently handed him her cellphone and sat down. Tindall then said "Hello and who is this?"

"It's your mother-in-law, Frank! And how are you doing?"

"I'm fine Mom and how's Dad doing?"

"He's fine and he's watching CNN." Mrs. Behnke sadly continued, "The reason for all of this was when your uncle Matt went to The University of Michigan my niece Stephanie Meldrim attended at the same time. They fell in love with each other and she became pregnant. Matt didn't want the responsibility of fatherhood or marriage at that time, so he pressured Stephanie to get an abortion. This was pre-Roe vs Wade so abortion was illegal in Michigan. I knew that Stephanie was pregnant but I didn't know she was going to get an abortion."

"Weren't the two of you old enough to be sisters?"

"Correct. I was just ten years older than Stephanie so our relationship was more like sisters than aunt and niece. Originally, we found out that she passed away due to an internal hemorrhage. But when it turned out that she died due to a back alley abortion and Matt was involved, all hell broke loose. My brother Peter confronted your grandfather and the confrontation was so vicious that they had to be prevented from killing each other. For about a year Peter was so angry that he refused to speak to me, believing that I knew about the abortion. I advised her to step away from school during the pregnancy and put the child up for adoption."

"I think that I know where this is going, Mom."

"Yes. Your grandfather and grandmother had an ugly confrontation with Matt and basically told him to get the hell out of their house and their family. They and the other Tindalls completely cut him off. To them, a real man married the woman that he got pregnant and took care of her and the child."

"Based on what you told me, Uncle Matt reaped what he sowed."

"That's right. But it also looks like that your grandparents didn't want to see him rotting away in the gutter."

Tindall cleared his throat. "I have a question for you, Mom, and if you don't want to answer it I understand. What kind of relationship did Stephanie had with her parents?"

"Difficult if not awful. Peter was domineering and not to be trifled with. His wife Kerstin was the same way, though she knew how to tow the line when necessary with Peter. In that household Stephanie would have been crushed if she was passive and compliant. She was a rebel, a wild child, and neither of them knew how to deal with it. Stephanie was shipped off to expensive boarding schools because of all of that. I couldn't intervene because she wasn't my child and no abuse was involved."

"That's terrible to hear."

"It is. Barbara loved her parents and they loved her but they didn't know how to relate to each other, and when she died, it was too late to try to work things out. That, I believe, was why Peter was so angry at your grandfather and me."

"You can't reconcile with the dead."

"Sad but true. I hope that I've answered any questions you had." In a brighter tone, Mrs. Behnke added, "It's better when people can talk about happy things and not depressing things."

"I agree and thanks for the information, Mom. Do you want to speak to Kathleen again?"

"No, we'll talk about brighter things tomorrow. Good bye!"

"The same to you!" Tindall concluded. Walking over to Kathleen, he reached out and hugged her. "I don't want what happened to Barbara to happen to our kids if we have any. I want our house to be a place where our kid is safe with talking to us and they're not afraid of us. That doesn't mean that the kid runs the house but that they can be heard."

Shuddering, Kathleen murmured, "I didn't know that the relationship between Barbara and my aunt and uncle was so bad. He was never like that with me but with Amy he had no use for her."

"Well, you have relatives who don't like each other or even hate each other. It's tragic, and I've seen quite a few cases of it at work. Let's talk about something else."

"The Harvest Festival is coming up at All Souls, so we'll need some volunteers," Kathleen said with a smile. "Would you like to volunteer?"

Laughing, Tindall replied, "You ask me every year and you get the same answer, yes!"

"I have to ask since it wouldn't be polite to assume," said Kathleen with mock seriousness. "After all, you always ask me every year regarding the Oktoberfest Festival."

"Agreed, and we volunteer for both. I'm talked out and the library will be closing at 6:00. Do you want to come?"

"But of course!" Tindall and Kathleen then went to the library together.

17

Sundays in St. Marys were mostly quiet, particularly in the early part of the day. Some St. Marians slept in through the morning after a night of fun in one of the local bars or nightspots or just because they didn't have to wake up early due to not working on Sundays. Others woke up early, beginning at 5:00 am, in preparation for attending church. The church bells began to ring throughout St. Marys and its surrounding towns and villages at 7:30 am and continued to do so through 11:00 am, surrounding the entire county with the message of announcing the Gospel and the holiness and purity of its message.

All through this time, men and women, old and young of different races and backgrounds walked into the First Methodist Church, St. Marys Presbyterian Church and the other local churches, some willingly to quench their thirst for the Gospel and to spend time with God, others only at the urging of their mate or at the order of their parent or parents. Still others came to find a pretty girl or a handsome boy or maybe to drum up some business for themselves or their company. A few spectators came for the novelty value or just curiosity. Everyone was welcome and maybe even a few got their souls and minds right with God for the first time.

But what about the sermons, you may ask? The

sermons encompassed a wide variety of themes based on the man or woman delivering it from the pulpit and the parishioners who put them on their payroll. In one church, the sermon may have a modern, New Ageist theme in which God is within you and the world is basically a good place with good people who merely have issues. In another church, the sermon may consist of God wanting you to live the good life and you can have it all if you just name and claim it from Him. The only sermon worth listening to and meditating on today, the Lord's Day, and future days, would be the sermon that preaches man's inherent wickedness and depravity and states that the only way to avoid Hell and the Lake of Fire is through the Gospel revealed to man by the Bible. Some may scoff and others may yawn, but it is what it is.

University Lutheran Church on 1000 University Ave, was Tindall's church and the only time he didn't attend it was when he was up in East Lansing at MSU. While he was there, he attended Martin Luther Chapel close to the MSU campus. He was neither shocked nor surprised that some of his contemporaries didn't want to attend church, since this was a time that they were away from home and they had to learn for themselves on whether or not they truly believed in the Gospel.

Tindall began to question his faith in his mid-teens, which wasn't an unusual time to do so. Other people began to question their faith once they went off to college. He finally realized that he had to make a choice on whether or not Christianity was true or not. After long, hard thinking, he came to the conclusion that it was true based on the fact that the Bible was true and it wasn't a book of fairy tales. Over the years, he liked to read books written by people like Lee Strobel, who knew how to defend Christianity in a way that ordinary people could understand and comprehend. Tindall read <u>Concordia: The Lutheran Confessions: A Reader's Edition of the Book of Concord</u> from cover to cover and it was a real meat and potatoes book, but you had to exercise your mental muscles to read it. That was why he appreciated writers such as Strobel.

As for University Lutheran itself, the parish and the church dated back to 1872. Prior to that time, the Lutherans living in what became St. Marys County in 1876 worshiped in each other's homes, with travelling ministers and in emergency cases laymen performing baptisms and Holy Communion. The church itself, a lovely red brick structure with a tall steeple crowned with a cross, still had the original bells that were rung on Sundays and whenever services were held. Over the years, some in the parish wanted to build another church on the site and the requests were rejected at large. It served the university community and the neighborhood that surrounded it. Traditionally, the area was a mix of upscale and middle class, and on any given Sunday you would see students, professors, blue collar and white-collar employees from Hamilton University and the surrounding neighborhood, and members of St. Marys' elite such as the Hedermans. From time to time, Meghane Hederman would be seen in one of the pews with her family and no one would ask for her autograph or disturb her. The Hedermans and Tindalls knew each other since the latter were prominent at the university and both were prominent at University Lutheran. It was an open secret that two of the Vestry Board seats would always be reserved for the Hedermans and Tindalls if they ran. There was some grumbling about this, but the naysayers' complaints were easily dismissed as sour grapes.

Since his cousin Elaine wasn't interested in the Vestry Board, Tindall ran for it and not surprisingly won it. He was active on the Vestry Board, and it didn't hurt that he worked for the Police Department and was married to one of the Meldrims. The congregation was about 1,500 members, which meant that Sunday services occurred at 8:15 am, 9:30 am, and 11:00 am. The parish was healthy in terms of finances and population. Tindall recalled the late Rev. David Eberhard of Historic Trinity Lutheran Church in Detroit advising that a church needed at least 350 members in order to be viable for the long term.

University Lutheran also had a grade school, from preschool to the 8th Grade. Some of the parish children went to the grade school, others went to the University School at Hamilton University and still others went to the St. Marys Public School District. Those living outside of the city attending public schools went to the St. Marys County School District. The parish along with other Lutheran churches in the county supported St. Marys Lutheran High School, which was one of the two county wide high schools for the Lutheran community.

As you walk inside University Lutheran's front entrance, you see pews filled with hymnals, communion cards and offering envelopes. Directly above the front entrance is the loft where the organist plays music and the choir, consisting of men and children of all ages and backgrounds, singing chorales, cantatas, and hymns that lead God and His angels to weep with emotion. Ahead of you on the right is the baptismal fount, dating back to 1905 and set in the floor, where hundreds if not thousands have been baptized, some here and some no longer here. Directly in front of you is the altar, covered with a clean, patterned white cloth. This is where on Communion Sundays the Mystery of Holy Communion manifests itself when Christ's Presence becomes part of the bread and wine through the Words of Institution spoken by the pastor.

On the wall behind the alter hangs a large, empty cross, symbolizing the defeat of sin, death and the power of the devil by Christ's death and resurrection. Above the altar and on the stained-glass windows are depictions of incidents from the Bible such as Moses at the burning bush and Jesus healing the sick and demon-possessed. To the altar's left side, you can see the lectern where laymen and laywomen read from the Old Testment, Epistles and the Gospels. On the altar's left side is the pastor's lectern where the sermon is given. Birth and death, marriage and hope, are present along with the hopes, dreams, and sorrows of all those who enter here and leave refreshed by God's gifts.

Tindall and Kathleen went to each other's church one a month, and this was the Sunday to spend together at University Lutheran. Next Sunday would be spent at All Souls Episcopal Church, which was also the spiritual home of the Peppiatts, owners of St. Marys Bank and Trust. Tindall wasn't a fan of Episcopalianism, Anglicanism, or whatever it was called, but he held his tongue to keep peace in the family home. He didn't have any problems with the rector there, Rev. Samuel Sholes, who was also a cousin of Pat Sholes, the person in charge of the Crime Lab on the weekends as well as when Chuck and Ann were on vacation.

After the first part of the service concluded and the sermon hymn was sung, Pastor Geoffrey Dingle began his sermon. One of things Tindall found interesting was that he could listen to his sermons with rapt attention and ten minutes after the sermon had concluded, he couldn't remember anything except for brief snatches of verbiage. Others within the parish probably could say the same thing.

The pastor was the same age as Tindall and was married with two cats and no children. He and his wife, Mrs. Dorothy Dingle, lived in the pastor's house located on the same property as the church. It was built a few years after the church in the same red brick manner. Tindall and Kathleen had dinner at the pastor's house and the Dingles had dinner at their house. They all considered each other as friends. In terms of doctrine, Pastor Dingle was well within the bounds of what was acceptable in the Missouri Synod. He didn't have a problem with the theological liberals at University Lutheran as long as they weren't open about their views. Most of the of the other parishioners, conservatives to a man or woman, had the same viewpoint.

Today's service didn't include Holy Communion so it was done in just under an hour. Neither Tindall nor Kathleen liked to stay after the service for Bible Study or for the refreshments in the lounge. They normally said hello to their friends and acquaintances before the service began. Fellowship with other Christians was one of the things that Tindall liked about going to church. The main reason for him was to worship and praise God and also to publicly affirm his faith.

After they greeted Pastor and Mrs. Dingle, Kathleen asked Tindall as they walked back home, "So what do you want to after we get home?"

Yawning, Tindall replied, "I don't want to do anything but just relax since it's work again for us tomorrow."

"Agreed. I don't want to do anything now myself. I may do some reading or TV. I don't know right now. There's nothing around the house that needs to be done except to cook—"

"And we can wait until about two or three to do it."

"Right. It's so nice that we can walk back and forth from here. Of course, we can also do so to All Souls."

"Yeah, I know that it's my time to come to All Souls. But I do like Sholes and the people there. They've been as nice to me—"

"As the people here have been nice to me. And that's how it should be."

"Isn't it so nice and sunny out here?" Tindall cried as he looked at the sky. "The birds are still here flying around. I just hope that none of them plops on my car. Bird murder in that case would be justified homicide."

Kathleen agreed. "I feel the same way about slugs in my garden. I just love to pour a little salt on them and watch them dissolve into gooey slime. Used to do that quite a bit as a kid."

"I also loved to do the same thing with flies. Such filthy creatures! I was quite skilled as a kid in smashing them with the curtains without staining them. Grandpa and Grandma would've had a conniption fit if the curtains were damaged!"

They both laughed. One of the things that Tindall and Kathleen liked about each other was that they made each other laugh in a manner that wasn't crude or boorish. Though sometimes they did like crude humor. They also never laughed at other people. Both Tindall's grandparents and Kathleen's parents made it clear to them when they were younger that it wasn't acceptable and it wouldn't be tolerated for them to laugh at other people, particularly due to a mental or physical disability.

One of the few times that Grandpa and Grandma Tindall were angry with him was during one Oktoberfest at St. Matthew's when he was twelve and an old pal of his named Jake Finazzo, who was the same age, mocked a deaf boy who was still dancing when the Oompah Orchestra had finished playing their music; the deaf boy had apparently turned off his hearing aid or aids for a moment. When Tindall's grandparents heard what had happened, they forced him to apologize to the deaf boy and his family in public and sent him home with no dinner. The same thing happened to Jake, who was now a teacher in Missouri. They still kept in touch with each other via Skype and Facebook.

As far as Tindall knew, nothing like that every occurred with Kathleen. Even though he was embarrassed as well as being angry over it, once he became older he appreciated what Grandpa and Grandma Tindall did to him. They wanted him to "walk a mile" in that other kid's shoes. Ironically, he and the kid, Bradley Eichhorst, became friends and still were to this day. If more parents disciplined their kids and taught them Christianity and knowing right from wrong he wouldn't have a job as a cop. Most of the people in prison, Tindall knew, came from broken or dysfunctional homes. People with stable, safe and healthy homes with married mothers and fathers tended not to end up in prison, the streets or dead.

"Well, we're home," Kathleen said as they arrived back to their house. "Are you okay, Frank? You looked out of it."

"I'm fine," Tindall replied, "I was just lost in my thoughts. Well, let's relax before we have to get back to work tomorrow."

"Yes, master!" Kathleen said with a laugh as she and Tindall went inside.

18

Ernie Davies sat in his living room on a bright Monday morning. It was almost 11:00 am and he was planning on running a few errands in the afternoon. He was scheduled to return back to work on Monday next week and following wise advice from the policeman whom he previously spoken to, he severely cut back on his drinking.

Davies also scheduled the date of Barbara's funeral with Hay & Daughters Funeral Home on Main and Third in St. Marys. He received a call from Tindall as he was calling people to give them the funeral date and time. "Have you caught Barbara's killer?"

"Not yet, Mr. Davies," replied Tindall, "but I do have an additional question or two to ask."

"And they are?" was the angry answer.

"Did you know that Mrs. Davies' original name was Linda Severinsen and that she came from Ironwood in the UP?"

Surprised, Davies replied, "I knew nothing about this. I've always known my wife as Barbara Davies."

"I'm restricted on what I can say due to this still being

an open case, but I can advise that what I've just said is true. Do you know of any of Mrs. Davies' friends and acquaintances that knew her prior to college and St. Marys?"

"No, all of the people that know her are only from college like Gwennie Nancarrow or the people she met after she moved to St. Marys."

"Thanks. If you can think of anyone else please call me back."

"Okay." Davies then hung up and went back to making his calls. He was angry at Tindall for calling him back with nothing further to tell him. But he also was angry at Barbara for not telling him fully about her past. He knew that something had happened due her evasiveness but he didn't know that she was a completely different person. What else was she involved in that I didn't know about, Davies wondered. I hope that her past didn't catch up with her at the end.

Davies' next call was to Gwennie Nancarrow. "Hello Gwennie, this is Ernie."

"Hello Ernie!" Gwennie replied. "Is everything okay?"

"It is and I hope that I'm not calling at a bad time."

"You're not and what do you need?"

Davies heard the concern in Gwennie's voice. Clearing his throat, he answered, "I'm calling to tell you that Barbara's funeral will be at Hay & Daughters Funeral Home on Wednesday of this week. I also wanted to ask if you wanted to play the music at Barbara's funeral."

After choking sobs, Gwennie replied, "I would be delighted to do so. I also have some of my own music that I can play if you wish. Do you want me to send it to you?"

"No need to do so, Gwennie, since you always have good taste and I trust your judgement."

"Still, I don't want to assume so I will e-mail the music file to you right now. It will take a minute or so. What's your e-mail address?"

Davies gave it to Gwennie. He received the file in about a minute and said, "I'll call you back today after I listen to the music and I'll have an answer for you then." Davies then asked, "Gwennie, did Barbara ever talk about someone named Linda Severinsen?"

"The name does not sound familiar. Is she a relative of Barbara's?"

"No, Linda Severinsen was Barbara's original name. The cop in charge of Barbara's case—Tindall—told me that she legally changed her to Barbara Russell name prior to moving here."

"I knew nothing about this. I always thought that Barbara Russell was her name."

"Thanks for your help, Gwennie."

"Of course. I will talk to you later. See you!"

"Same here." After hanging up Davies felt guilt at his attraction towards Gwennie. Barbara had only been dead a week and he wanted to bed her best friend. Actually, he had been attracted to both Barbara and Gwennie when he first met them—he had actually met Barbara for the first time through her friend Melanie Hunter. The reason that he chose Barbara was due to religion. Neither of them were religious and Davies quickly found out that Gwennie was and in a deep and thoughtful way. For starters, someone who was a church organist tended to be more religious than someone who worked for a regular band. Also, Gwennie was up front about only dating and marrying someone who was a Christian. He didn't know if Gwennie was attracted to him and he would never ask due to his respect for Barbara and her. Well, that's something I don't have time to deal with right now, Davies sighed as he returned to his calls.

Gwennie never admitted to Barbara and she certainly wouldn't admit to Ernie that she had been attracted to him from the moment that she saw him. Something held her back and led her to encourage Barbara while she was dating Ernie. It was a wise move, since Barbara and Ernie were an excellent fit. Gwennie was a Christian who wanted to marry a Christian man. Ernie wasn't religious but it wasn't in a nasty Bill Maher type of way. It just wasn't for him. Barbara had the same attitude, though sometimes she would ask Gwennie questions about her faith.

She knew that Barbara did receive some religious training in the past based on her questions. She loved discussing her faith to those who were interested and she didn't have any patience for those on either side of the fence who tried to cram their views down other people's throats. Gwennie wasn't terribly shocked about the news that she just received from Ernie. She knew that Barbara was hiding something and that was why she was so secretive. When it comes to murder investigations, she thought, the police will find out everything that's hidden. She also felt guilty because Barbara had been dead just a week and she had strong feelings of attraction towards Ernie. Those feelings had been checked due to her friendship with Barbara and her respect for another woman's marriage. Gwennie decided a long time ago that she wasn't going to have sex until marriage and she thanked God that He gave her the strength to persevere. Now I have to get back to work regarding the music for next Sunday's services, she thought, there's so much to do and so little time...

Tindall figured that Davies didn't know about wife's name change but he had to ask. Earlier in the morning he briefed Capt. Carter on the status of the investigation and he merely nodded in approval. The police chief and Mrs. Bruschetta were receiving everything that was available. Neither Perez nor Parkins had any new information to report.

Tindall was still waiting to hear from Ann and Chuck regarding if there were any e-mails or calls from Mrs. Davies' old high school chums on her computers or iPhone. He talked to them today and all Ann said was that they were still working on it. And she gave no time frame on it. Sighing, all Tindall and the team could do was to wait.

Out of curiosity, Tindall decided to go online to see if he could find any information regarding Lesley Blandick's funeral. He knew that her parents had predeceased her so a relative or relatives would have handled the funeral arrangements. Typing in Lesley's full name, Tindall noted that her funeral took place at St. Mary's Catholic Church in Ironwood earlier this year per the Ironwood Daily Globe.

Since she had been in a coma since the age of eighteen the information about her life was brief. He also noted that a sister named Ali was listed. No last name nor Ali's location was listed.

Highly odd, Tindall thought, I'm going to do a further check on Ms. Ali Blandick. The Ironwood police did note that Ms. Blandick's parents were killed in an auto accident while on their way to visit Lesley in the nursing home five years prior to her passing. He decided to do a check on Lesley's parents, Bibiana and Dominus Blandick, and found out that their funeral was also held at St. Mary's in Ironwood. Their two daughters, Lesley and Ali were listed, but there was no last name or location for Ali.

Tindall decided call St. Mary's and speak to the priest there regarding any information pertaining to the Blandicks. After a few rings, the call was answered by a woman.

"This is St. John's and how can I help you?"

"This is Lt. Frank Tindall from the St. Marys Police Dept. May I speak to the priest in charge of St. John's? I need to speak to him regarding a case that we're working on."

"Oh! I'll get Fr. John. One moment please."

Tindall quietly waited for a minute until he heard a warm, genteel voice say, "This is Fr. John. Cassie told me that you're from the St. Marys Police Dept. Are you located in Michigan?"

"Yes, we're located in the Michiana area."

"Heard of it but never been there. Pleased to talk to you, Lieutenant. What do you need from me?"

"As I advised Cassie, we're working on a case that may involve a Lesley Blandick and her family. Specifically, we need to know what information you have regarding her sister Ali."

"Well, I've been the parish priest here for about ten years and I knew Mr. and Mrs. Blandick well prior to their passing. As for Ali, I didn't know her that well. She was close to twenty years older than Lesley. When she came to visit her parents and Lesley she would attend church here. She was polite but distant, and she really never talked about herself. I didn't even know that she was a doctor until Mrs. Dobbins, one of the parishioners here at St. Mary's, had a heart attack and she treated her until the ambulance arrived. Fortunately, she survived."

"Fr. John," Tindall asked, "Did Ali ever come with her husband and kids and do you know what kind of doctor she was?"

"Sometimes she did and I don't know what kind of doctor she was. Her husband's first name was the same as mine but I can't recall their last name. It wasn't a regular last name such as Jones and he owned a retail store selling watches, jewels or something of the sort. I can't recall the names of her children, though."

"Is there someone else at St. Mary's who would have any additional information about the Blandicks?"

"The only other person who may have some more information would be Mrs. Kaiser, who was our office manager for thirty years. She retired about a year or so ago and still lives in Ironwood. My predecessor, Fr. Rocco DiPonio, passed away about five years ago. You'll receive a call back from me in about a day or so."

"Thanks, Fr. John. By the way, what is your last name?"

"It's Halloran. H-a-l-l-o-r-a-n."

"I have one more question, please. Do you know if Ali lives in Michigan?"

"She did say that she liked the part of Michigan she was in because she and the family could do day trips to Chicago if they wanted to."

Tindall gave Fr. John his callback number and thanked him again. After hanging up, Tindall noticed some progress. After a few minutes jotting some items on a scrap of paper, Tindall walked out of his office and down to Perez and Parkins' cubicles. Grinning like a Cheshire Cat, Tindall announced, "We've gotten some more info regarding the Blandicks!"

Skeptically, Parkins asked, "What info did we get?"

"I was able to get some information from Fr. John Halloran at St. Mary's Catholic Church in Ironwood. The Blandicks went to that church. They also had another daughter, Ali, whom Fr. John stated was close to twenty years older than Lesley. She was also a doctor per the good father and she also said that in the part of Michigan she and her family lived in they could take day trips to Chicago if they wanted to."

"Sounds like Ali may live around here," Perez noted.

"Correct," replied Tindall. "Now, in regards to Ali's name it could be her actual name—I've known cases of people with the names of Kristie, Jamie, or Tina and those were their actual names—or it could be a nickname for Alison, Alix, Alicia, Alisa, Alis, Alexandra or Alice."

"So that means we're going to have to check under all of those variants?"

"Right. And thinking further about it, Ali could be her first or middle name or it may not even be her legal name at all. Also, she could have a new name due to marriage or divorce."

"One of the nice things about the Net," mused Parkins, "it that it sometimes reduces some of the grunt work time."

"Sometimes," Tindall said, "and sometimes not. I'll do the search under Ali, Alisa, Alis, and Alexandra and you and Mike'll do the search under the other names. Good luck to all of us!"

Tindall walked back to his office and began his search on a database only available to police departments. Twenty minutes later he found nothing and walked out of his office over to Perez and Parkins. "I didn't find anything under my names," Tindall wryly noted. "Have you guys found anything yet?"

"I'm looking right now under Alison," said Parkins. "Mike and I weren't able to find anything under the other names. Looks like we found something."

Moving over to Parkins' computer, Perez replied,

"There's a Judith Alison Blandick who married a John Bruschetta in 1990. The marriage license was issued by the St. Marys County Clerk's office."

"My, my, my," Tindall purred, "Dr. Bruschetta of Rothmann is Lesley Blandick's big sister. I'm waiting to receive a call back from Fr. John Halloran at St. Mary's in Ironwood regarding the Blandicks. Now we need to get all of the information available regarding Dr. Bruschetta."

Parkins asked, "Do you think that Dr. Bruschetta was involved in Davies' murder?"

"Possibly. Considering her status in the community, I don't want to go there until we have enough evidence. I don't want anyone's job to be on the line regarding this. Mike and Jim, I want you to find everything you can about Dr. Bruschetta from birth to present. Also find out if she had any connections to Davies and company."

"We'll take care of it," said Perez. Glancing at the wall clock he announced that it was lunch time. Tindall grinned over it, since he was so busy he completely missed the time.

Tindall thanked them and walked down to his office. He turned on his radio and listened to some music while eating his lunch. Have to buy a mp3 player soon, he said to himself. He also had to follow up with Ann and Chuck regarding Mrs. Davies' items. Too bad he couldn't just enjoy a nice sunny day but you can't laze around during a work day.

Yawning, Tindall saw that it was time to get back to work. He walked down to the Crime Lab and said hello

Chuck and the rest of the staff. Tindall then asked, "Where's your better half, Chuck?"

"Oh, she stepped out for a minute," replied Chuck. I know what you're here for and sad to say, none of Mrs. Davies' items have anything on them regarding the other three women you asked about."

"That's fine. Thanks and also give my thanks to Ann when she gets back."

"I will and see you later."

Tindall considered it a crap shoot and wasn't disappointed at Chuck's information. If Mrs. Davies had contact with the three women, she could have easily done it using one of those disposable cell phones. No trace as long as you paid in cash and bought it outside of your area. He saw that Fr. John from St. Mary's left a message on his voice mail once he returned to his office.

After reaching Fr. John, Tindall said, "Thank you for calling me back so quickly, Father John. What information was Mrs. Kaiser able to give you?"

"She told me that the Blandicks arrived in Ironwood from Marquette after Lesley, the youngest daughter, was born. Pretty little child, according to Mrs. Kaiser. A tragedy what happened to her. Ali, the oldest daughter, only lived here until she graduated and went to NMU. She used to come back often during the weekends and summers. Prior to the move here, Ali was sick for a year or so before the move."

"Did Mrs. Kaiser know what the illness was?"

"She didn't know what it was but she also told me that during Ali's illness she and Mrs. Blandick were together."

"And Mrs. Blandick was pregnant at the same time?"

"Yes, it's sounds odd but that's the information I was given."

"Did Mrs. Kaiser have any information about the relationships between the Blandicks?"

"She said that they were very warm and loving with each other, though she did say that Ali behaved in an odd way towards Lesley, sometimes more like a mother than an older sister. She told me that when Ali found out about what happened, she was devastated in a way that you only see with a mother."

"I see. Well, thank you for your information, Fr. John. I'll call you back if I have any further questions."

"Please do so."

Tindall hung up the phone and thought for a few minutes. After making a few calls and a few requests, he walked out to Perkins and Perez and gave them the information received from Fr. John.

Parkins replied thoughtfully, "It sound real odd what Fr. John was told by that Kaiser lady. Real odd."

"Agreed," replied Perez. "What do you think Frank?"

"I don't want to say right now but I'm waiting to get some further information before I tip my hand," Tindall answered. "Hopefully, it won't take that long."

"We still getting all of the information available regarding Dr. Bruschetta and we should have all of it by the end of the day or early tomorrow."

"That'll be fine. We'll go through everything tomorrow in our daily meeting. Thanks."

Perez and Parkins did a thumbs up as Tindall walked back to his office.

Sitting down in his chair, Tindall took some notes, made a few calls and leaned back in his chair with an air of relief in his face. He needed to find out if Heather Rowlands had any close friends in the Metro Detroit area at the time of her passing, so he decided to call Insp. Charlie Watkins of the Detroit Police Department. After a few rings, Tindall was greeted by a gruff "Insp. Watkins, Detroit Police Department."

"Hello Charlie, this is Frank Tindall from the St. Marys Police Dept. How's the wife and kids?"

"They're fine. I heard that you recently got married. Congrats."

"That's true and thanks. My team and I are working on a homicide case and I need some info about a Heather Rowlands. She was found drowned in the Detroit River about three years ago."

"I remember the case well. It was handled by 'Sloppy Joe' McIssac and he didn't get that name from a favorite kind of food."

Tindall knew perfectly well what Watkins was hinting at. "So you didn't think that it was handled as it should have been?"

"No, but it wasn't my case and you know the rules."

"I know them well and I don't ask any questions. Well, can you find out if Ms. Rowlands had any close friends in Detroit when she passed away that we can contact?"

"I will and you'll get a call back no later than next week."

"Thanks, Charlie."

Tindall checked his watch and saw that it was 5:00 pm. "Time to go home," he said to himself as he put on his coat and shut everything off. He then locked his office and said goodbye to Perez and Parkins. Calling Kathleen as he walked to his car, he asked, "Do you need for me to pick anything up from Koditscheks?"

"No, we're all set here until the weekend," Kathleen replied. "See you soon!"

"Same here," Tindall replied as he hung up. Supposed to rain tomorrow, he thought. Well, that's what umbrellas are for, chucking inwardly as he drove home.

19

Perez noted that Tuesdays sometimes moved quickly and sometimes they were long and drawn out. Everything was going well at home with Sheila and the kids. As for Parkins, it was just Millie and him at the house since their kid was grown and living on her own and he didn't care either way about Tuesdays. Tindall shared Parkins' sentiments and kept his focus to Fridays as the most important work week. Sundays were very important to him for obvious reasons.

It was 8:30 am and the daily meeting regarding the Davies case began with Tindall. "Jim, what information did you and Mike get about Dr. Bruschetta?"

Flipping through their notes, Parkins replied, "Dr. Judith Alison Bruschetta was born on 12/12/63 to Bibiana and Dominus Blandick at St. Luke's Hospital, in Marquette, Michigan. She graduated from Marquette Senior High School in 1980 and graduated from NMU in 1984. She enrolled in Wayne State University's medical school and received her doctor's license in 1992. Dr. Bruschetta did her residency at Rothmann and after completing it and after receiving her degree she was hired there full time."

Picking up the thread, Perez continued, "In 1990 Dr. Bruschetta married John Bruschetta, the owner of Bruschetta Jewelers in St. Marys and they had two children, Veronica and Mark."

"Have either of you heard of Boult Hospital?" Tindall asked.

"The name sounds familiar," said Perez.

"I vaguely recalled the case until yesterday," answered Tindall. In the Nineties, there was a scandal involving Boult Hospital, which was in a suburb of Detroit called Canton. There were allegations that for the right amount, they would issue fake certificate of births to the local registrar in violation of the law."

"To people who bought babies on the black market?"

"Yes, as well as for families who wanted to cover up their daughters birthing illegitimate children. Some families didn't care, but others would due to scandal concerns. Do you know where I'm going?"

"You think that Dr. Bruschetta was Lesley Blandick's mother," answered Parkins.

"Exactly. I don't believe that the father was a family member or relative. She probably got involved with some boy her age and had to go to her parents when she got pregnant."

Perez jumped in. "From the info we received, Mrs. Blandick lived in Hamtramck prior to her marriage, which is also a Detroit suburb. So when Dr. Bruschetta became pregnant, Mrs. Blandick could ask a few questions and get the answer she needed."

"Yes, and the answer was Boult Hospital," replied

Tindall. "The cover story for the relatives and friends in the UP was that Mrs. Blandick suddenly became pregnant after so many years and at about the same time Ali came down with a sudden illness that couldn't be treated in the UP. The best special treatment hospitals in this state are in the Detroit and Ann Arbor areas."

"And of course, Ali's illness lasted about the same time as her mother's pregnancy."

"That's right. Since Boult Hospital was a private clinic that would churn out fake records for both mother and daughter for a price."

Shaking his head, Parkins asked, "What evidence do we have?"

"We don't. What I'm saying is strictly a theory on my part. If we can prove it, then I will be able to say who I believed murdered Mrs. Davies."

"You remember what you said a while ago about Edith Dowling?" asked Perez.

Frowning, Tindall replied, "Yes, I said that Red Friman and his team found signs that someone tried to pick Dowling's back door lock."

Perez handed a printout to Tindall. "Take a look at this." Tindall read it for a few minutes and replied with surprise, "I didn't know that Dr. Bruschetta was a locksmith in her previous life."

"I was surprised too when I saw this piece online from Michiana Living's website. It's dated March 2012 and she talks about working in a locksmith shop starting in high

169

school and through college. Dr. Bruschetta also talked about she still picked locks for fun that she bought from the local hardware store. She's even a member of Associate Locksmiths of America and on a few occasions, gave her husband advice on the best type of locks to use at Bruschetta Jewelers."

Tindall drummed his fingers for a minute or so before he replied. "I think that Edith Dowling was murdered and her murderer was the same as Davies'. Once we get further information regarding Rowlands and we have a further chat with Dr. Bruschetta, I'll tip my hand further."

"Are you going back to Rothmann to talk to Dr. Bruschetta?"

"She has to come down here. Can you call her regarding it? I have to talk to Capt. Carter for a few minutes."

"I'll take care of it. But why do you want her to come down here?"

"We need something that only the good Dr. Bruschetta can provide us regarding the case," replied Tindall mildly. "We wouldn't be able to get it if I went to her office."

After a second, the penny turned for Perez. "You're talking about—"

"Yes."

"All right, I'll call her and get her down here."

"Thanks." Tindall walked down to Capt. Carter's office. The latter was busy on a call when Tindall stepped in and he motioned Tindall to sit down. Tindall sat quietly as Capt. Carter talked amiably about this or that, hither and thither to the other caller. It wasn't a business-related call. After a minute or so, Capt. Carter announced, "Well, I have to go since I have some work to catch up on. Talk to you soon and bye."

Capt. Carter then said, "Do you have anything new regarding the Davies case?"

"I believe we do, but we need to get some additional information. I have to speak to Dr. Bruschetta here and Mike's calling her to see when she can come down here."

"Something's going on Frank. Do you want to tell me now or do you want to keep it close to your chest?"

"I want to keep it close to my chest. I have a theory that may or may not pan out. And since it's a theory, I don't want to say anything more. But I believe that we are getting close."

"Rothmann's down the chief's back and he's down my back. You get my point?"

"You don't want to have to come down on my back with sharp spurs."

"Exactly."

"Point made, but we can't go to the County Prosecutor's office with a garbage case. Julie Pettersson and the rest of the gang down there love me with the possible exception of Robitaille, but they'll throw us out the door if we don't have the goods."

Sighing, Capt. Carter replied, "Okay. I'll tell the chief that we're still working on it. But you gotta give me something soon."

"I promise," Tindall sweetly said as he walked out. He almost skipped his way down to the Crime Lab, avoiding knocking down two uniformed policewomen passing by. Walking in, Tindall asked Ann, "Good morning. Have you received the package yet from Ironwood?"

"We did and it's in the lab. Once you get your stuff we'll test everything."

"You'll get it when I have it. My apologies, how's Chuck and the kids doing?"

"They're fine as usual. And how's Kathleen?"

"She's fine." Checking his watch, Tindall said, "I gotta go since it's lunch time. See you later."

"The same here."

Arriving back in his office, Tindall read a note on his desk from Perez saying that Dr. Bruschetta would be here tomorrow at 10:00 am. Tindall made some notes and went to lunch. Calling Kathleen, he asked, "Are you doing any special right now?"

Kathleen laughed. "No, I'm just working. But I will be going to lunch in a few minutes. If I don't eat I don't work."

"I always thought that if you didn't work you didn't eat."

"Whatever," Kathleen mocked with a fake Valley Girl accent. "I'm surprised that you didn't make the crack that I didn't have to work to eat." They both laughed. Continuing, Kathleen asked, "How is the Davies case going/"

"It's still going. By the end of the week everything should be going well in regards to it."

"Sounds great. Well I have to go now. My boss wouldn't like it if I came back to lunch late."

Tindall laughed as he hung up. After finishing his lunch, he saw that Perez was at lunch and Parkins was still working. While working on paperwork from other cases, he received a call. "St. Marys Police Dept., this is Lt. Tindall. How can I help you?"

"This is Charlie Watkins from the Detroit Police Dept. I'm calling back, Frank, to tell you that I'm going to fax the information we previously discussed. You'll receive it in a few minutes. "

"Thanks, Charlie. How's the wife?"

"Good and yours?"

"The same."

"Call back if you need anything else."

"Thanks."

Tindall hung up and waited until 1:15 pm. He then walked down to Anne-Marie Simonini's office. After saying hello to Anne-Marie and receiving Watkins' fax,

Tindall walked back to his office. It took just a few minutes for him to go through the information and divide up into three sections.

At 2:00 pm Tindall walked out to Perez and Parkins. After handing their part of the information, he said, "We're going to do about five contacts each regarding Rowlands' friends and acquaintances in Detroit. Based on the time right now, we'll probably be spending the rest of the day working on this and maybe tomorrow."

"Hopefully, this doesn't bleed into tomorrow," noted Parkins.

"This is part of police grunt work," sighed Perez.

"If either of you get any interesting information, don't worry about disturbing me or vice versa," replied Tindall as he walked back to his office.

Tindall had some Pine Bros. throat lozenges in case he had to soothe his throat. Oddly enough, whenever he had to do any kind of talking for an extended period of time his throat dried up. It was annoying but it never led him to not being able to do what needed to be done. Gritting his teeth, he began to make the calls. If he was a policeman thirty or more years ago, he would probably have a cig in the corner of his mouth and a cup of stale coffee on his desk while doing the calls.

Going through the calls, he left one message, had two disconnected phone numbers and spoke to three nice people who advised him that Heather Rowlands was a sweet but guarded person who didn't talk about her life prior to the Detroit area. One of them met her at Narcotics Anonymous and they quickly became best friends. This same person stated that she was hooked on prescription drugs, not street junk. Tindall knew through work how destructive booze and junk were to individuals and families. It wasn't as bad in St. Marys as if was, say in the Detroit area, but you could buy street junk in and out of the city and throughout the county if you knew the right people. There were also stories of some doctors and pharmacies in the county who would write out prescriptions and sell the legal stuff to junkies if the price was right. Tindall hoped that Parkins and Perez found more than what he got.

Sludge, Perez silently noted as he went through his calls. Four of the calls panned out as disconnected phone numbers and the fifth didn't give that much information about Rowlands. While going through his calls, he missed a call from Sheila. In between the third and fourth calls, Perez called her back and said that he may be coming home from work and not to wait up for him regarding dinner. Sheila sighed in a mock way and said, "Oh well, I'm going to have to tell your children that their father may miss their dinner. You'll break their heart!"

Perez laughed and replied that "you wouldn't say that and I know that you're joking!"

"Do you know that?"

"We both do!" Sheila and Perez had a hearty laugh as the latter hung up. Clearly, Perez had a happy marriage and wanted to keep it that way. He hoped that Tindall and Parkins found more than what he got.

It took Parkins longer that Tindall or Perez to go through his five calls. Two of three callers wanted to have a long, drawn out chat with him that focused very little on Rowlands and much on the weather, traveling, whether cats or dogs made the better pets, and other nonsensical items. Parkins had to use all of his charm and tact to get off of those calls quickly. The other two numbers were no longer in service so he was relieved not to have to go through another long and drawn out conversation.

Grimacing, Parkins wondered how the fifth and final call would pan out. "Hello, this is Fr. Casey's Kitchen. How can I help you?"

"This is Detective Jim Parkins from the St. Marys Police Department. Can I speak to Ms. Regina Dahl please?"

"You're speaking to her," the same cheerful voice replied. "What do you need, Detective?"

"I'm calling you regarding a case that we're working on. We received information that you knew a Heather Rowlands."

Sadly, Regina replied, "I knew Heather well. We were friends and coworkers at Fr. Casey's. Actually, I was her boss. She worked in the office and purchased and maintained our supplies. What information are you looking for?"

"Well, I'm looking for information about if anything was bothering Heather at the time of her passing."

There was a pause for a moment before Parkins received a reply. "There was something on Heather's mind at the time she passed away. She didn't talk about her time prior to moving to Detroit and I didn't press her. Her record was excellent and she worked well with others and the community we serve."

"So Fr. Casey's Kitchen, is it some kind of soup kitchen?"

"It is. It's run by people who want to serve others in the tradition of Fr. Solanus Casey, the founder of the Capuchin Soup Kitchen in Detroit. We're an interfaith organization of Christians who provide food for the poor. You can always come down here to volunteer on a weekend if you wish."

"Do you know what was on Heather's mind when she passed away?"

"She didn't say except that she did something terrible and she had to be held accountable for it."

"Did she have any personal items at Fr. Casey's Kitchen?"

"After she passed away, we sent what we thought were her personal items to her family. It turns out that in a cubbyhole that old buildings like ours have, there was a leather bag with a mp3 player with a recording of her speaking to someone else."

"Did you listen to it?"

"I did, once Sandra, the person who found it gave to me today. It was very disturbing and I'll give it to the police."

"If you don't want to say anything about the conversation I understand. Please give the mp3 player to Insp. Charlie Watkins of the Detroit Police Dept. He's been working with us regarding this."

"We'll contact him today regarding it. Do you have any further questions for me, Detective?"

"No, and thank you for your time."

After hanging up, Parkins told Perez and Tindall what happened. Tindall replied, "I'll call Watkins tomorrow afternoon and ask if he can send a transcript of what was on the mp3 player. It may or may not be relevant to Davies but we still need to know it. Look how time flies! It's already 5:30 so we can wrap it up. See you tomorrow at 8:00."

"Same here," replied Perez and Parkins. Within minutes all three men left for warm houses and hearts, apologizing for the late delay.

20

Based on their schedule, some members of the St. Marys Police Department enjoyed Wednesdays due to it being the middle of their workweek and close to their Saturday and Sunday off days while it was a matter of indifference to others due to their different work schedules. As for Tindall, Perez and Parkins, it all depended on what cases they were working on. Hopefully, Tindall thought, he wouldn't have to do any work either or Saturday or Sunday. Tindall also hoped that he would get the transcript or a copy of the recording from Watkins sometime today.

Tindall checked the clock on his wall and saw that it was a quarter to ten. Almost time for the chat with Dr. Bruschetta. He had a few things to take care and meetings with Capt. Carter and Perez and Parkins. Tindall literally twiddled his thumbs until 10:00 am arrived. As on a cue, Dr. Judith Bruschetta arrived. They greeted each other politely yet formally and Dr. Bruschetta sat down.

Dr. Bruschetta began first after accepting a glass of water from Tindall. "I was surprised when I received a call from one of your men to come down here for a meeting. I thought that you would come to my office, Lieutenant," she concluded with a trace of irritation.

Pained, Tindall replied, "Normally I would have, but we've been so busy on the Davies case I decided that it would be best if you came down here. My apologies."

Mollified, Dr. Bruschetta said, "There's nothing to apologize for. You have a lot of things on your plate at this time. I'm working on my end to ensure that everyone in the city and county continues to have confidence in Rothmann."

You really mean confidence in you, Tindall replied with a silent laugh. But he said, "I understand completely. Rothmann is the pride of St. Marys and all of us want to keep it that way.

"I appreciate your understanding, Lieutenant. Do you have any further information regarding who killed Davies?"

Soberly, Tindall answered, "I believe that Davies' murder and the possible murder of another woman in Klingsburg may be connected to your family. Do you recall the names of Linda Severinsen and Edith Albanese?"

A flicker of rage briefly flashed in Dr. Bruschetta's eyes before she responded in a thoughtful manner, "The names sound vaguely familiar."

"The car that they and some others were in was involved in a hit-and-run accident involving your sister Lesley. According to the Ironwood police, their car was stolen at the time at the time of the accident."

"Now I know why the names sounded familiar. Those poor things. Lesley never had the chance to have the life I had," tears forming in Dr. Bruschetta's eyes while she spoke. Tindall handed her a box of tissue and waited for a few minutes. "Please, Lieutenant, I don't want to talk about Lesley. It's too painful. Forgive me for saying this, but it's was more painful when she died than when my parents died."

"I lost my parents, Dr. Bruschetta, when I was very young," Tindall answered softly, "so I don't have the pain that you have. But my grandparents and other people in my family had that pain. My apologies for bringing it up but we have to find Ms. Davies killer."

Wiping her eyes, Dr. Bruschetta agreed. "The killer has to be found and has to be held accountable for what they did. Excuse me, but I have to go now please."

"Of course." Tindall waited until Dr. Bruschetta put on her coat and escorted her out of her office and out of Police Headquarters. He then walked back to his office, grabbed Mrs. Bruschetta's glass with a tissue and walked down to the Crime Lab. Seeing Ann, Tindall asked after he handed the glass to her, "How long will the DNA test take?"

"We should be done by tomorrow evening at the latest," Ann replied. "You're lucky because we don't have a lot of things to test, 'cause if we're really busy it could take weeks."

"I know that, and it's fortunate that Ironwood still had some of Lesley Blandick's DNA on file that could be tested. It's also good that we received the DNA material from them so quickly. Thanks."

Tindall walked back to his office. In an about thirty minutes it would be 12:30 pm, time for lunch. He hadn't heard back from Watkins yet and decided to call him back tomorrow afternoon if he hadn't heard from him. Yawning, he finished up some paperwork and went to lunch at 12:30 pm. After enjoying an excellent lunch, Tindall decided that he would have a meeting with Perez and Parkins once he received the DNA results from the Crime Lab.

Perez spent his time going through some old case file notes and checking to see if anything was out or order or place. He checked his e-mails for any important news. Nothing but ordinary departmental notices. The same old same old. Shaking his head, he continued his work before going to lunch at 12:00 pm.

Parkins received a call from his wife Millie which he was reviewing his file notes from previous cases. "Hello Millie! Do you need for me to bring anything from Koditscheks before I get home today?"

Millie laughed. "No, we're all set here. I just wanted to tell you that Mrs. Otis' daughter is getting married next year and we'll be getting further details in a few days."

"It sounds like we got an invitation to the wedding from the bride and groom to be."

"That's right, which means you have to be on your best behavior."

Parkins laughed. "Me! I'll have you know, Mildred, that I'm always on my best behavior," he concluded with mock shock.

"Oh really?" was the response. "I've known you long enough, James, to say that you always keep the lights on, you never let the seat down in the bathroom, you sometimes snore so loud that the dog howls...." Millie and Parkins then broke out laughing.

"On a serious note," Millie concluded, "will you be coming home late?"

"Based on the current case load, I should be home on time."

"See you soon them." After Millie hung up, Parkins rose from his chair to stretch his legs. The Davies case was coming along as it would be expected with Frank having someone in mind as the person of interest. Parkins knew Frank well enough that for something as serious as this he always kept his cards in his vest until arrest time.

5:00 pm came and Peres and Parkins were getting ready to go home. Parkins walked to Tindall's office to see how much longer he was staying. When he saw Tindall on the phone, Parkins waved good bye. Tindall returned the favor and resumed his conversation. Almost all of the Police Department's day shift had either left for the day or were on their way out the door. In a few hours the cleaning crew would be through to ensure that the place was neat and tidy for tomorrow's work. Perez and Parkins had other things on their minds as they went home.

21

Aileen's Attic was the most popular morning radio show in St. Marys. The host, Aileen Pottier, had been at WSTM AM radio for about fifteen years and listeners ranging from prisoners in the county jail to the mayor loved listening to her during the 6-9 morning time slot. None of the other morning shows had her high ratings, which pleased the Evening News Co., WSTM AM's owner, along with Aileen, who could ask for, and receive, an excellent salary and lucrative product endorsements.

There had been talk of her moving perhaps to a larger market such as Grand Rapids or Kalamazoo or even syndication, but Aileen had discouraged it. She enjoyed living in St. Marys for its charm and people, having originally grown up in Crown Point, Indiana. Living in Crown Point was fun due to it being so close to Chicago with its museums and other attractions such as the Cubs and the Bulls. Aileen didn't like the Black Hawks since they didn't do that much for her.

Another attraction St. Marys had for her was that she was a big fish in a large pond. Because she was a money maker for WSTM AM, her situation was set provided she didn't act like a diva. Aileen wasn't stupid since she always made sure that she had good relationships with those above and below her along with the community. If someone didn't like her, that was their problem, but she preferred to walk away from confrontations unless she was cornered. If that occurred, then the other party quickly found out what she was capable of. Fortunately, those incidents rarely occurred and didn't continue.

Since today was Thursday, it was "Ask the Police" in the third hour. People would call in with questions and issues and other callers would provide suggestions and tips. Aileen's producer, Howie Ekman, screened out the crazies and such. She trusted Howie completely since he knew the business up and down; and he was also her man and not management's. Aileen loved her callers and the feelings were reciprocated. All in all, it was a good life.

Her guest, as usual for the "Ask the Police" segment, was Lt. Hannah Gildersleeve, the community affairs specialist of the St. Marys Police Department. Gildersleeve's job was to be the liaison between the police and the community. Some cynical souls would call the dear lieutenant a PR flack but Aileen would never use that term since she operated from the Mike Donal-Merv Grace school of talk show hosts in which you didn't ask guests when they stopped beating their wives if you wanted to get a steady stream of politicians, celebrities and movers and shakers of varying kinds on your show.

Aileen loved the police since quite a few of her relatives were cops on both sides of the Michiana border. She had a great deal of respect for Gildersleeve and a close personal friendship emerged out of their five years of doing the segment together. "Well, one of the things that makes St. Marys pure pleasure on this side of heaven," Aileen purred, "along with Hunnibell Dairy stuff and Koditscheks groceries, is the exceptionally low crime rate in the city and county."

Laughing, Gildersleeve agreed. "We're proud that we're all working together, from the Police Department to the community, in making St. Marys a safe place to work and play. Shall we take another call?"

"Of course!" Aileen said. "Hello Eli! What question or comment do you have?"

"Hello Aileen and Officer Gildersleeve. Well, I'm concerned that we haven't heard anything about the murder at Rothmann. Have you guys caught anyone and not told anyone about it? I don't want my wife and I to be murdered there if we have go there."

"I can assure you," Gildersleeve answered in her most definitive voice, "that—"

Tindall turned the radio off. He liked Gildersleeve, though they weren't friends. He also thought highly of her work as the department's community relations liaison. Well, the caller would probably be dissatisfied with Gildersleeve's answer but you can't please everyone. He along with everyone else liked Aileen Pottier's show and even met her a few times in a professional setting. Tindall even saw her once or twice at Koditscheks. Tall for a woman, about 6 feet, thin with light brown hair and gold-rimmed glasses. He never said hello to her due to him being occupied with shopping.

Nothing yet from Ann, Chuck or Watkins yet, so he would do the walk this afternoon regarding Ann and Chuck and the call regarding Watkins if he didn't hear anything from them at that time. Kathleen decided to wake up later than usual, a very rare thing for her since she always liked to get to work early so she could leave early. She also liked to set a positive example for her staff since "fish rot from the head," as she cheerfully liked to say.

All in all, Tindall mused, home and work were going well for him and Kathleen. Nothing to worry about in their marriage either. He had a meeting scheduled with Perez and Parkins at 9:00 am regarding the Davies case and he briefly updated Capt. Carter regarding the status of the Davies case. Capt. Carter merely grunted his consent and Tindall walked back to his office a happy camper. When he worked on a case the waiting for the different forensic tests, obtaining the needed information regarding the case could be long and the irritation while waiting could be immense. But that was the world of police investigations. Everything had to be done right so that the guilty received their just punishment and the innocent didn't spend time in prison for crimes that they didn't commit. And to avoid policemen losing their jobs.

The Davies case team meeting began at 9:00 am. "I haven't heard anything yet from the Crime Lab about the test I requested nor have I heard from Watkins," Tindall dryly noted. "If I don't hear from the two of them by this afternoon I'll have to do the hall walk and the phone call. Yipee for both."

Parkins asked, "Did you hear Gildersleeve having to take a call regarding this case on Aileen Pottier's show?"

"I did, and I didn't want to hear the answer, so I shut the thing off. Gildersleeve's a pro at this. She's skilled in answering questions her and not the questioner's way."

"Well, there's nothing that she could say about the case," Perez mused, "since it's still ongoing. And we know what you would tell her if she asked you."

Yawning, Tindall replied, "I would just tell her that the case is still ongoing and that we're diligently working on it. I'll come back if I hear anything from either party."

"That's fine," both Perez and Parkins replied.

Tindall hated to twiddle his thumbs during a case. To him it didn't seem like he was earning his keep at work. He never like to appear that he wasn't working, even if there wasn't any work to do. It was a matter of pride. Tindall noted that there would be a long wait before lunch. To ease the time, he decided to turn on and listen to his shortwave radio. There was one classical music station he could pick up during the day and they played some really good music. Too bad most people didn't like to listen to it. At one point, Tindall mused, classical music was so popular that MGM made popular movies from the Thirties through the Fifties based on operas and operettas.

Fortunately, noon arrived and Tindall went to lunch. Sometimes he and the rest of team took a 30-minute lunch and other times a full hour. Normally he took the full hour only if he wanted to walk around before he ate or if he had errands to do. Today, Tindall decided to take a walk. The air was fresh and cool outside and since it was lunch time for most people, people were busy walking to the different restaurants along Main St. and its side streets.

The non-fast food restaurants such as Verdonckt's and Winternitz's had excellent food at reasonable prices. In terms of quality, the University Inn Restaurant equaled the previous two restaurants in terms of quality. Tindall and his grandparents usually had dinner at the University Inn either on Fridays or Saturdays. He did like a chicken place called Chicken Shack in the Metro Detroit area. Although he only had the food there a few times, it was good since unlike the items at other chicken places the food was cooked to order and wasn't stuck under a heat lamp for hours on end.

Tindall also saw some of the beautiful shops and offices along Main St. along with such venable old churches such as First United Methodist Church and St. Marys Congregational Church. All Souls Episcopal Church was also on Main St., and he and Kathleen were scheduled to attend there this coming Sunday. On most Sundays Tindall went to University Lutheran and Kathleen went to All Souls but there were two Sundays out of the month in which they attended each other churches. Neither held contemporary services and both used traditional liturgies.

He also greeted some of the passersby who knew him, ether friends or people who worked in the different offices in the Central District. Tindall could have walked for far longer but he saw that fifteen minutes had passed so he walked back to Headquarters. After arriving back at his office, he saw that someone left a voice mail message on his phone. He decided to check it after lunch and had a hearty appetite after his walk. Tindall turned on the radio again and listed to the news on NPR. Though leftist, NPR did have some interesting pieces on if that were quite entertaining aside from the leftism.

At 1:00 pm Tindall listened to his voice mail message. He then walked down to the Crime Lab and after Tindall and Chuck exchanged greetings, the latter replied, "Here's the test results. You're lucky we were able to get it done so quickly."

"Yeah, I really appreciate the quick service," Tindall replied. "Tell Ann that I said hello."

Chuck nodded. Tindall walked back to his office and read the test results. As he read the results, he smiled. The final piece of the case was in place. Now all that was needed was hard, solid evidence. Capt. Carter would have to sign off on what further action was necessary and it would probably have to go all the way up to the mayor.

Perez and Parkins were chatting about aspects of the Davies case when Tindall motioned them to follow him to his office. After everyone sat down and the door was closed Tindall said to Perez and Parkins as he handed them copies of the test results, "Mike, Jim, I want the two of you to take a look at this."

After a minute or two, Parkins replied, "Looks like we have a person of interest."

"Right." Perez mused. "You'll second it, Frank?"

"I already knew it. And I also believe that Dr. Bruschetta murdered Edith Dowling, though it looks like there won't be enough evidence to get an arrest warrant. I'll call Red regarding it. He may be able to find additional evidence in her house, though whatever evidence was there may be lost."

"When would we be able to speak to Judge Carlile about a search warrant?"

"It'll have to wait until I speak to Capt. Carter and get clearance from him regarding this. Considering how high-profile Dr. Bruschetta and her family are, it may take a while to get approval or it may not even be granted." Looking at his watch, Tindall continued, "I'll be in Capt. Carter's office for a few minutes. Get me if it's something serious."

After a few minutes listening to Tindall's review of the Davies case along with his request for getting a search warrant regarding Dr. Bruschetta from the county prosecutor's office, Capt. Carter muttered, "The police chief and the mayor will have a very nice chat with Rothmann's brass regarding this. There's also no way that they can avoid talking to Dr. Bruschetta regarding this. So how long, Frank, were you suspicious of her?"

"Not from the start," replied Tindall, "but I knew that Davies' murder was an inside job. For someone to have waltzed in and commited murder at Rothmann they would have had to have either cased the place beforehand or they have to had knowledge of the place either as a worker or ex-worker or as a contractor. It was also confirmed by the info Mac McElroy gave me.

"Now in regards to Dowling, when we found out that she was connected to Davies and Lesley Blandick's hit and run, I thought that it was perhaps possible that their deaths were connected, particularly when Red told me there were signs that someone tried to pick Dowling's lock on her back door. I believe that it was a ruse and that the killer got in by picking her French doors on the side of her house or even the front door. Red'll have to investigate that as well, since from the <u>Michiana Living</u> article I talked to you about she's a skilled locksmith and she even likes to pick locks for the hell of it.

"Finally, when I asked Dr. Bruschetta to come in, she feigned irritation over it when we met, but I sensed that it was a ruse to see exactly how we knew, specifically how much I knew. Also, when I spoke to her about the women involved in Lesley's hit and run, I saw a flash of anger in her eyes, although she tried to play it off. That's when I said to myself, 'She did it.' She's also a very clever woman."

Capt. Carter sensed the tone of compassion and respect in Tindall's voice as he spoke about Dr. Bruschetta. He also knew that Tindall's view of Dr. Bruschetta was like the bear hunter who respected bears but would do everything within the bounds of legality and sportsmanship to have the bear's head on his wall. He asked Tindall, "Do you think we'll find anything in Dr. Bruschetta's house or the store or in her office?"

"Probably not, since she has had ample time to destroy or get rid of any evidence of the Davies and Dowling murders. If I was a betting man beyond the lottery, I would say that she probably disposed of the evidence quickly after she committed the murders. But I still want to do a thorough job regarding this."

Chucking, Capt. Carter replied, "You sound like the good Dr. Bruschetta will get an O.J."

"Probably yes in that we probably won't be able to charge her with anything due to a lack of evidence. Still, there's no statute of limitations regarding murder and if there's any new evidence, we'll arrest her. But I believe that she's finished regarding Rothmann. They'll get rid of her to remove the smell from the place. She could set up her own practice or live off of the profits from Bruschetta Jewelers. I heard that she's entitled to receive a cut of the profits from her husband's estate."

"I noticed that you haven't said anything about Heather Rowlands and Dr. Bruschetta's possible connection to it."

Frowning, Tindall replied, "I don't want to say too much about Rowlands until I hear from Watkins. I'll just say for now that her passing was suspicious in my humble opinion."

"There's nothing to be coy about since Rowlands isn't connected to the Davies case."

"Maybe and maybe not."

"Have it your way, then," Capt. Carter sighed. "I'll be glad when we're done with this case since it's more trouble than it's worth."

"I second it," Tindall wearily said as he walked back to his office. He saw a message on his phone and reviewed it. It was Watkins telling him that he sent a copy of the mp3 recording plus a transcript of it via overnight mail to him and it should arrive no later than tomorrow afternoon.

Tindall called Watkins back and left a message thanking him for the quick service. There was nothing further to do until he received the recording and transcript except for one little thing. He called and left a message on Cecelia Killian's phone asking if she could call him back regarding any further information she could think of regarding her two deceased classmates. After he did so, he checked his watch and saw that it was close to 4:00 pm.

One more hour to go, he lazily thought as he went through some dreary paperwork. One of the nice things about working in a small city like St. Marys was that the crime was not as out of control as in some of the larger cities in the state such as Detroit or Flint. Most of the crime consisted of walking in unlocked homes and garages and stealing DVD players and lawnmowers or doing a smash and grab at a car to get someone's laptop or purse that was left out in the open. A few rapes were reported from time to time along with terrible cases of children being abused. Those two kinds of cases tended not to be reported as they should due to their sordidness.

Tindall called Red Friman and was surprised to find him still in his office after 4:00 pm. "Hello Red, this is Frank Tindall. I was calling to ask if you could do a further check regarding the Dowling case? We think that it may not have been an accident."

Surprised, Friman asked, "You think that it may have been a murder?"

"Possibly, only because she was connected to the Davies case."

"Well do a further check but I can't promise anything. The site wasn't secured and the ME already ruled it an accident and they're not going to change it unless they have serious evidence."

"It is what it is and thanks."

Tindall hung up and went to the bathroom for a few minutes.

Cecelia Killian left a message for Tindall two minutes before 5:00 pm. It lasted about two minutes and Tindall listed to it intensely. Afterwards, he played the message back and recorded it on a sturdy mp3 player he had. He wrote a brief note detailing the time and the length of the message and put it along with the mp3 player in a small Manilla envelope. Locking his desk, Tindall put on his coat and other items and walked out of his office after locking his door.

He said goodbye to Perez and Parkins and as he walked out the door he called Kathleen. She asked, "Any new Davies details?"

Tindall laughed. "You know that I can't say anything about it! We're still working on it and how has your day gone?"

"Busy, busy, busy as usual. But I love it. It's a part of me and I wouldn't change it."

"I think the same way about being a cop. It's who I am. I'll see you in a few minutes."

"Righto, lover boy."

Tindall laughed again as he hung up. Really, life was good and he hoped that it would continue to be that way as he drove home.

22

"Thank God's it's Friday," Pete Messinger in Records said to his assistant manager, Thomasina Hill, as they recorded incoming evidence involving cases. It was early in the morning and the items were a bit much. Fortunately, Pete had three other team members in the back busily working like beavers.

"Shouldn't you say, Pete, TGIF? Some people may not like the use of the word God," Thomasina concluded with a laugh.

Pete laughed too. "They can go stuff themselves if they don't like it. Maybe their friends in Venezuela'll like it. You know that they're eating their pets and zoo animals down there due to no food?"

"Yeah. Communism at work."

"Amen, sister, amen."

They continued to banter in this vein until they saw Perez walk over to them. "Hi, Mike!" both Pete and Thomasina yelled. "Are you here on business or to say hello?"

"Just to say hello," Perez replied, "and how are you and the crew doing?"

"We're doing fine," Thomasina replied. "Not too busy now but you never know about later in the day. You got any info regarding Davies?"

"You know perfectly well, Ms. Hill, that I can't discuss an open case," Perez said mockingly. "Unfortunately, you'll know about everything once it's done."

"Just a little hint?" asked Messinger wryly.

Perez merely shook his head and said, "Well, I have to go now. See you later."

Thomasina murmured as Perez walked back to his cubicle, "He's as tight-lipped as Frank is."

"It comes with the territory," remarked Messinger. "They want to make sure that whoever's involved doesn't get off. You know that."

"I do but there's nothing's wrong with us asking!" The two of them laughed and resumed their work. The Records Department had to be open seven days a week since criminals didn't take vacations. Thomasina was the manager on Saturdays and Sundays so when she was off or on vacation Pete deputized one of the others to fill her spot. No one in Records had any complaints about Pete since as long as they did their jobs well and didn't cause him or anyone inside or outside of the department any problems he didn't bother them.

He enjoyed working in Records and it was the only department he worked in after being a street cop for a year after being hired. The person whom he replaced wasn't able to return from a medical disability leave so his temporary position became a permanent one. It was an easy life and it suited him and his wife quite nicely. They didn't have children but they did have a few nieces and nephews and one great nephew. Frank sure knows how to avoid trouble, Pete silently noted as he returned back to work, since some of the cases he had could have been sticky if he wasn't blessed with the good common sense and the good common touch he had.

Regretfully, I can't have a nice little visit with the sole remaining bitch Cecelia Killian. There's too many bright lights surrounding her. Tindall knows that she's connected to Davies and he's probably connected her to dear Edith's passing. He's probably even contacted the Klingsville police to do a further investigation regarding her death. It's likely that they won't find anything because I was very careful in killing her. In fact, I didn't lay one hand on her except to confirm that she was dead. I haven't heard any additional information yet about the status of the investigation. I have to be careful about tipping my hand since I wouldn't want to incriminate myself. The things that I would love to do to dear, sweet Cecelia are just not printable. Though I wouldn't be stupid enough to put anything in print. And any incriminating information in print would go straight to my delightful heavy-duty confetti shredder.

I only decided to go after the three lovelies after someone who knew them quite well confessed to their part in Little's death. After I found out the truth, I had to use all of my self-control to avoid a violent outburst. People, including my family, marvel about how calm and even tempered I am. Nothing seems to ruffle me. And that is true most of the time. But when it comes to Little, the most primitive and savage instincts rise to the surface, forcing me to use my self-control to the utmost.

When I was told that I couldn't keep Little, I went into a deep depression and I even began to mutilate myself. The modern term is cutting. When I did it, it was like having sex. I still have a few minor scars from it and I use creams to conceal them if necessary. The persons who became known as Little's parents were my own parents. I became Little's big sister. Many times, I wanted to cry out to her and the world, "You're mine!" But I couldn't since it would be damaging to myself and my parents. Also, it would be damaging to Little as well. Small towns didn't tolerate unwed motherhood and families mixed up in it lost the respect of the community.

I finally found out the truth about what happened to Little when I received an e-mail letter from someone named Heather on a busy Monday morning who said that she had information regarding Little's accident because she was present on the scene. The meeting would be in Detroit on the following Saturday at 7:00 pm. I agreed and I drove early Friday morning to Detroit.

I met Heather in her apartment in the Wayne State University area. Since I had only been to Detroit a few times I had to make sure that I didn't get lost. I also had to book a hotel in the Downtown Detroit area. The neighborhood was clean and safe looking so I didn't have to worry about being robbed or worse. I parked my car on the one of the side streets and ranged her bell. I opened the main door after being let in and walked up the stairs to her apartment on the second floor.

When necessary, I can control my face and emotions

very well. "Hello," I said as Heather let me in. The place was spacious yet simple. It was tastefully furnished and its occupant was about my height with light brown hair and a thin, wiry build. She was around Little's age.

"Please sit down, Dr. Bruschetta," Heather said after escorting me to her living room table. I felt the tension in the air and waited for what I knew was going to happen.

After a few minutes of silence, Heather began to talk. "I won't ask for your forgiveness because I don't deserve it. You probably know from the police report that the car involved in your sister's hit and run was reported as stolen by all of us—me, Edie, Ceci and Linda. We also stated that we were drinking beer in the woods at the time it was stolen. All of it was a lie because all of us was in the car when we hit your sister. The lie and the hit and run wasn't the worst of it. The worst of it was that the driver deliberately sped up to hit your sister when we saw her."

Dry mouthed, I quietly said, "Who was the driver?"

"It was Ceci."

"You mean Cecelia Killian. Why?"

"Jealousy and resentment. Ceci was jealous that everything she wanted your sister always got it. She was tired of the leftovers. Also, she was angry because she thought that your sister thought she was better than the rest of us since your parents were well respected and ours were considered trailer trash."

"There's more to it. What was it?"

"All I will say is that there were other things involved

but I won't say anything else. You can kill me, but I won't discuss it."

I figured where she was going but I let it pass. "So, why would you invite me to your apartment when you barely knew me and I could have gone postal on you after this?"

"Because I'm tired of the guilt and lies. Since your parents are dead I couldn't give the information to them so that's why I contacted you. If you want to kill me, it would be your right. I do have to say that I'm planning on going back home tomorrow to confess to the police."

"Do the others think the same way as you?"

"No, they don't. They're living in denial. I don't know if you're a Christian but I'm one and I have to walk the walk and talk the talk, so if I have to go to prison then so be it."

There was nothing more to be said. I knew that we would never see each other again. Heather walked me to the door but before I left I hugged her and stroked her hair. Both of us began to cry and I walked out into the corridor with tears in my eyes.

As I walked downstairs and out into the darkness, I noted that I wanted to kill her for a second after she told me what really happened. But I didn't want to go there because I sensed that she was guilt ridden. She had compassion for me and my family. And she was willing to take her punishment like a woman. I also noticed a Narcotics Anonymous pamphlet on one of the tables when I first walked in. So, she was a recovering drug addict. Heather looked clean and I didn't see any needle marks on her arms. Her eyes were clear and focused.

When I returned home, I found out a week later that Heather was found dead in the Detroit River. I already knew even before I met her that her last name was Rowlands and the others were Linda Severinsen and Edith Albanese. Those names had floated around my mind for years. Both my parents and I were suspicious about what actually happened but the police couldn't prove anything and we couldn't risk harassment charges if we confronted them. There were others who were suspicious of them, which led to all of the girls leaving town permanently.

I didn't believe that Heather's death was an accident. The coverage on the online versions of The Detroit News and The Detroit Free Press stated that her death was an accident but I noted the concern in her voice when she told me that her friends were in denial about what happened. If she told any of them of what she was going to do, it would be an excellent motivation for murder. Still, I didn't want to get involved and I couldn't contact the police regarding what she said. Who would believe me? There was no evidence other that what Heather told me and she was dead. It was neither recorded nor written down. So, I had to let it go. Besides, Little was still living, my parents having been killed in a car crash while they were driving to see Little.

What led me down to the eye for an eye path was when I was notified by the long-term care facility that Little was dying. As I rushed to her, crying as I hugged and kissed her, I thought why this couldn't have this happened to me instead of her. I wouldn't have had a problem with it, since a mother should be more concerned about her child's life than hers. "Goodbye, Little, you'll be with Mom and Dad,"

I said as she passed away while I held her hand. I still had to keep up the pretense of being the older sister. It wasn't about me, it was about Little and my parents. No one needed to know about what really happened.

As for Little's father, I never told him anything about her and I vividly remember when I had to tell my parents when I found out through a cheap pregnancy kit that I was pregnant. Sixteen going onto seventeen and I had to tell them. Within a short period of time I would show and I wouldn't do anything to harm my baby.

A few days I said to my parents after dinner in the kitchen, "Mom, Dad, I have to tell you something. I'm pregnant."

Their faces fell when they heard the news. Then Dad said, "Were you--"

"No, it was consensual and it was someone my age."

"Is it anyone we know?"

"No, Dad, it was someone I met when I went to that summer science project in Marquette. I don't want to talk about him nor what happened."

Then Mom came and held me tight. We both cried while Dad sat at the kitchen table, head bowed. It was only few minutes, but to me it felt like hours. I thought that they would hit me or curse me or throw me out of the house.

Finally, Dad said, "You can give the child up for adoption or we can raise him or her as our child. You're not old enough or mature enough to take care of a child and I don't want you to be condemned as a slut."

"Thank you, Dad," I said with tears streaming down my face. "I let you and Mom down."

"The only One whom you let down was God, and He forgives. You didn't do anything to us and you have to forgive yourself." Mom nodded. "Do you want to keep the baby?" I nodded yes.

"Then your mother and I have some plans that we have to make," Dad replied. "We'll go through everything with you in a few days."

Within a few days everything was planned. Mom and I would go to the Lower Peninsula under the guise that I was ill and needed special treatment. While we were gone, it would turn out that Mom was pregnant and after nine months, I would come back cured and Mom with a lovely newborn child. My illness part would of course be vouched for by Dr. Olson, our family doctor. Until he died, I always kept in touch with Dr. Olson.

Little grew into a lovely child and a beautiful young woman. Since by the time she was born I was close to graduating from high school I wasn't able to spend as much time as I wanted to with her. Then it was college and medical school and then my marriage to John and our own children. I spent as much time as I could with Little and our relationship was the typical little sister-big sister relationship.

By the time Little became a teenager, she began to ask questions about who she was. One time, as I was visiting her, Mom and Dad, she pulled me aside and asked, "Am I adopted?"

Surprised, I said, "Why would you say something like that?"

"Well, I don't look like Mom and Dad and I love them and vice versa, but there's something missing. And you sometimes act like a parent than a big sister."

"Not everyone in a family looks the same and I do have to admit that sometimes I may come across like a mother than a sister. But that's because I'm your big sister and I don't want anything bad to happen to you and we all love you. Have you talked to Mom and Dad regarding this?"

"Oh, no, I've only spoke to you regarding it. Please don't tell them."

"I won't and remember, we all love you and want the best for you." I kissed and hugged her.

I never told Mom and Dad about it because I didn't want to hurt them. They had done everything right for Little and I and it would never be forgotten. When we heard about Little's accident, parts of us died. Until their own accident, Mom and Dad visited Little every day and because of the distance, I was only able to visit her every month. And when it was her birthday, I always made sure that I was there. I would have gone postal if someone had tried to stop me.

One of the things that I loved about my husband was that he respected my connection to Little. I couldn't tell him everything and he understood. There are things within families that outsiders would never be privy to. He had things within his family that he wouldn't discuss with outsiders, even with me. But I always made sure that he and our kids knew that I was always there for them. When he died, the kids and I were devastated. I was even more devastated when I found out that his death was due to a criminal he did business with. The business was hurt for a brief time but it recovered. The manager, Homer Formby, was skilled and honest. He didn't use our family tragedy to "make hay while the sun shines," and I respected him for it.

Based on Tindall's progress, I will probably be seeing him again, and when that happens, he will probably have a search warrant. I would be thrown to the wolves if the powers that be considered me a liability. I've cleaned my trail as much as I could but there could still be enough traces for him to get an arrest warrant from the Prosecutor's Office. Robitaille, the County Prosecutor, would only grant it if he thought that the case was tight enough not only to get a conviction but to avoid a backlash from the well-connected elements of St. Marys society. It would be something that Chief Assistant Prosecutor Julie Pettersson would have to clear with him first. I knew Pettersson, and she was aggressive but pragmatic. She knew her place in dealing with Robitaille.

Tindall knew that I killed Barbara and that it was likely that I also killed Edith. But I also saw understanding and dare I say it, respect. He wouldn't hesitate to arrest me if he could but he didn't see me as trash that needed to be incinerated.

The door opens and my administrative assistant comes in. I have to put on my happy face and not let her see that her boss is a multiple murderess and that she may have a new boss soon. Ce la vie.

23

"Have you heard anything yet from Capt. Carter regarding the search warrant?" Perez asked Tindall before the two of them along with Parkins went to lunch.

"I haven't heard anything yet," Tindall sighed. "Since it's noon on a Friday, we may not hear anything until Monday. "I'm still waiting to receive the package from Watkins today. Hopefully, it'll arrive at a decent time this afternoon. If not, I'll have to go through it tomorrow. Kathleen won't like it, though." After a pause Tindall concluded, "I'm dropping work for about an hour for lunch. I'll see you and Jim in about an hour."

"Same here and enjoy."

Tindall walked down to the break room and walked back with his salad. Headquarters didn't have a cafeteria, just a break room with some vending machines and two refrigerators. Most people brown bagged their lunches since it was cheaper to do so. A few went to the fast food and other regular restaurants in the Central District. Tindall wanted to save as much nickels, dimes and quarters that he could.

Along with his salad he had some sesame snack sticks. Thank God for Trader Joe's, both he and Kathleen thought. They loved it for some of the items stocked there. Some people called it the poor man's Whole Foods but they didn't care. Tindall and Kathleen only went there for certain items that they couldn't find in the Farmers' Market or Koditscheks. They also bought some items at the local health food store in St. Marys such as the hot whole grain cereals and the fragrance-free soap. Tindall particularly loved the Dr. Bronner's soap brand.

If he was able to review Watkins' information today, then he would be able to spend all weekend with Kathleen. Tindall and Kathleen were alike in which they enjoyed spending time with each other but they also needed considerable "my time." They both did an excellent job in balancing both aspects and strengthening their marriage in the balance. Early in the marriage, Tindall asked for help from Elaine and Phil and Kathleen from her parents. Marriage wasn't something that you could learn from a book, mused Tindall, it was something that you had to learn from experience and from relatives and close friends who had strong and stable marriages. Plus, you had to put in the sweat equity to make it work, similar to what you had to do on your job and in your work and personal relationships.

Perhaps I should have been a philosophy professor, Tindall thought, though I probably would have ended up in tens of thousands of dollars in debt and serving lattes at a coffeehouse. Not a pleasing or productive prospect. Still, it would have been interesting.

As he brushed the crumbs off of his clothes and put his salad contained into his backpack, he continued to muse while listening to Alex Jones on his shortwave radio. Rather interesting character, noted Tindall, a good portion of what he says I agree with. No so with Kathleen. After listening to Jones for about a few minutes, Kathleen laughed and asked, "Do you really believe any of his nonsense?" Tindall replied, "And do you really believe any of the nonsense that your NPR crowd spews out?" "Touche!" And they both laughed at each other.

At 12:30 pm Tindall walked for about thirty minutes outside. The streets of downtown St. Marys were busy as usual this time of the day. The sky was overcast and looked like it was ready to rain at any time, which was why Tindall walked with his large umbrella that he bought from the Barnes and Noble next to Pioneer Square Mall. It was big and sturdy and strong enough to handle heavy winds without falling apart. It was also stylish, which Tindall liked very much. He also had a smaller and just as sturdy umbrella in his backpack. Since he was a kid Tindall always had a backpack. He could hold different things in his hands while he was walking and he could sit down on a bus or train seat while wearing it, which prevented theft or forgetting it when he stepped off of the bus or train.

Refreshed, Tindall went back to work at 1:00 pm. He called Kathleen back in response to her message and got her voice mail. Phone tag day, Tindall silently thought as he left his voice mail telling her that he may be late coming home. He also saw that someone had put a FedEx package on his desk. It was what he was waiting for from Watkins. Opening the package, he noted that it was a flash drive inside it along with a transcript of the flash drive's contents.

Tindall called Watkins and got his voice mail. He left a message telling Watkins that he received the package and thanked him for it. Funny that Charlie didn't put a cover note or letter in the packet, Tindall mused. Whatever. He walked the package down to the Crime Lab along with another item that he wanted to be tested along with the flash drive.

Ann and Chuck greeted Tindall warmly as usual. "What do you have for us today?" Ann playfully asked.

Shaking his head in artificial disapproval, Tindall replied, as he handed over to them the items in question, "Dear Ann, dear Chuck, I want you to make a copy of this flash drive for me and send the original along with this transcript to Records. I'll also have a copy of the transcript as well. I also want you to test the copy of this message from my voice mail on this mp3 player against the voices on the flash drive. Please make one copy for me and send the original to Records."

"Is all of this in regards to the Davies case?" Chuck replied.

"Possibly or possibly not, which is why I'm asking if you can do all of this asap."

Sighing, Ann replied, "You really like to make a girl's job difficult, don't you?" She then smiled. "It'll be done no later than tomorrow. We'll call you if we're done before."

"Thanks. Don't you have my cell number?"

"We do, but why don't you use a Smartphone or IPhone? They do so much."

"I don't need any more issues involving hacking or identity theft."

"Understandable. You'll hear from us."

"Thanks."

Tindall walked down to Perez' and Parkins's cubicles and sat down at an empty spot next to them. People said hello to him and vice versa. The area was busy as usual with policemen, policewomen and civilians walking to and from different offices and departments.

Parkins asked, "What news do you have for us?"

"I received a package from Charlie Watkins at the Detroit police which had a flash drive in it along with a transcript of the conversation on it. I requested Ann and Chuck to compare the voices on it to the recording of a message that Cecelia Killian left on my voice mail. I also requested that they make copies of everything for me and to send the originals to Records. They told me that everything should be done no later than tomorrow."

"So that means we'll be on standby?"

"Correct. Once I get the info and review it, I'll call you and Mike and you'll get what I have. Based upon what we learn, it'll probably be something that'll concern Detroit and Klingsburg and not us."

"What will you be doing for the rest of the day?" Perez asked.

"Waiting to see if I hear anything from Ann and Chuck. Going through crap cases. Scraps, basically. And what will you guys be doing?"

"The same."

"Call me if you get anything important."

Tindall walked back to his office and went through some employee background checks. As part of the Investigative Division, among his and the other detectives' tasks was to perform employee background checks. For jobs involving money, the public trust or minors, along with the regular drug tests that most companies required, prospective hires also had to submit to a background check to make sure that there no convictions involving any of those three areas.

Tindall didn't have a problem with investigating cases involving money or public trust issues but he was squeamish regarding cases involving minors. Some of those convictions were so graphic that he didn't want to even discuss them in general terms with Kathleen. But it had to be done to prevent child rapists from being able to clean toilets or worse in St. Marys' public or private schools. One creepy bastard was a real nasty piece of work, Tindall shaking his head in disgust over thinking about it.

One bright case, if you could call busting people trying to fly under the radar in the hiring process, was a case in which a guy was trying to get a job as a bookkeeper in a heating and cooling place. It didn't take Tindall long to find out the guy previously did five years in Jackson for embezzling $10,000 from a company he worked at as an accountant under another name.

God only knows what other crimes this guy was mixed up in, Tindall noted dryly. People always forgot that with the new technology it was very difficult to get away with different crimes in different jurisdictions. And as for people who ranted and raved about a national ID card, well we already have a de facto one, Tindall would say mildly, and then conclude by saying that the Social Security number that you have to give to set up a bank account, to apply for a job, even to obtain certain kinds of utilities, was a de facto ID card. Case closed and have a nice day.

The last part would only be said by Tindall if he was dealing with a nasty piece of work who deserved their comeuppance. Usually he walked away from arguments since he always liked to say that you don't win arguments by getting into them. Most people learned either through hard experience or through them seeing and witnessing the hard experiences of others. Sad but true in Tindall's book.

Turning away from his philosophical thoughts, Tindall continued to work. He liked to say partly in jest and partly seriously that computers could replace dogs as man's best friend. Research that used to take hours, days or weeks now only took a few minutes online. Background checks were done quicker and cases were solved faster. Tindall recalled reading in one book about security that a private investigation was able to solve a case while she was cooking via her computer.

After finishing the background checks, Tindall sent the information to Ann-Marie Simonini and she and her support staff would mail out the information to the employers. Since the employers were within the city they would receive the information no later than two business days. Smiling, Tindall checked his wall clock and saw that it was 3:00 pm. He had no other work on his plate for the rest of the day so he would have to look like he was doing something. He hadn't heard anything from Capt. Carter regarding the search warrant and he wouldn't have been surprised if he didn't receive a yea or nea until Monday. Capt. Carter sometimes left as early as 4:00 pm and sometimes as late as 6:00 pm or even 7:00 pm. It all depended on how busy he was with meetings and work that had to be done.

At 5:00 pm Tindall hadn't heard anything further from Capt. Carter or the Crime Lab so he decided that it was time to go home. He wished Perez and Parkins a good evening along with those still at Headquarters and drove home.

Kathleen was reading The Case Against Sugar in the living room when she heard the door open and Tindall walk in. "Hello Frank and how did your day go?"

"It went well, Katy and yours?" Tindall replied as he sat down next to Kathleen.

"My day went well and I was busy as usual. I also had a few meetings today. Boring but necessary. You look like you have bad news for me. What is it?"

"Well, I'm waiting to receive news from the Crime Lab tomorrow, and if I do, then I'll have to go down to Headquarters."

Kathleen understood. "That happens. You're a cop and that means you may not have a nine to five situation."

"Thanks for understanding. I know that sometimes you may have to stay late in the office or go out of town for conferences. It comes with our work."

Kathleen leaned over to Tindall and held his hand.

"That's why I love you so Frank! You care about your job and the people you work with and help."

"I think the same way about you, Katy. I appreciate how much you care about other people and it's good to see that when you sometimes have to deal with the worst of the worst."

"No more shop talk. We're going to eat and enjoy the rest of the evening," Kathleen said as she led Tindall to the kitchen. Looks like everything's going to be okay tonight, he lazily thought as they walked to the kitchen.

24

"That was truly a deelicious breakfast, Millie!" Parkins said to his wife as he cleaned up the kitchen. "You sure know how to cook Saturday breakfast!"

Millie laughed. "You say that to everyone, Jim. I believe that you used to say that to my mother and your mother."

Parkins grinned. "So what? It's true that you, your mother and my mother were excellent cooks. I also can cook, as you very well know."

"You're right. The last time you baked a cake we had to throw it out because it was like rubber, another time the corned beef was like boot leather because you didn't put it in enough water to cook…"

"You've made your point. Now you know that we're going to meet Ike and Ophelia at Drewry's Bar around noon so you won't have anything to complain about."

"I won't since I love seeing the two of them. Really, the only time that all of us get to meet is during vacations and weekends."

Parkins met Ike Grigsby in the service while Millie and Ophelia, Ike's wife, had known each other since childhood in Gary, Indiana. Parkins hailed from Chicago, but Ike came from St. Louis. Both Ike and Ophelia worked for the City of Chicago, the former as a maintenance department head and the latter as an office manager. Their pay was excellent along with their pension plans.

Neither Millie nor Parkins had to face the prospect of eating dog food in their old age. Parkins did a full twenty years in the Army, retiring honorably with a full pension. He had already worked fifteen years with the St. Marys Police Department, so he would be eligible for a full pension there. Combined with his investment plan, Parkins was set since he didn't have any addictions or bad habits. Millie also had a good pension plan from Koditscheks along with her own investment plan. And their daughter Alice was an assistant professor at a university in Mississippi. Life was good to them and they enjoyed it thoroughly yet thoughtfully.

Looking at his watch, Parkins saw that it was 11:00 am as he sat in his recliner, noting mentally that it was almost time for him and Millie to hit the road to Drewry's. It was a nice bar, the oldest in St. Marys, dating back to 1890 and still owned by the descendants of the founder. Politicians and downtown workers flocked there during the day while students arrived at night. It tended to be slightly busy at Drewry's on the weekends. At 11:30 pm Millie called out to Parkins from the kitchen, "Jim, it's time to go."

"Alright," Parkins replied with a yawn as he got up from the recliner. "You just woke me up. I nodded off for a bit." He put on his shoes, fetched and put on his coat, and waited for Millie at the front door. Parkins let Millie go out her and they left after locking their front door.

"Looks so cloudy out here," Millie said as Parkins drove to downtown St. Marys. They could see the usual people out and about on a late Sunday morning jogging and power walking. Parkins was careful with bikers on the street, taking care not to be in the same lane with them. Like Tindall and Perez, they were both concerned about being too close to bikers due to safety concerns—what would happen if the biker lost control of their bike and was too close to their car?

Parkins and Millie like most married couples, were a two-car family, sometimes three cars when Alice came home during the holidays. She was never married and had no kids. Alice was too focused on her career and her personal growth to think about marriage and family. Parkins wasn't sad about not having grandchildren since he had witnessed firsthand children living in households where they weren't wanted. Usually it was a recipe for abuse or death and cops like him and others along with the legal system had to pick up the pieces. Very destructive for the children involved. He knew that Millie wanted grandchildren but he knew that if Alice didn't want to marry and have kids then it was her decision to make.

Millie enjoyed the fresh air, calm yet sweet. Both she and Parkins preferred Fall, with its crisp, cool air. After Alice went to college and moved out of their house, they could take vacations in the Fall. Sometime they hung around the house either to relax or to do projects around the house or they went out of town for a few days either to visit relatives or for fun. The only foreign country they had every travelled to was Canada, spending time in Toronto and Montreal. Millie in particular liked Montreal since she could practice her French. She was fluent in it and was proud of it. Parkins was proudly monolingual and wasn't interested in changing it.

"We're finally here," Parkins noted as he parked their Buick in one of the downtown open-air parking lots.

"We're not <u>there</u> since Drewry's is about four blocks from <u>here</u>," Millie retorted.

Parkins laughed. "You know perfectly well what I'm talking about, Millie. You should be ashamed of yourself."

"I know what I'm talking about and I'm not ashamed of myself," Millie said as she playfully hugged Parkins.

"Let's went, as my father used to say." Parkins and Millie walked the four blocks down Main Street to Drewry's. Since it was close to noon, there was people walking to and fro from different shops, restaurants and bars. The bars and restaurants really didn't begin to become crowded until late Saturday and since most of the bars and some of the restaurants closed at 2:00 am, there was only a few hours between then and people going to the downtown churches. The only synagogue was on the outskirts of town. Fortunately, St. Marians didn't have to worry about adherents of the religion of peace disrupting their town or county.

It was ten to noon according to Parkins's watch. Better to be early than late was his and Millie's policy. They disliked tardiness in other people and raised Alice in the same manner. Since Parkins drove he had to get either soda water or pop. Drinking liquor in all of its forms never impressed Millie and smoking turned her off. Parkins didn't like smoking either and the only kind of liquor he drank was beer.

While she and Parkins waited for the Grigsbys to arrive, Millie asked, "So can you tell me anything about the case that you and the guys are working on?"

Sighing, Parkins replied, "It's still going on. We can't say too much until the case is finished. And even then, we have to stay mum until the person's convicted."

"Sounds like it's interesting."

"It is. You never know what you'll find when the police get involved. Anything that's secret we'll find it out."

Millie knew better than to press Parkins regarding a case that he was working on. He didn't like to discuss the nastier cases that he worked. Most of the time, she would find about a case that he was involved in when she would discuss a notorious case in the Evening News and Parkins would quietly say that he was one of the police involved in it. Up until five years ago, he worked in the Patrol Division as one of the uniforms. He liked being on the street working directly with the community, particularly in the rough part of St. Marys, located in the southern part of the city. There the crime rate was higher than the rest of the city but it wasn't a bloodbath like Chicago.

There were a few times in which Parkins faced bad guys that wanted him dead. One time he avoided a premature harp and pearly gates due to his Kevlar jacket. Out of respect for Millie's concerns, Parkins decided to transfer over to the Investigative Division. To his surprise, he liked the different change of pace. The hours were more reasonable unless he was working on a big case and a good part of the job involved office paperwork. Millie loved the schedule change, though she knew that she could still find someone from the Police Department at her front door at any time with bad news about Jim.

Millie and Parkins continued to chat away until they looked up and saw Ike and Ophelia walking towards their table. They both looked healthy and fit, enjoying life and doing good in the world. Looks like it's going a nice weekend, both Parkins and Millie thought.

Perez enjoyed reading a nice book and listening to the radio in peace and quiet early Saturday afternoon in the living room. A rare time indeed! Though it was a bit cool outside, he decided to open up a window or two to get some fresh air. Birds chirped in the air along with sounds of cars driving down the street and lawnmowers cutting grass. Some of his neighbors used old-fashioned lawnmowers to cut their grass. Perez preferred the regular gas lawnmowers.

This month would be the last that he and Kevin would have to mow and edge the grass. Sheila and Angelica handled the garden part. The kids enjoyed it and also learned responsibility and completing a task successfully. Sheila and the kids were out and about doing errands and they would be back by about 3:00 pm. Afterwards, everyone was going to the movies and dinner afterwards. Other diners regularly praised Perez and Sheila for how well-behaved Kevin and Angelica were. He was delighted by the praise because had seen too many cases of kids ending up in prison as juvies or adults because their parent or parents didn't teach them to respect authority and other people and their stuff.

Perez hadn't heard anything yet from Tindall regarding the Crime Lab. Pat Sholes, Ann and Chuck's fill in on the weekends and some holidays, was as good as they were. He heard rumors that Sholes was thinking about moving over to the county's crime lab or even the State Police's crime lab in Grand Rapids. In special cases, both city and county used the Grand Rapids lab if necessary. Perez knew that Sholes would be a good fit in either of those departments and he wouldn't be surprised if he left.

People come and go from where you work, Perez ironically mused as he read his book. Sad but true. You work with someone for years, you build a relationship with them and either they or you leave for greener pastures or to enjoy a happy retirement. You keep in touch with them for a few months or a year or so and either you or they get tired of it and the contact dries up. Things change in life and everything dies or comes to an end. Only God is eternal and unchanging.

Geoffrey Wawro's book <u>A Mad Catastrophe</u>, a book on the first few years of Austria-Hungary's military activities during World War I on the Eastern Front, impressed Perez very much. Reading through it, he was surprised by how incompetently the Austro-Hungarian government and military conducted its war campaign against Serbia and Russia. Even though he was only into the first seventy pages of the book, there was enough information to make it clear that Austria-Hungary should have done everything it could not to get into a war it wasn't prepared and able to fight. Normally, Perez wasn't enthused about military history, but Frank encouraged him to read it. Since neither the Public Library nor Hamilton had a copy of it, Perez had to order a copy of the book from Amazon.

Feeling drowsy, Perez decided to take a nap on the couch in the living room instead of upstairs so he could hear out for Sheila and the kids. If he snoozed upstairs, he wouldn't hear anything but he would be woken up by Sheila calling out for him. Normally, he didn't have to take a nap during the day and even if he wanted to do so, he was either too busy working or running errands to have the time to do so. He laid down on the couch and promptly went to sleep.

Since Tindall and Kathleen didn't have cable or dish services, when they had free time on Saturdays and Sundays, they liked to channel surf or watch DVDs. Neither of them wanted to pay for cable or dish services since they were already paying for Internet service and it alone was Godawful expensive. This time early Saturday afternoon Tindall was in the living room channel surfing. Nothing particularly interesting was on but he hadn't finished yet. WSTM had acquired two HD frequencies and one was the affiliate for a network that showed old TV shows and the other was the local affiliate for an all movie channel. He and Kathleen enjoyed both channels due to their excellent content.

Tindall was on the verge of changing to the movie channel when his phone rang. "Hello, this is Frank Tindall and who is this?"

"Hello Frank, this is Pat Sholes from the Crime Lab. We're done with the recording and I can give you the results now or at Headquarters."

"I'm on my way now, Pat. See you in about twenty minutes,"

"Ok."

Tindall then called Kathleen on her cellphone. Not being able to reach her, he left her a voice mail message saying that "I'm going down to Headquarters and I should be back in a few hours." They were planning on having dinner with mutual friends in the early evening and he hoped the he would be able to show up for it. If he wasn't able to, Kathleen and their friends would be disappointed but not upset over it. One of the drawbacks of police work, Tindall ruefully noted as drove down to Headquarters.

Walking inside Headquarters, Tindall saw that there was a skeleton crew as usual on the weekends and holidays. Everyone else were off on weekends and holidays. There were still people manning the Crime Lab, Records and certain other departments. And twenty-four hours a day, seven days a week year-round, including weekends and holidays, there were patrolmen and women out on the city streets simply because criminals didn't do holidays.

Tindall greeted Pat Sholes in the Crime Lab. He was around his age with dark brown hair and beard, sporting a pair of designer glasses. "So, what do you have for me Pat?" Tindall asked jovially.

Sholes walked to his desk and handed to Tindall a report and a recording. "Frank, this is our report regarding the recording that you received from the Detroit Police Department along with a copy of the recording. Do you want me to brief you regarding it?"

"No. I'll take everything back to my office for a review. How long will you be here?"

Sholes thought for a moment. "I'll be here until about 5:00 'cause I want to get to the Symphony Orchestra concert at Peppiatt Hall on Hamilton's campus by 6:00. Have you ever gone to one?"

"I've gone quite a number of times with Kathleen. It's a very good symphony for a city of this size and everyone should be proud of it."

"Well, I don't want to hold you up, Pat. Enjoy the rest of your day."

"Same here."

Tindall went back to his office and read through the report. It was 3:00 pm and as he read the report, a Cheshire Cat grin slowly spread across his face. Steve in Appleton's going to love this along with the police in Ironwood, Tindall wryly noted. I wonder if Watkins has called him yet regarding this, he mused as he called Perez and Parkins.

"Sounds like the information you got from the Crime Lab was very important," Perez said as he sat down in Tindall's office. Parkins was already seated by the time he arrived.

"It is, though not for us," Tindall replied as he handed out copies of the Crime Lab report. He said nothing further as Perez and Parkins read the report. Finally, Parkins replied, "The Ironwood and Detroit police departments are gonna want to know about this."

Tindall smiled. "But of course! Ms. Killian's voice on my voice mail matches the voice of the person Heather Rowlands spoke to on the conversation she recorded on the

MP3 player submitted to the Detroit police. The report also includes a transcript of the conversation stating that Ms. Killian was very, shall we say, unhappy about Ms. Rowlands going back to Ironwood to confess."

Without saying another word, Tindall played back the recorded conversation between Cecelia Killian and Heather Rowlands. When it was over, Perez said, "This would be damning to Ms. Killian and the rest of her friends in a court of law."

Parkins agreed. "It sure would be. When will we be sending all of this to Ironwood and the other police departments?"

"Since today's Saturday and it's after 4:00, the earliest that we would be able to send this stuff out would be Monday. So, early Monday morning I'm going to prepare all of this for Anne-Marie to send out and I'm also going to have to call everyone so they will be aware of what's coming."

"By the way," Perez asked, "have you heard from Capt. Carter yet regarding Dr. Bruschetta?"

"Not a thing and the earliest that I'll probably hear from him regarding it would be Monday."

Parkins nodded. "The mayor, chief and the powers that be at Rothmann are probably discussing Dr. Bruschetta right now."

"I agree," replied Tindall. "Too bad that we're not flies on the wall wherever they're meeting regarding this. Well, we've done all that can be done today. My apologies for taking up part of your weekend. We'll have the rest of the day and tomorrow for R&R."

"We'll see you again on Monday," Parkins said as he and Perez left Tindall's office. Tindall decided to stay for a while. Just for the hell of it he decided to listen to the Rowlands-Killian conversation again:

Killian: Hello, who is this?

Rowlands: This is Heather.

Killian: What do you want? Money?

Rowlands: I wouldn't try to blackmail a schoolmarm like you, Cece. Edie would be worth far more. No, I'm calling to tell you that I'm going back to Ironwood to tell the police what really happened.

Killian: So you want to ruin our lives and careers? Not surprising, considering that you're an ex-smackhead. You don't have shit.

Rowlands: Yes, I am. And I've met people at NA meetings and other places far better than you. You always had a mean streak, even in grade school. Did you ever care about anyone other than yourself?

Killian: I do care about some people, two people in particular. You want to play games, I can too. I know about the shitty little soup kitchen you work at, Fr. Casey's. The neighborhood's not nice—come to think of it, Detroit's not a nice place, period. Some little crackhead could slit your throat open and with your purse and money missing, the cops would think that it was just a robbery gone bad. Another stupid white woman killed in the 'hood.

Rowlands: Ha, ha, ha. I've known that you been watching me for quite some time. Why haven't you tried to do something?

Killian: It's simple. You've been a loser hooked on legal junk for quite some time. Who would believe a strung out dopehead? But now, you've cleaned yourself up and you're sort of nice and presentable. You're a liability to all of us. The weakest link.

Rowlands: Are Edie and Linda involved?

Killian: You'll never know, will you?

Rowlands: Goodbye.

Disgusted, Tindall shut off the recording. What a piece of work. The worst criminals in Tindall's book were those who tried to hide behind a respectable façade like Killian. He didn't have that attitude towards criminals such as Tom Ridste, John Bruschetta's killer, since the guy reeked of thug the moment you dealt with him. What arrogance, so arrogant that she didn't even think that she could be recorded. Tindall felt sympathy for Killian's family. Pretty soon they were going to find out that their wife and mother was a monster who would probably do life in the state pen.

Sighing, he made copies of everything and after typing up cover letters, he then placed all of the items in three secured, padded envelopes along with cover letters, one to the Appleton Police Department, the second to the Detroit Police Department and the third to the Ironwood Police Department. Tindall then called all three police departments and left messages stating that the packages would be mailed out on Monday and they should receive them by the end of the week.

Tindall pondered about Heather Rowlands' murder, since he had no doubt that she was murdered. He had no doubt about Killian's involvement, since it was clear from the recording that she wanted Rowlands permanently silenced. The question was if she did it or if she hired someone else to do it. Considering the distance between Detroit and St. Marys, there was no way that she could have kept tabs on Rowlands directly.

Someone had to have been working for her. That kind of surveillance cost money, since people in that field didn't work on the cheap. Even though high school teachers didn't work for peanuts, they didn't have the kind of salary to hire a professional to watch someone on a long-term basis or to do a contract hit. But Killian did have an old high school chum who had money. Was Dowling involved, and if so, how deep? Killian mocked Rowlands in the recording stating that she would never know if Dowling and Severinsen were involved.

Tindall doubted that Severinsen aka Davies was involved. Considering the lengths she went through to cover her past he didn't sense that she wanted to be pulled back into it. She also probably didn't know that Dowling and Killian lived in the same county as she did. And Dowling's involvement could have just been providing money to keep track of, as Killian sneeringly noted, "the weakest link."

Tindall decided to call it a day and go back home to Kathleen. Sholes gave him and idea regarding the St. Marys Symphony Orchestra. Since he and Kathleen were going to be busy at the same time as their performance, they would have to find out the next time they're playing at Peppiatt Hall. Kathleen enjoyed going to the Symphony.

Kathleen was listening to the radio when Tindall came in. "Looks like you're done for the day," she noted with a grin.

"You're darned tootin'," Tindall laughed as he hung his coat in the coat closet. "Hopefully, I won't have to do anything further regarding work until Monday. Tomorrow, I want to have some peace and quiet with you after church. Just some little down time."

"Same here, tiger," Kathleen cooed as she and Tindall grabbed each other on their nice, comfy couch. Looking at their wall clock, she cried out as she drew back, "But we have to meet Leah and Nate in about an hour so we won't have any snuggle time until afterwards."

Sighing, Tindall replied, "You're right."

25

Luke Barrat didn't mind walking in the rain even if it was storming since he figured if it was his time to go, then it was his time to go. Every day, rain or shine, summer or winter, he liked to walk in downtown St. Marys. He preferred to do so in the early morning, just as the day began to start. Barrat didn't want to be bothered with crowds. This Sunday was no different and he wasn't walking to go to church since he was agnostic. His wife and daughter were Catholics who attended St. Anselm's in downtown St. Marys.

Barrat wasn't hostile to religion, he simply didn't believe in it since the age of 15. Despite the religious differences between him and his wife they both loved each other and he deeply grieved when she died a few years ago. The end of more than thirty years of marriage leaving him and their daughter alone.

Barrat sometimes went to St. Anselm's with his wife and daughter and even now sometimes still attended services. Sometimes jokingly and sometimes seriously he liked to call himself a Catholic agnostic or a cultural Catholic, since he was formed and shaped by the Catholicism that he left many years ago. He and the parish priest, David Boughal, were very good friends and were the same in age. Sadly, Fr. Boughal would have to step down from St. Anselm's once he turned 75, Barrat mused as he walked down the street.

Even though it was damp and chilly, Barrat didn't feel the cold since he was bundled up. As part of his Sunday walk, he was going to walk down to the Hunnibell Dairy Mart to pick up a copy of the <u>Evening News</u>. Most people read the <u>Chicago Tribune</u> rather than the Detroit newspapers since Chicago was far closer than Detroit. The Dairy Mart also sold the Detroit papers. Barrat had never been to Detroit and he wasn't unusual since most St. Marians either went to Chicago or Grand Rapids if they wanted to see the bright lights, bypassing Benton Harbor-St. Joe completely. He had been to Chicago numerous times with his family and enjoyed the scenery there.

As Barrat walked to St. Anselm's, he saw the policeman Perez and his family. Very nice family, he noted. Always a kind word for people and the kids always well-behaved, not bratty at all. As he waved to them, Mrs. Perez called out, "Hi Luke! Coming in with us?"

Barrat laughed, "Not today! I'm taking a break from church."

"Too bad, Fr. Boughal's going to have a nice sermon today."

"I know, he always tells me in advance. Have a nice day and week!"

"You too!"

Barrat remembered that one time Fr. Boughal noted that his name was the actual name of the comedian Alan

Carney, who paired up with fellow comedian Wally Brown in a series of movies at RKO in the 1940s. RKO basically tried to rip off Universal's successful Abbott & Costello franchise. Both sets of movies were good, though by the late 1940s and into the 1950s the Abbott & Costello movies were basically recycling their comedy bits from their earlier movies. Life's so amazing, Barrat noted as he continued his rainy walk.

"Luke's such a nice man," Perez said to Sheila and the kids as they walked into St. Anselm's.

"That's true," replied Sheila. "I love chatting with him and it was terrible when Marion passed away a few years ago."

"It truly was. Denise, their daughter, comes here when she's in town."

Perez responded after they all said hello to the greeters Al and Betty Sinnott. "She lives in Chicago now."

"So many St. Marians end up in Chicago instead of Detroit," mused Sheila.

"Not surprising since most people around here are more familiar with Grand Rapids or Chicago. Since the two of us hail further east most people living in our area would go to the Detroit area."

"Shoosh!" Perez quietly said with a smile, "don't you know Mass's going to start in a minute? You're setting a bad example for the kids!"

Angelica laughingly said, "Dad, Mom, why do you have to put us kids in the middle of this?"

"Okay, let's all of us stay quiet for the next hour or so."

After the Mass, Perez, Sheila and the kids walked out of St. Anselm's after saying hello to old friends and acquaintances. Sheila only saw a few since most of the teachers and parents that she worked with at St. Anselm's High School went to the later services. She and Perez liked going to the early service at 8:15 am since they had to rest of the day to relax before returning back to work on Monday. Angelique and Kevin didn't mind since they tended to be early risers. In fact, the entire family tended to be early risers and only stayed up late during some weekends and holidays. Quite a few old and beautiful churches resided in downtown St. Marys other than St. Anselm's.

St. Anselm's looked more like a New England Congregationalist Church than your typical Catholic church because it was originally home to a Congregationalist church that moved to a neighborhood close by the downtown area in the 1890s. St. Anselm's growing parish needed a larger church and their present location fit the bill. The parishioners tended to be those who worked or attended Hamilton or the Law School, those who lived in or close to the downtown area, and the few prominent Catholics who lived in the county such as the Bruschettas. Perez saw the Bruschettas once or twice during the morning services. Even with the tragedy and the ensuing scandal that affected the family, Bruschetta Jewelers was still the jewelry store for the members of St. Mary's elite such as the Meldrims and Peppiatts as well as ordinary St. Marians.

"I hope that Sholes' sermon today is interesting,"

Tindall whispered to Kathleen as the service began at All Souls Church. Kathleen nudged him to be quiet. Personally, Tindall liked Sholes but didn't think that his sermons were interesting. Nice but not interesting. When Tindall attended All Souls Church with Kathleen, they usually went to the 11:00 am service, the latest that could be found since Kathleen wasn't an early riser on the weekends.

The music was lovely as usual and the choir gave everything from their souls via song. There was an annual choir competition between the different church choirs in the county held at Peppiatt Hall and All Souls usually won either first or second place. University Lutheran won a few and Memorial Lutheran in Klingsburg won a few as well. For a long time, Memorial Lutheran was known as Swedish Memorial Lutheran due to the bulk of the congregation being originally from Sweden.

Other than the sermons, Tindall liked All Souls. The people were friendly and most of the congregation's theological views were similar to his; the hymns were excellent as well. He met some good friends and acquaintances at All Souls. In fact, the couple he and Kathleen went to dinner last night with, Nate and Leah Paulson, were members of All Souls. Tindall and Kathleen didn't see the two of them today, which meant that they probably went to one of the earlier services.

Tindall waited quietly while Kathleen and those wanting to take communion went up to the altar rail for it. Most of the parishioners received communion and only a few like him waited for their friends and loved ones to return. Everything was beautiful inside All Souls. To him, a true church needed to be vibrant with God's Word and love. The same was true with University Lutheran. While Kathleen walked back to her seat, Tindall saw that it was becoming brighter outside through the stained-glass windows. The weather reports said that there would be off and on rain today so the dry spell may only last for a few minutes or an hour.

As Sheila and Tindall walked out, after greeting Rev. Sholes and saying hello to everyone that they knew, they walked home in peace and joy.

Parkins loved sleeping in late on Sundays, since it was one of the few chances during the week that he could do so outside of vacation or holiday time. By the time he woke up, Millie would already either be at Faith Baptist Church or on her way there. Parkins definitely wasn't a churchgoer. He considered himself a Christian, but one who preferred to observe the Sabbath in his own way; Parkins loved to note that going to church didn't save you. His daughter Alice was a churchgoer like her mother and the two of them went to church when she was in town.

At 9:00 am Parkins got up and fixed himself some breakfast. He ate three square meals a day and marveled at how Tindall went through the day with a light breakfast and lunch. Granted, Parkins didn't have the time on weekdays to fix a full breakfast but on the weekends, he fixed breakfast for Millie and himself and fixed his own breakfast on Sundays. Millie was like Tindall in having a light breakfast and lunch.

The fried potatoes with onions and the sausage was excellent, washed down with orange juice. Parkins didn't like milk but he did like butter, cheese and ice cream. Both

Millie and Alice loved all of those things along with milk, the former preferring skim. Parkins never gained weight because he was a very active man, working outdoors throughout the year shoveling snow and mowing and edging the grass. He also did long walks in the neighborhood almost every day, enjoying the scenery and the fresh air. Sometimes he walked in the morning and sometimes he walked after work. Even in the rain and snow he walked.

Parkins loved reading the paper while he ate. He only did so if he was eating alone, since he considered it rude to read when he was sitting with someone else. The <u>Evening News</u> was somewhat of a moderately thin paper during the week but it was thick on Saturdays since it wasn't published on Sundays, Christmas or Easter. The Christmas and Easter papers were actually published on Christmas Eve and Good Friday. He knew from Tindall that there was only a skeleton crew at the <u>Evening News</u> on Saturdays, Christmas and Easter.

Millie loved the Sunday supplements regarding the weekly sales at Koditscheks and other local and national retailers. She also liked reading the Parade supplement while he liked the comics. The <u>Evening News</u> still published the "old school" comics that both Parkins and Tindall loved, such as <u>Dick Tracy</u> and <u>Blondie</u>. He also liked the soap opera comics <u>Judge Parker</u> and <u>Rex Morgan, M.D.</u>

Parkins cracked his knuckles and began to read the <u>Evening News'</u> editorial section. It was too conservative for his taste, but he had to admit that on a few issues he had to agree with the different viewpoints. He and Millie also received the Sunday <u>Chicago Tribune</u>. Parkins hadn't had the chance to go through it yet. After going through the <u>Evening News</u>, he carefully put it back together and placed it on the living room table. Millie'll be back in about an hour or so and the rest of the day will begin, Parkins mused as he walked upstairs to get ready for the rest of the day.

26

Dr. Judith Bruschetta was enjoying a nice cup of coffee while reading her reports on a nice sunny morning at Rothmann Lutheran Hospital. Everything was fine and she was receiving regular reports on the status of the Davies case from the police chief. Tindall, the policeman in charge of the case and his team were diligently working on the case. Her mood was bright and clear, always charming and elegant.

Outside her office Valerie Stanley, her clever administrative assistant, was typing up the final draft of a speech Dr. Bruschetta was scheduled to deliver at the St. Marys Chamber of Commerce on Wednesday. The good doctor had timed the speech so that it would be exactly twenty minutes. Afterwards, there would be a delicious lunch scheduled in one of the banquet rooms at the University Inn. The Inn, as local St. Marians called it, was a favorite place for receptions of all kinds.

Different organizations literally begged for Dr. Bruschetta to do talks and panels with them, but she was careful about how many speaking engagements she had. For one thing, as Rothmann's CEO, she had a lot of things to do with so little time to do them. Second, too much publicity was a bad thing. It was 9:00 am and she was still reading reports when her phone rang. "Hello, who is this?"

She was answered with refined laughter. "You don't know who this is, Judith? You hurt my feelings!"

"I would never forget your voice, Paul. Is this business or pleasure?"

"Business, regretfully. Let's meet at noon for lunch at the University Club."

"You sound serious. Do you want tell me what's going on?"

"Not now. It can wait until lunch."

Dr. Bruschetta didn't like the tone in Paul Peppiatt's voice. Lightly dismissive, yet very firm. She wouldn't find anything out from him until they had lunch. People who thought that Paul and his family were light touches due to their charm and niceness did so at their own risk. As owners of St. Marys Bank & Trust, the Peppiatts were not to be trifled with. Almost all of the large companies in St. Marys County did business with them and they had a large customer base among St. Marians. The Peppiatts, along with others, also owned a large part of St. Marys Gas & Electric, the local publicly traded utility.

Dr. Bruschetta sighed. She knew perfectly well that Paul's invitation was an order and not a request. People like the Peppiatts were skilled in this area and only a fool wouldn't see what it was. Undoubtedly it was in regards to the Davies case. Given that Paul was the chairman of Rothmann's board whatever decision he delivered to her would be official with no right of appeal.

If push came to shove, Dr. Bruschetta noted, she would

simply have to step down under the guise of "family reasons" and either set up her own practice, become a consultant of some type, or live off of her share of Bruschetta Jewelers. Under the terms of her husband's will she was entitled to half of the proceeds for her lifetime and her portion would pass to her children at her passing. Prudently, Dr. Bruschetta lived off of her CEO salary and invested the bulk of her share in blue chip stocks and bonds, so at this point, she wouldn't have to work again unless she wanted to.

It would be sad if she had to go, but it would be what it would be. Valerie may or may not be kept on by the new CEO but Dr. Bruschetta could keep her on as her administrative assistant if she wanted to stay with her. She was very skilled in her job and if the relationship wasn't employee and employer they would be close friends. They both got along with each other and had the same interests. Already 10:30 am, Dr. Bruschetta glumly noted. At least, I'll get a good meal before the execution.

"The police chief advised me that you'll be able to contact the District Court to get a search warrant for Dr. Bruschetta's house, her car and her electronic home items only," Capt. Carter said to Tindall in his office. The clock on the captain's desk showed 10:40 am. He continued, "That's all I was able to get for us, Frank."

"It is what it is," Tindall mildly replied. "I'm not surprised that we wouldn't be able to get a search warrant for Dr. Bruschetta's office."

"There's no way in hell that Rothmann's board would allow that and as for the dear doctor, she's not going to be there for long."

"About the info regarding Rowlands and her old BFF Killian, I've sent the info regarding those two over to the Ironwood and Detroit police departments. I've also sent the info to Steve Gould over in Appleton since Killian lives there. He and his team'll keep a close watch on her."

Capt. Carter grunted in approval. "I'm not worried about it since it's not our cases. Hopefully, there's enough evidence to get that Killian woman off of the street."

"I hope so too." Rising from his chair, Tindall concluded, "I have get back and write up the warrant request for Judge Carlile. I'll call his office in a few minutes to get an appointment." Tindall then walked back to his office and wrote up a search warrant request. After a few minutes, he was done and then called Judge Carlile's office for an appointment. Ms. Hart, his administrative assistant, replied that "the Judge has an opening at 2:30 pm, Frank."

"I'll be there at 2:30 pm and thanks, Ms. Hart. I'm also faxing the request over so the Judge can take a look at it."

"You're welcome, Frank. See you then."

Tindall then walked out of his office to see Perez and Parkins. "I have an appointment with Judge Carlile at 2:30 to get a search warrant," Tindall said to them. "Capt. Carter was only able to approval to search Dr. Bruschetta's home, car and her electronic items there."

"Considering she's a heavy hitter at Rothmann, I'm not surprised that he wasn't able to get anything more," replied Parkins.

Perez jumped in. "The people on Rothmann's board are bigger in the juice department than the good doctor."

Tindall agreed, adding that "I just sent the info over regarding Rowlands and the Blandick case to Ironwood and Detroit. I also sent the info over to Appleton so they can keep a watch on Killian. She doesn't know anything yet and she won't know until the noose tightens around her neck."

"Do you want either of us to come with you to the Judge's office?"

"No, the two of you can hold down the fort here. It shouldn't take more than an hour. And since it'll be in the afternoon, we'll start tomorrow morning."

"Ok."

"We'll call Dr. Bruschetta today and advise her that we need to speak to her tomorrow regarding the Davies case at her house. Reading between the lines, Rothmann doesn't want us back there regarding Davies."

Perez asked, "Anything else, Frank?"

"That's it and I'll be in my office prior to lunch." Returning back to his office, Tindall focused on some employee background checks. Everyone in his stack so far looked clean after checking the different databases. He went through the information regarding other people on his list and saw that there were convictions for petty theft. Knowing the companies as he did, he knew that those employee wannabees wouldn't get the job, particularly if quite a few people applied for the same job.

Sometimes, he reviewed liquor license applications. Perez and Parkins were working on a stack of them now. Although convicted felons or persons convicted of non-felonious crimes involving alcohol were barred from obtaining a liquor license, there were still people from those two categories who tried to obtain liquor licenses. All Tindall did when he busted any of these folks was to shake his head. With the technology at their fingertips, the police, or anyone else for that matter, could find out a great deal of information that people didn't want others to know.

Tindall was looking forward to lunch time when his phone rang. "Tindall, St. Marys Police Dept. Who's this?"

"You know who!"

Laughing, Tindall replied, "This sounds like someone I know with a fake accent. I can do a far better accent, Katy."

It was Kathleen's turn to laugh. "You spoiled my fun! By the way, how is it going?"

"I'm doing some employee background checks. Sounds dull, but I have to earn my keep when I'm not solving serious cases."

"Me too. I'm going through some paperwork. The News editor wants me to sign off on some new presses and the TV and radio station managers also want to purchase some new equipment. That means I have to go through all of the paperwork and say yea or nea regarding all of it. "

"Sounds like you're going to be busy all day regarding it."

"Looks like it. Do you want to do lunch sometime this week?"

Tindall groaned. "Like during a work day? Jeez, can't we do it on Saturday?"

"You need to step out of your comfort zone, Frank. And you don't want me to cry since you've told me that you don't like hearing a woman crying."

"Alright, how about tomorrow?"

"Yes! Verdonckt's at noon?"

"That'll be fine. See you later at home."

"Bye for now."

Tindall hung up the phone silently chuckling. What does Katy have up her sleeve? She's planning something or she wants to tell me something big. Well, he'll find out tomorrow.

It's noon and time for lunch, Tindall noted with relief. He had his simple lunch as usual and listened to some classical music. For the past few weeks Tindall read Henry Handel Richardson's epic trilogy The Fortunes of Richard Mahony. It was the story of an English immigrant in 19th Century Australia who moved from place to place and from profession to profession, never being content with living in one place or practicing one profession for an extended period of time. The title character, Richard Mahony, was an unlikeable and unpleasant figure, but Richardson did an excellent job in holding the reader's interest in his fate.

The same was true with her first novel, which Tindall

also had read, <u>Maurice Guest</u>. The title character, Maurice Guest, was just as unlikeable and unpleasant as Richard Mahony, but the reader was hooked into finding out what happened to him. Tindall considered it a testament to a writer's craft if they were able to write a main character or characters that were repulsive yet interesting.

Another example Tindall thought about was the movie <u>Glengarry Glen Ross</u>, which was based on a David Mamet play of the same name. All of the characters in the movie were vile including one character played by the late Jack Lemmon, whom you initially rooted for, but found out at the end that he was just as vile as the others. Yet the movie was quite entertaining to both him and Kathleen.

Refreshed after his walk, Tindall noted that he had ten minutes left before returning to work. Close to four hours left if there weren't any complications, he regretfully thought, and an hour and a half before his meeting with Judge Carlile. In about five years the Judge's going have to step down due to age since in Michigan he won't be able to serve after turning 75, Tindall continued mentally. The thought had to wait since he had to return back to work.

"The board has decided, Judith," Paul Peppiatt noted gently as he and Dr. Bruschetta finished their lunch at the University Club, "that it would be best for you to step down from the CEO position for a bit."

Poker faced, Dr. Bruschetta asked, "For how long?"

Mildly Peppiatt replied, "Unfortunately, we'll have to wait and see. I knew that you would take it well, since you've always been focused on the hospital's success."

Dr. Bruschetta was neither shocked nor surprised. Obviously, someone had to be held accountable for what happened to Davies and since she was the captain of the ship, she would be the fall guy, or in this case, the fall woman. She noted that Paul was watching her closely to see if she would fall apart. Even if she wanted to, she wouldn't make herself a spectacle or a laughingstock in public. Both of them knew that she would be gone permanently.

Dr. Bruschetta also noted that Paul liked her, liked her a lot in fact. His behavior was discreet, but she knew that he would go to bed with her if she snapped her fingers. Dr. Bruschetta would never do that since she heard rumors about his womanizing in his younger days. There were also rumors that it led directly to the collapse of his first and only marriage. Considering all that, she didn't trust that it would work out. Friendship was far better.

"Obviously," Peppiatt continued, "it would be effective immediately, and you can give whatever reason you wish."

"Who will be in charge in the meantime?"

"Dr. Ankeney will be in charge temporarily."

What a slug, Dr. Bruschetta thought. Ankeney's incapable of running anything except into the ground. Still, he was the perfect seat warmer until the board decided on a permanent CEO.

Looking at her surroundings, Dr. Bruschetta marveled at how far she had travelled as a doctor. To be the head of a hospital and having to leave after being in charge for a brief period of time. Such is life. Obviously, the board was being gracious in letting her step down instead of firing her outright. It was likely that she was given a fig leaf of stepping down "temporarily" due to Paul's influence. Yet even Paul concluded that her position was untenable.

Dr. Bruschetta smiled. "Thank you, Paul for your help."

Peppiatt nodded. "We'll keep in touch and the bill's on me."

"Thanks." Dr. Bruschetta walked out of the University Club after hugging him. I'll have to tell the kids that I'm no longer at the hospital and I have to clear my things out of my office, she thought. By the time she arrived at her office she was prepared. Personal items had to be boxed, paperwork handed to different departments, goodbyes said to staff and colleagues.

After an hour or so, Dr. Bruschetta was ready to leave. Valerie, her administrative assistant, was surprised to see her boss's items in boxes. Concerned, she asked, "What's going on, Judith?"

"I'm stepping down temporarily for personal reasons. Dave Ankeney will be in charge."

"Dr. Ankeney? What a joke." Valerie began to laugh but was silenced by Dr. Bruschetta's stern attitude.

"Valerie, please don't do that again. Dr. Ankeney will be you new boss and you're going to be working with him closely. You won't keep your position here if you're disrespectful towards him."

"You're right and I apologize. Please keep in touch, Judith."

"I will and keep yourself out of trouble."

Valerie left and while Dr. Bruschetta was packing there were people in and out of her office wishing their goodbyes and requesting to stay in touch. One person whom she was surprised to see was none other than Dave Ankeney. "Hello Dave. It looks like you heard the news?"

Ankeney agreed. "Yes, I've heard it. Too bad that you're stepping down temporarily."

"And you'll be manning the fort until I come back."

"It's be an interesting challenge, particularly regarding the Davies case. We haven't received any information from the police regarding it yet."

"The last that I heard was that they were still busy with their investigation."

After saying goodbye to Ankeney, Dr. Bruschetta finished up her packing. She locked her office, left the keys with Valerie, and drove home. Once Dr. Bruschetta arrived home, she noted that for the first time in years, except for vacations and holidays, there was no work for her to do. It was depressing in the sense that she no longer had the status power position that she previously had but it was also liberating in that her schedule was completely free to do or not to do something. The sky was the limit.

Since Dr. Bruschetta considered idle minds and hands the devil's workshop, she decided that the first two weeks she would use as vacation time. Afterwards, she would do something productive, such as charity or volunteer work. Doing the day to day running of Bruschetta Jewelers was out of the question since Homer Formby, the manager, was clearly doing an excellent job. Dr. Bruschetta discussed the business with Formby on a weekly basis and checked the financial records on a monthly basis.

Laying on her couch while drinking lemonade, Dr. Bruschetta reviewed her life with a mixture of pain and joy. Pain because of what happened in the past and joy due to what was happening now. Her kids were doing well in college and they were healthy and happy. True, they had to deal with the loss of their father, and it wasn't easy to cope with it, but there were doing fine and he would be proud of them.

Dr. Bruschetta decided to take a nap and have dinner around 4:00 pm. Normally she ate dinner around 6:00 pm or thereabouts since usually came back home around that time or sometimes even later. She could stay on the couch or go to her own bed. Dr. Bruschetta decided to nap on her bed so she went upstairs, changed into her pajamas, and had a pleasant nap for a few hours.

27

Working for Judge A.T. Carlile was interesting and rewarding for Alice Hart, who was usually called Ms. Hart throughout the St. Marys County Courthouse. As the judge's administrative assistant, she was responsible for handling his scheduling and maintaining his direct paperwork among other items. Ms. Hart and the Judge had worked so long with each other that she knew what he wanted even before he asked.

In person, Ms. Hart was trim and in her early fifties. Well-groomed and of regular height, she kept herself fit through exercise and healthy eating, and always credited Jack LaLanne as her inspiration. Dietary supplements she disdained since her attitude was that they weren't needed if you ate a nutritious and well-balanced diet on a regular basis. Ms. Hart slept well and was unmarried, though she did receive proposals earlier in her life and even now. There were rumors that she had a crush on Judge Carlile but she didn't act on it due to not wanting to upset her nice position on the District Court.

Ms. Hart was finishing up some paperwork for the judge when Tindall walked in. "Hello, Frank! You're here right on the dot as usual."

'I always like to be on time, Ms. Hart," Tindall replied with a smile. "And how are you doing?"

"I'm fine and thanks for asking. I'll tell the judge that you're here." Ms. Hart called Judge Carlile and informed him that Tindall was here. After about two minutes, Ms. Hart said, "You can go in now, Frank."

"Thanks."

Judge A.T. Carlile was reviewing notes on a case he was currently presiding over when Tindall walked in. Standing up, he shook Tindall's hand and said, "How are you and the family doing, Frank?"

"I'm doing fine, Judge, and you and yours?"

"We're doing fine." Gesturing toward his conference table, Carlile motioned Tindall to sit down. "Do you want coffee or tea before we begin?" he asked.

"No, I'm perfectly fine."

Carlile was brief and to the point. "I'm going to grant your request for the subpoena on Dr. Bruschetta's house, car and all of the electronic and communications equipment connected to her house. It also includes any picking tools or other items used to fix or pick locks."

"Thanks, Your Honor," Tindall said as he rose from his chair and shook the judge's hand. He then said good bye to him and Ms. Hart after retrieving his coat from the coat closet and the subpoena from Ms. Hart. Tindall noted that it was a bit warm in both parts of the judge's office. Sometimes, people are more sensitive to cold or heat either when they are younger, older or both, he thought. He also knew that people who had more meat on their bones tended not to get cold as quickly as those who were thin. Dr.

Bruschetta was in for a big surprise tomorrow.

As he returned to his office, Pete Messinger stopped him in the hallway. "You've heard the news?"

Surprised, Tindall asked, "What news? I just came back from Carlile's office at the courthouse regarding the Davies case."

"Well, just a few minutes ago WSTM had a breaking story about your old friend Judith Bruschetta. Seems like she's stepping down from Rothmann temporarily for personal reasons."

"I see. Well, this is the first time I heard about it. It won't change anything about the Davies case except that I'll speaking to someone else. Did they say who was going to fill her spot?"

"They didn't say."

"Thanks for the info, Pete." Tindall stopped by Perez and Parkins' area and Perez confirmed that they heard the news.

"I'm not surprised," Tindall noted wryly, "since I knew that they would probably throw her to the wolves after their little meetings with the mayor and police chief."

Perez asked, "You got the subpoena from Carlile?"

"It's in here," Tindall said as he tapped his coat pocket, "and tomorrow morning we're going to pay Dr. Bruschetta a little visit. I'll call her in advance to make sure she's there. I always like to make sure that someone other than us is on the premises to avoid fake charges."

"We'll take one of the fleet SUVs?"

"Only because we don't know how much stuff we'll be hauling out of there. I'll also make copies of the subpoena so everyone will have one and I don't think that we'll need any additional people."

"So we'll be over to Dr. Bruschetta's house by 10:00?"

"Yes."

"Allright and I'll give the info to Jim when he gets back."

"Fine with me, and if I don't see the two of you later, then have a nice evening and we'll see each other tomorrow." Tindall walked back to his office and called Capt. Carter.

"What's going on, Frank?"

"Captain, I just got the subpoena from Carlile for Dr. Bruschetta's house, car and everything in them."

"I'm not surprised that Carlile authorized the subpoena. You probably heard about Dr. Bruschetta?"

"Pete Messinger told me about it. She was thrown to the wolves."

"They're cutting their losses. I hope that you don't think that she will be coming back."

"Not really. Tomorrow morning Perez, Parkins and I will be going to Dr. Bruschetta's to do a search. If we find anything I'll be surprised, since she has had plenty of time to cover her tracks."

"See you tomorrow."

Tindall hung up and looked outside of his office window. The was a bit of traffic both on the street and on the sidewalks. It was close to 4:00 pm and it was almost time for him going home. He called Kathleen regarding Dr. Bruschetta. "Katy, this is Frank. I'm curious about Dr. Bruschetta."

"I don't have any info regarding what went down regarding Dr. Bruschetta. I'm not on Rothmann's board and even if I was, I wouldn't be able to disclose any information."

Tindall laughed. "I thought you were cozy with the Peppiatts and the other board members?"

Kathleen laughed in response. "I'm friends with some, on cordial terms with others and still others we agree to disagree. I wouldn't presume to ask questions regarding Dr. Bruschetta since it could damage relationships and even prevent me from being nominated to the board in the future. I'm not joking—I was advised that a seat would be open for me when the next vacancy occurred."

"Aren't you on enough local boards?"

"Ha ha. You know very well how many boards I'm on. And they all do useful work. Will you be home soon?"

"I'll be leaving at 5:00."

"Remember our lunch date tomorrow. Oh, I almost forgot, we will be having lunch at home instead of

Verdonckt's."

"Fine with me. I'll see you soon."

"Hugs and kisses!" Kathleen hung up.

Tindall knew for a fact that Kathleen was planning something big. And true to form, she wouldn't tell him until tomorrow's lunch. The light-hearted way she proposed lunch as well as what she said just a moment ago struck Tindall as meaning that whatever she was going to spring on him wasn't shocking or unpleasant. He would find out tomorrow.

Oh, Tindall almost forgot, he and the team had to search Dr. Bruschetta's car and house. It could take all day and everyone would have to have lunch onsite if it did. He called Kathleen back and left a voice mail message advising her that lunch would either have to be on Wednesday or it could be dinner tomorrow after work due to the Davies case.

Relieved, he returned back to work, finishing up some paperwork and reviewing a request from Lt. Hannah Gildersleeve to do a tag team with her at one of the local schools regarding drug and alcohol abuse two weeks from now. The fellow she normally tag teamed with, Symonds, was out on disability leave. He e-mailed a quick note to Hannah, stating that he would be able to do it only if the Davies case had been wrapped up by that time.

Satisfied with his efforts, Tindall prepared to go home. Cleaning up his desk as usual, he walked out of his office after shutting everything off. He didn't see a soul in the hallway, Perez and Parkins had already left and there were only a few uniforms at the front desk. Waving goodbye to them, Tindall walked out into the graying light.

Ernest Davies just closed a sale on a 300k property on the outskirts of St. Marys at the same time as Tindall walked in the graying light. He was back in business as a real estate agent and that was the second sale that he closed since Barbara's passing. Her memorial service at Hay & Daughters Funeral Home on a sunny Saturday went well and all of Barbara's friends were there. Davies decided after careful thought not to contact Barbara's relatives in Ironwood. Let sleeping dogs lie, he thought.

All of his friends and relatives were there and Gwennie Nancarrow played some hymns. Although Davies and Barbara weren't religious, there were certain hymns that they liked. Gwennie played the electric organ very well and she even played a hymn that she composed herself. As Davies saw her play, he was attracted to her yet felt guilt over doing so. She was Barbara's friend and Barbara had only been dead for a short time. He turned away from her in guilt. It wasn't proper to lust after one of your dead wife's best friends and she hadn't been buried yet.

Gwennie and Barbara's friends did heartfelt and moving eulogies regarding Barbara. Almost everyone either cried or had tears brimming in the eyes while listening to them. Davies and some of his relatives also gave eulogies. After he said his farewells to everyone leaving who had paid their respects it was just him and Gwennie. They both wanted to say something but the current situation stopped them from doing so. Finally, all they could do was to comfort each other as best as possible in silence.

Returning to the present, Davies smiled as he handed the

paperwork to the office secretary. He had other things to do before going home. A Realtor's day was never over. They had to be on the call around the clock, and evenings and weekends were very busy for them since most house hunters used those times for their searches. Networking was also very important to Davies, since it was an excellent way of finding out about houses that people wanted to sell even before they actually went to an agent.

He was back in his mojo, and it felt good. He had to earn his commissions in order to eat and to keep his job. Bill Abbott, his manager, wouldn't keep him on the payroll if he wasn't producing. Glengarry Glen Ross, the David Mamet play and movie, while vulgar and over the top in some ways, was a good view of how brutally competitive the real estate business could be. Only the strong survived, he mused.

If he still had his thoughts regarding Gwennie after a few months, he could call her, make some kind of excuse regarding the call. Davies didn't know how she would respond. After all they had different views regarding religion and he didn't know what her attitude was regarding having children. Barbara said early on that she didn't have a maternal bone in her body whereas he was ambivalent about having children. Some days he felt like it and other days he didn't. But he knew that if you married someone who made it clear that they didn't want children you had to respect their choice. Davies was still young enough to have children without having to worry about being Social Security eligible while the children were still underage.

Sighing, he decided to call it a day. Everything was done that needed to be done and he could go home.

Tomorrow was the mandatory Tuesday staff meeting and afterwards there were houses to show along with other things. Life's a grind or sunflowers, Davies concluded as he went home.

Gwennie Nancarrow spent most of her time during the week either composing or preparing for Sunday services and today was no exception. Yesterday was a success as usual at St. John's United Methodist Church with an excellent service and joyous music accompanying it. The choir was in full session and Gwennie as the church's music director was responsible for ensuring that everything ran smoothly.

She had always been interested in music since she was a child and beginning in her teens she began to compose songs and hymns. One of her songs was performed during the homecoming parade in her senior year. She knew she wanted to be a professional musician once she entered high school and she chose Marygrove College due to its excellent music program.

While still at Marygrove, Gwennie had composed some hymns that received some critical attention and once she graduated with full honors, she received more than one job offer. Gwennie decided to accept the organist position at St. John's because she wanted to move out of the Metro Detroit area and to see how it was to live in a different part of Michigan. She considered Michigan to be her home and since she was an only child, she wanted to be in the state in case something happened to her parents. They were still healthy but things could change in an instant.

Gwennie liked to publicly credit her parents with encouraging her in her musical talents along with

Professors Eleanor Grover and Sue Ann Vanderbeck at Marygrove College for encouraging and strengthening the academic side of her music. She kept in touch with the two professors as often as she could along with her parents and friends.

Gwennie sensed that Ernie was interested in her but she didn't want to encourage him because of her loyalty to Barbara and because he needed time to grieve. She thought that it would be wise for him to wait for about a year before considering dating anyone so that he would be ready to move on. Gwennie knew of friends and acquaintances who tried getting back into the dating scene too early after the loss of spouse or boyfriend or girlfriend and it was a disaster for them as well as the people they were dating.

Sighing, she returned back to work, preparing for next Sunday's service. Normally, Rev. Howard Calkins, St. John's minister, would give Gwennie an outline of what the following sermon would be by early Monday afternoon. She liked how Rev. Calkins would give the information as early as possible so she would have as much time as possible to plan the music since things could change and she along with everyone else had to be prepared. They had a good professional and personal relationship. She had the knack of working well with people without ruffling their feathers or making enemies.

Composing music came easy to Gwennie and she enjoyed it. Mentally, it all fell into place suddenly and she usually quickly wrote everything down to avoid losing it. The sources were numerous: dreams, birdsong, rain, a beautiful painting or a tragedy. Right now, she was working on a Requiem Mass based on Barbara's passing.

Once she finished it, she would discuss it with Ernie and get his consent before it was publicly performed.

Checking her watch, Gwennie saw that it was close to 5:00 pm. Being an early person, she normally arrived at her office at 7:00 am and left at 3:30 pm. And because St. John's had a silent piano, she could compose and practice her music at any time without disturbing anyone. She also had a silent piano at home. The miracles of modern technology, she mentally mused as she finished up her day. A nice bath, dinner, some good reading, music, and then bed, she thought with contentment as she left St. John's.

"So how did it go at school today, Shawn?" Cecelia Killian asked her daughter as the two of them and Jeff ate dinner.

Shawna made a face and replied after chewing her food, "It was ok. We did the usual stuff and we had to talk about a book we read. Some of the books the other kids read were soo boring!"

Cecelia smiled. "Well, you have to respect other people's choices even if you disagree with them."

"I know," pouted Shawna, "but that doesn't mean it's fair."

"One thing that you'll find out even now, Shawna," Jeff gently replied, "is that life sometimes isn't fair."

Changing the subject, Cecelia said, "Thanksgiving is coming up soon and because of it we get to work together to do the Annual Killian & Stevenson Thanksgiving Dinner!"

Laughing, Shawna replied, "So I'll stuff the turkey?"
"Yes."

"And get to make the pies and cookies?"

"Yes."

"And get to drink Grandpa's Hamm's and Grandma's Mogen David?"

"No."

"I thought I had you, Mom!"

"You didn't, Shawn.   Don't try to trick tricksters," Cecelia smiled as she hugged Shawna.

Jeff laughed. "Your mother's right some of the time."

"Some of the time?" Cecelia said in fake surprise. "You really hurt my feelings."

"No, I didn't.   I know that you're right most of the time."

"That's better. Do you and Shawn want anything else?"

"No, we're done," both Jeff and Shawna said.

Cecelia, Jeff and Shawna took their plates to the sink and Jeff washed the dishes after putting the food into the refrigerator.   Cecelia did the cooking with Shawna's assistance and Jeff cleaned up.   It was important to her for her family to share dinner together, since it was the only time that all three of them were able to eat together. Breakfasts were too busy and Shawna was at school for lunch. She also enjoyed Shawna helping her fix dinner since it was important for her to learn that as a member of a household or community she had to give and not just to take.

The glow of family dinner was dimming in Cecelia's heart due to there being no additional news regarding the Davies case. The <u>Evening News</u> revealed no new information nor did its sister radio and TV stations disclose any new information. The policeman who briefly interviewed her, Tindall, she heard nothing further from him. Even though she had nothing to do with it she was still nervous about the entire thing because it could open up things from her past that she didn't want opened.

If worst came to worst she would have to come clean with Jeff. He may or may not leave her at that point, but she wouldn't lie to him. He didn't deserve it. He believed that he married a semi-hard, semi-sweet young woman who may have had a slightly troubled past. I don't know how much Jeff knows or suspects about me, Cecelia thought, and I don't want to find out. She also didn't want Shawna to be hurt. A young child doesn't deserve pain or to lose a parent or parents.

"Did you hear me, Mom?"

"My apologies, Shawn, I was thinking of something else. What did you say?"

"I was asking you and Dad if we could have a goose instead of a turkey for Thanksgiving."

"Did someone at school bring it up?"

"Yeah, Robbie Stevens said that her family had goose last year and they liked it. Can we?"

"What do you think, Jeff?"

"They do sell geese at the Farmers' Market around Thanksgiving and Christmas. However, Shawn, we would have to ask all of our guests if they like goose. You don't want to invite a large group of people and give them food that they can't eat."

Shawna cried out, "Yippee! We're going to have goose!"

Wryly Cecelia concluded, "We <u>may</u> have goose and it's time for you to go to bed."

Shawna pouted. "I can't stay up until nine? I'm ten!"

"You can go to bed at nine when you turn twelve. Let's go to bed."

Cecelia walked Shawna upstairs to her room, Jeff looking at them lovingly. He was happy to be married to Cecelia. There was something about her that was soft yet hard, a mixture that was complete and whole in a warm manner. Cecelia didn't like to discuss her past and Jeff didn't press. He also noted that she was tenser than she usually was. No one else knew about it, not their neighbors, coworkers or friends. But Jeff knew since husbands and wives know things about each other that outsiders wouldn't comprehend.

After Shawna was fast asleep and Jeff was waiting for her to come upstairs to bed, Cecelia, trembling, made an outside call on her iPhone. Hoping to not get a response, she held her breath. When the other line was picked up, Cecelia said as she sobbed, "Mom, Dad, we need to talk…"

28

"Early to bed, early to rise, makes a man healthy and wise" was one of Dr. Judith Bruschetta's favorite expressions derived from Ben Franklin and she practiced on a regular basis. Since she stepped down "temporarily" as Rothmann's CEO, she didn't have to worry about rising early and going to bed late. This was the first day during a work week that she could laze around all day if she wanted to do so.

But Dr. Bruschetta wasn't that kind of person since she was an active person who wanted to live life in an honorable and productive way. She had, in fact been awake since 5:00 am and already had plans on what she was going to do with her life. She hadn't told her kids and she was going to have to tell them soon before they heard about in from the news or from someone else.

It was now 9:00 am and Dr. Bruschetta was listing to the Radio Classics channel on Sirius/XM when she heard the doorbell ring. She knew that Tindall called her yesterday to see if she would be home today. He had some kind of news to give her that needed to be delivered in person at home and she agreed. Undoubtedly it was related to the Davies case, though since she was no longer Rothmann's CEO she wouldn't need to know anything further regarding it.

Walking to the front door, she noticed that there was an unmarked police SUV parked in front of her house. Amused, she suppressed her laughter and walked confidently to her door. Opening it, she wasn't surprised to see Tindall and two other men, one black and one Hispanic, clearly plainclothes policemen on her front porch, carrying empty containers.

"Come in, officers," Dr. Bruschetta motioned Tindall and the two officers inside. "Would you any of you care for something to drink?"

"No, thank you, Dr. Bruschetta," Tindall mildly replied. "The policemen with me are Sgt. Perez and Detective Parkins." All three policemen showed their badges to Dr. Bruschetta.

"Looks like you're here on serious business, Lieutenant," Dr. Bruschetta briskly said. "Would you care to sit down in the living room?"

"Of course," replied Tindall in the same brisk tone. After everyone sat down, Tindall fished through his coat pocket and handed over some folded papers to Dr. Bruschetta, saying, "This is a search warrant for your car, house, and electronic equipment such as your cell phone and computers. It also includes any objects used to pick or fix locks. We'll wait while you review the paperwork."

"Oh no, I'll have to call my attorney so he can take a look at it." Tindall handed his phone over to Dr. Bruschetta and waited for a minute or two as she went back and forth with her attorney. She then hung up the phone and handed it back to Tindall. "He'll be here in a few minutes. You must have loved the Michiana Living article about the lock picking to include it."

Twenty minutes later, the doorbell rang. Dr. Bruschetta got up from her chair and went to open the door. Neither Tindall nor his team were surprised to see Neil Baron, one of the best criminal defense attorneys in the county if not the Michiana area. He and Baron knew each other very well, though they weren't friends. They had a high regard for each other's abilities and always spoke of each other with respect if not warmth.

After greetings, Baron reviewed the search warrant for a few minutes and said, "The warrant's cut and dried, Judith. Carlile does his job well. I'll keep watch here until they're done and I told my office I'll be over here all day today. I'll also advise you not to say anything regarding this without clearing it with me."

Dr. Bruschetta nodded. Tindall wasn't surprised by what Baron said. Turning to him, Baron asked, "So this is in regards to the Davies case?"

"It is, and we're restricted to what we can say regarding this, Ken."

"Is my client a person of interest?"

"We can't say at this time, though I would advise Dr. Bruschetta to be careful about what she says to us."

Baron nodded. He and Dr. Bruschetta sat down in the living room and quietly waited while Tindall and company began to search. Baron didn't worry about Tindall or his team trying to do anything outrageous, since Tindall was a by the book policeman. If you weren't a piece of shit and if it was within the law Tindall would try to help you and if you were, he would let you twist in the wind with no remorse.

Baron also sensed that while Tindall was sympathetic to Dr. Bruschetta, his teammates Perez and Parkins were neutral, not caring either way about Dr. Bruschetta. He noticed that Radio Classics was playing on the doctor's Sirius/XM radio. The last car he bought had a one-year subscription on it. Baron let it drop because he just didn't want to spend the money on it. It was one of his favorite channels. Too bad most of the actors and actresses on those old-time radio shows were dead.

His father, may God rest his soul, used to love to talk about listening to one show in particular, The Whistler. It was a mystery show with a sneering narrator who functioned much like an ancient Greek chorus of old. Most of the protagonists on the show ended up badly and the endings themselves usually ended in a twist. Baron's father also noted that the show could only be heard on the West Coast and was sponsored by Signal Oil, a long defunct oil company. His attention was brought to The Whistler because it was playing and both he and Dr. Bruschetta were drawn to the story, mainly because it was interesting and partly because they had nothing else better to do at this time except to wait.

Breaking the silence, Baron asked Dr. Bruschetta, "Is The Whistler one of your favorite old-time radio shows?"

"It is," replied Dr. Bruschetta, "along with a few others such as Yours Truly, Johnny Dollar. That show along with Suspense, were the two last remaining old-time radio shows standing when CBS Radio cancelled them in 1962."

"Some of the broadcasts are quite sharp and clear considering that they were recorded or taped at least fifty years ago."

Dr. Bruschetta smiled at the remark. "Yes, the miracles of modern technology. You know what, Neil, if the two of us were living in 1900 and someone told us about all of the things that we would be able to do today in science, communications and other things, we would have written them off as being mentally ill."

Laughing, Baron replied, "You're right! And we probably would have had a good laugh at their expense. I wonder how Tindall and company are doing."

"I hear them in the back, so it sounds like that they haven't reached upstairs yet. How long do you think it will take?"

Frowning, Baron said, "I don't know. It may take time since they're going to search everything from top to bottom to make sure that everything has been thoroughly searched. Don't say anything to me right now regarding this. We can talk about this either later today or tomorrow, say at 10:00 am."

Dr. Bruschetta agreed. "You also know that I've temporarily stepped down from the CEO position at Rothmann, so it won't be difficult for you to reach me here if you need to."

"My sympathies, Judith," Baron somberly mused. From the grapevine, he knew that her departure from Rothmann was permanent, probably due to the fallout from the Davies case. That was why he needed to talk to her immediately about her involvement with Davies, since it was clear to him that Dr. Bruschetta was a person of interest in the case.

Baron also knew from the tone of her voice when she asked for him to come over that she wasn't shocked when Tindall and company came ringing at her door. Which meant to him that she was involved in some way. He wasn't surprised that she was mixed up in it since years as a criminal defense attorney taught him not to be surprised or shocked over anything.

Baron noticed that it was close to noon and knowing Tindall as he did the latter probably brought a cooler full of lunch food for him and his team. Which was obvious since he didn't want to give anyone the opportunity to try to hide or destroy evidence. Sure enough, when noon arrived, Tindall walked into the living room and out the door. After a few minutes, he came back with a small cooler full of sandwiches and soda. Baron saw that the sandwiches were carefully wrapped to avoid sogginess and he also saw Parkins and Perez walk into the living room.

Tindall asked Dr. Bruschetta, "Do you mind if my team and I eat in your living room?"

"Be my guest," was the smiling response.

Baron had to laugh at all of this. Both sides being so genteel, with one side trying to get enough evidence to put the other away and the other side being amused about the whole thing.

"By the way, Neil," Dr. Bruschetta continued, "since it's lunch time and you'll probably be here for a while, I'll make some lunch for us. If you wish we can even have a nice chat with Lt. Tindall and his team while we all eat."

Smiling, Baron replied, "It wouldn't bother me at all."

Dr. Bruschetta and Baron chatted with each other and with Tindall and his team. By unspoken agreement nothing was discussed about the search or about the Davies case. The conversation was easy and interesting, everyone being able to talk about interesting and diverse subjects. Everyone discussed the upcoming Thanksgiving holiday and what they were going to do regarding it.

"We all love ham and turkey in our house," Baron noted with satisfaction as he ate his sandwich, "and it has to be the good stuff. Not the crap in the can but the kind like Honey Baked."

"Agreed," Perez replied. "Honey Baked is where my wife and I get our ham and sliced turkey breast. All we have to do is to cook the side dishes. My wife cooks a green bean casserole to die for."

Tindall grimaced. "Yuck! I can't stand cream dishes or mayo or creamy salad dressing. The thought of any of that stuff makes me nauseous."

Dr. Bruschetta asked, "Did you have a bad case of food poisoning?"
"Yes, and from then on I can't eat any of that stuff."

Dr. Bruschetta nodded in sympathy. "I had a bad experience with one of the fast food chicken places so that's why I can't eat anything from that particular chain. Even smelling it makes me ill."

"Well, I can eat whatever what I want," noted Parkins.

I've never had food poisoning and I'm glad that I never had it."

"The same here," replied Perez.

Baron asked Tindall as the latter ate an apple and some sesame sticks, "Do you eat real food, Frank?"

Laughing, Tindall replied, "I do for dinner, Neil. It keeps me fit and trim to eat light for breakfast and lunch. You should try it."

"Not me! I like hearty meals and a full stomach."

Lunch was over by 1:00 pm and Tindall and his team went back to work. Dr. Bruschetta and Baron turned the Sirius radio back on and continued to listen to Radio Classics. The former noted how quiet Tindall and company were regarding their search. She had nothing to worry about since there was no evidence to point to her involvement in the Davies case. Glancing at one of the wall clocks, Dr. Bruschetta noted how slowly or fast time could pass based on one's perspective.

For the search, Tindall examined the basement, Perez explored the first floor and Parkins combed upstairs. They carefully went through the rooms, collecting any electronic equipment they found. Perez had to disturb Baron and Dr. Bruschetta when he checked the living room. He saw traces of amusement on the doctor's face as he checked everything wearing latex gloves. That was standard operating procedure when doing searches to avoid smearing any possible fingerprints.

Dr. Bruschetta was doubly amused when he asked for

her Smartphone, which led Perez to conclude that she believed that they would never find any information to pin the Davies murder on her. Perez couldn't say anything but if he could he would advise her to be very careful about any steps that she took and since there was no statute of limitations on murder, the police had all of the time in the world. True, over time the case would be put on the back burner in favor of more recent crimes, but it would still be there and the criminal would still need to worry about facing their judge and jury in court.

Perez found Dr. Bruschetta's laptop in her office, a quality HP snug in a secure and padded bag. The office itself looked comfortable and cozy, with two file cabinets and two bookcases among other items. The doctor's desk was neat and clean. Perez easily opened up the desk using a special skeleton key and checked it, going through bills and letters. Nothing incriminating was found.

Moving over to the file cabinets, Perez opened the first one to his right. After a few minutes, he saw nothing incriminating. The same was true regarding the second file cabinet. Whistling, Perez admitted that the doctor was wise to not leave any traces.

He then checked the paper shredder to the right side of the desk. It was a heavy-duty office shredder, the good kind that cost around $200 and shredded the paper, credit cards and CDs into confetti. Far better than that cheap crap that just shred the paper into strips, Perez noted wryly as he examined its bin. Easy work for policemen like him and the black hat boys to put damning documents together. Nothing incriminating. The office itself was located in the back of the house, and the windows in it had a commanding view of the backyard. It looked like it may have been a bedroom at one time, with nice blinds shutting out the harsh and warm glare of the room on bright and hot summer days.

Perez would have loved to watch a bit more of the scenery in the backyard but work called. He walked outside of the office and back to the front with the laptop, the doctor's Smartphone and some flash drives he found in her desk. Dr. Bruschetta and Baron were still there, listening to Sirius Radio. Looking at his watch, Perez saw that it was almost 2:00 pm, time for <u>The Stan Bilkos Show</u>. Bilkos was a former Cleveland cop who ended up with his own daytime talk show. Both Perez and Sheila cherished the show since they gleefully loved it when Bilkos dressed down some little pukepuddle who did horrible things to his woman and children. The high point was when particularly nasty guests were told to "Get the hell off of my stage!"

One noteworthy episode was when some human toxic waste decided to turn his long-lost daughter into his girlfriend. One of Sheila's relatives said after watching it that "that little piece of shit should be taken to a bare field, tied to a stake, something flammable poured on 'em and a lit match flicked on 'em. I'll laugh at his screams."

Sheila said "Damned right!" when she heard it. Tindall and everyone else said the same thing. It disgusted everyone when they saw it or heard about it, though everyone knew that evil took many forms. Brushing that aside, Perez walked to the dining room and went through it and the kitchen.

Carrying his container to the top of the stairs leading down to the basement, he called out to Tindall, "Frank, do you need any help down there?"

"No, I'm fine and thanks for asking. I'm almost done down   here."

"Ok. I'll see if Jim needs any help. "

Perez walked to the bottom of the stairs leading to the second floor and then called out, "Jim, do you need any help?"

"No, I don't need any help up here but you and Frank can check out the attic if your done with your stuff."

"We will, Jim and thanks."

After giving the information to Tindall, Perez then went up to the attic and began to work there. It was clean yet filled with all sorts of junk such as baby furniture, old pictures and clothes, and unused athletic equipment. The old pictures consisted of Bruschetta family members either singly or multiple. There were also pictures of Dr. Bruschetta with whom it appeared to be members of her own family. Some of the pictures she was with Lesley, a mother's pride clearly emanating through.

Perez wondered how many if any in Ironwood suspected the real relationship between the two. It was something that would be discussed openly but in the shadows. Tindall interrupted his thoughts. "How much more do we have to do up here?"

"It's about half done," Perez replied. "Did you find anything in the basement?"

"Not a thing," said Tindall, "and I wasn't surprised. I didn't think that Dr. Bruschetta would make it easy for us.

Something like this she would have planned long and hard about. We may find something on her Smartphone or laptop."

"You may be right. On the other hand, I don't think that she would be stupid enough to leave any traces on her office computer or phone. It would be too easy to trace."

"Let me stop talking and start working." Tindall began to work his side of the attic. He found the same things as Perez, old Bruschetta family heirlooms and junk that the Bruschettas didn't want to throw away. Kathleen had the same kind of stuff in her house and he did as well. You didn't want to throw or donate any of those things away because on some irrational level you felt like you were throwing a relative away. It was irrational but it was a very powerful emotion to feel.

Using his skeleton key, Tindall opened up two chests and a strongbox in his area. Some valuable looking jewelry and coins in the strongbox but nothing of value in the chests except for old school books, reports, essays and report cards. Tindall even saw the college theses of Dr. Bruschetta and her late husband. He closed and relocked the chests and strongbox and called out, "Mike, have you found anything?"

"Nothing but different letters from Bruschetta family members. Some are even in Italian. There's a few love letters from the doctor and her husband."

"I didn't find anything useful either. Let's see if Jim needs any help." Very carefully, Tindall and Perez walked down the stairs with their containers to the second floor. They found Parkins in the bathroom and Perez asked, "Did you find anything, Jim?"

Parkins mopped his brow before answering, "I didn't find anything. Did you?"

"We didn't find anything but we'll be taking the doctor's laptop and Smartphone to the Crime Lab for testing."

"Let's go. I don't want to say anything else until we get back to the office. Walls sometime have ears."

"You're right," Parkins replied. The three policemen walked back to the ground floor in silence. Tindall then said to both Baron and Dr. Bruschetta, "We're taking Dr. Bruschetta's Smartphone and laptop for further examination. Can you give us the passwords?"

Dr. Bruschetta got up and went to a side table in the living room and wrote on a note pad for about a minute. Afterwards she gave the slip of paper to Tindall. "Here's the information to open up my laptop and phone. When will I get it back to reset the passwords?"

"All I can advise now is that both items will be returned back to you as soon as possible. We'll be gone once we examine your car and garage."

"Take your time," replied Dr. Bruschetta mildly.

Tindall walked outside and examined Dr. Bruschetta's Lexus while Perez and Parkins examined the garage. The car itself was in good condition both inside and out, and Tindall didn't find anything suspicious in it. Frowning, he walked over to the garage to help in the search. It was a typical garage, filled with lawn and garden equipment along with garbage cans and assorted junk.

Silently, Tindall began to work in the area of the garage that Perez and Parkins hadn't reached yet. A few minutes later, Perez said after the garage had been searched, "Nothing here!"

Both Parkins and Tindall agreed.

"Let's get back to Headquarters," Tindall wryly replied. The three policemen walked back into the house and Tindall then said to Dr. Bruschetta, "Thank you for your time today and we apologize for disturbing you."

Smiling, Dr. Bruschetta said, "It's nothing to apologize for, Lieutenant. You and your men are doing you jobs. I hope that you catch the person or persons who killed poor Davies quickly."

"There's no statute of limitations on murder. Good evening."

Both the doctor and her attorney said good evening. Once they were safely alone the attorney asked, "Judith, you have to be completely honest with me. Did you have anything to do with Davies' death?"

"Please sit down, Neil and I will tell you," the doctor calmly said. After the doctor and her attorney sat down in the living room, she told her story.

"So how long will it take for you guys to examine Dr. Bruschetta's Smartphone and laptop?" asked Tindall to Chuck Roberts in the Crime Lab.

Chuck thought for a moment before replying. "Based

on our current backlog, it should be done no later than the end of this week."

"Good. Well, I hope that you and Ann have a nice evening."

"The same to you and Kathleen."

Tindall walked back to his office and left after shutting everything down. He had previously said goodbye to Perez and Parkins a few minutes prior to him leaving. Tomorrow will be hump day, Tindall thought with relief.

29

"As of right now," Tindall said to Capt. Carter in their Wednesday meeting, "unless there's anything on Dr. Bruschetta's Smartphone or laptop she'll walk. We also didn't find any lock picking equipment."

"For now," Capt. Carter noted.

"That's right since there's no statute of limitations on murder, at least regarding Davies. And there's nothing we can do regarding Dowling since Merewether ruled it an accident and there's no evidence of any foul play. Still, she's no longer at Rothmann and that's the best thing that may come out if it."

Capt. Carter grunted. "Also, given how prominent the Bruschettas are and given the fact that Davies and company were involved in the death of the doctor's biological child, the Prosecutor's Office mayn't even get a conviction."

"Or Robitaille would probably plea bargain the charges down to second degree murder or even manslaughter if he thought that he could get an easy conviction."

"Probably right." Everyone knew, including Tindall and Capt. Carter, that St. Marys County Prosecutor Arthur Robitaille wanted quick and easy prosecutions since they were cheap for the taxpayer and they led to positive publicity and automatic reelection. Now if the case involved rape, child abuse or the murder of children, law enforcement officials, the mentally/physically disabled or the elderly, torture murder or serial murder, Robitaille would push for the max. Even those cases were too vile for him to try to plea down and he could wrap himself up in the law and order mantle.

It was a standing joke among St. Marys' political and social elite that Robitaille toyed with moving on, preferably to the State Senate or House and that it would be very tempting for him to ditch the Prosecutor's Office for either of those two positions. The drawback would be that those positions, along with the state-wide positions, such as governor, were term limited and Robitaille would have to start over on the local level afterwards, possibly having to contend with a sitting county prosecutor even more popular than him. Also, the prospect of doing criminal law in the private sector disgusted him since he saw himself as a prosecutor and not as some sleazy shyster defending an O.J. Simpson clone. So, it served his interests in staying put and not stepping up. For the time being.

"Keep me posted if you have further news regarding the Davies case," Capt. Carter concluded. Taking the hint, Tindall returned back to his office. What he said to Capt. Carter was the same news that he, Perez and Parkins discussed yesterday. Sitting down at his desk, he noticed that someone left him a voice mail message. It was from Charlie Watkins requesting a call back.

Tindall called Watkins back and got him after a few rings. "Hello Frank! How are you and the family doing?"

"Fine, Charlie and yours?"

"The same. I'm calling to tell you that I received your package and it doesn't look too good for Ms. Killian. We'll send the stuff over to the ME's office and the Prosecutor's Office for review. Thanks for the info."

"You're welcome, Charlie. Keep me posted."

"Will do. Bye."

Tindall hung up and thought for a moment before going through his paperwork. More background checks to take care of. He figured that it would probably take the rest of the hour to go through all of it. Tindall was going through his pile when his phone rang. Picking up the phone, he said, "Lt. Tindall, St. Marys Police Department."

"Good morning, Lieutenant, this is Sgt. Beth Graham from the Ironwood Public Safety Department. We received your information regarding the Blandick case and thanks for sending it."

"Thanks for the call, Sergeant. Have a nice day."

"Same here."

I wouldn't want to be in Cecelia Killian's shoes, Tindall wryly thought. Still, it wasn't his problem or business. Ironwood and Detroit would handle her and if there were indictments in either jurisdiction, the prosecutors would have to draw straws to see who would get prosecution rights first. Killian and her attorney or attorneys would cop a plea only if the evidence was so damning that there was no chance that she could get off.

Tindall figured that he would probably hear from Gould in Appleton sometime today or tomorrow. If Killian was arrested, then the Appleton police would be responsible for it since she lived in their jurisdiction. Then she would be transferred either over to the Ironwood or Detroit cops. Knowing Gould liked he did, Tindall calculated that he would keep a close watch on Killian to prevent her from bolting.

But Tindall quickly sized Killian up at their first and only meeting. He knew that she wasn't a runner because it wasn't her personality and also because she had enough common sense to know that a person of interest in a serious crime case was automatically admitting guilt by running. No, she would face it to the bitter end and even if she went to jail, Tindall reckoned that she would take her punishment like a man without whining or complaining.

One case he thought of was the Dr. Krekorian case. The good doctor was finally convicted of participating in an assisted suicide. He had evaded prosecution for other assisted suicides through his skillful attorney Gerard Feigenson and sympathetic jurors. Krekorian made his fatal mistake when he ditched Feigenson and decided to play the martyr card and defend himself in court. Needless to say, he was duly convicted. Then he tried to have the conviction overturned but that maneuver failed.

In fact, Tindall had a grudging respect for Krekorian due to his attitude, not because of his peddling of assisted suicide, which Tindall thought was nothing more than an attempt to legalize euthanasia by stealth, but because he was standing up for a principle and was willing to face the consequences. He only turned on Krekorian once he tried to play the poor victim that so many criminals tried to do once they were behind bars. If you violate the law for a principle such as animal rights or abortion, then you should be prepared to do you time like a man, Tindall thought.

Tindall noted that it was 11:30 am. Almost time for lunch with Kathleen at noon. He already cleared it with Capt. Carter who didn't mind him staying out for a bit longer lunch since Tindall rarely if ever spent more than an hour at lunch. Sometimes he only spent a half hour at lunch. It all depended on how busy he was or if he wanted to leave Headquarters early.

At 11:40 am he left Headquarters and walked home after wishing everyone a good lunch. The day was lovely and crisp, and he enjoyed it, walking in his coat and wearing a cap and earmuffs on top and alpaca gloves on his fingers. Not a cloud in sight and birds still flying around. There were people walking their dogs and sometimes it looked like the dogs were walking the people. A few squirrels were running from tree to tree. Quick little devils, Tindall noted. I wouldn't touch them because I don't want to have to get ten stomach shots to avoid rabies.

Tindall saw a few Canadian geese walking around, proudly showing the black, grey and white plumages. He considered them to be nice looking birds but he also considered them to be pests of sort, fouling up lawns and sidewalks. Tindall felt sorry for anyone having to clean up sidewalks with that kind of stuff on them. Only once he saw a blue jay or a cardinal outside. They were even more beautiful than the Canadian geese, though toucans, puffins and peacocks were colorful birds.

Tindall read someplace that Icelanders ate puffins. He knew that they ate rotting shark and that the taste of it was described as a very strong blue cheese, which he enjoyed along with gorgonza and other fine cheeses. While walking home, Tindall didn't see any rabbits, possums or skunks. Normally he only saw those creatures when he walked early in the morning. Those kinds of animals made good pets provided that you acquired them when they were young. Raccoons could be difficult to raise since they had very sharp claws that could cut through a variety of different things.

Kathleen wanted to get a cat, preferably two cats, and Tindall was inclined to agree. Cats were cleaner than dogs since you could train them to do their business in a kitty litter box. Dogs, on the other hand, did their thing anywhere and you had to clean up after them. He remembered when he went to someone's house as a little kid and it was disgusting how the homeowners didn't clean up their front and back lawns.

Tindall was now back in his neighborhood and close to home. Since it was noon, the streets were quiet. Only retirees and people on vacation were out and about. He didn't see Mrs. Forbes or any other familiar faces. Probably running errands or something else. He also saw a van parked in front of his house.

Home at last! Tindall walked up the steps to the porch, slowly walked to the front door and opened it. Inside, the living room was decorated with bunting, Nat King Cole's "Caroling, Caroling," was playing from the boom box and Kathleen was nowhere to be found. Tindall walked to the dining room after shedding his coat and saw that a table for two had been set. Very fine and elegant setting, Tindall noted as he sat down, while also noticing that there were sounds of someone in the kitchen.

Checking his watch, he noted that it was 11:55 am and lunch would begin in about five minutes. The smell of food moved into the dining room as Tindall quietly waited.

At noon, Kathleen came out of the kitchen and ran over to Tindall to hug him. Surprised, Tindall asked, "What's going on? Is it some kind of anniversary that I missed?"

Kathleen laughed. "No, I'M PREGNANT!"

Surprise and joy flooded Tindall's face. He rose from the dining room table and hugged Kathleen. "How long have you known?"

"Since last week. I went in for my annual checkup and Dr. Crouse told me that I was pregnant. I was shocked! I didn't have any symptoms and my periods usually don't occur until the end of the month."

Tindall knew it well. Kathleen became morose and depressed during those times and he did everything he could to make as easy as possible for her during those times. "So we're going to have a little one in about nine months?"

"You got it right, buster. We'll have to tell everyone and we'll have to prepare the house to make it kid friendly."

"I admit that I'm a bit nervous about this. I'm 45 and you're 40 and we're going to have a kid for the first time. We've never been parents so we're going to have to ask for help."

Kathleen squeezed Tindall's hand. "I know that you will be a good father. You're kind and decent and sweet.

287

And we can ask Elaine and Phil for advice and my mother would be willing to stay with us for a few weeks to show us the ropes."

Smiling, Tindall replied, "I know that you will be great mother, since you're also sweet and kind. Before you know it, we will have to figure out if the little one will go to the University School or the Lutheran school system."

"Well, I'm a bit biased since Amy and I went through the University School. The only people that I know of who didn't were the Bruschettas and some of the Hedermans." Checking her watch, Kathleen continued, "How rude I'm being! It's 12:15 and you have to get back to work by 1:00. Let's eat!"

Tindall asked, "What are we eating?"

"You'll find out."

Lunch was excellently prepared and served by the University Inn caterers. Tindall enjoyed the Biff a la Lindstrom, mashed potatoes, lingonberries, and beef barley soup; he and Kathleen loved Swedish food. Dessert was an opera torte. Both he and Kathleen ate silently, savoring the food and the time together. It was one of the few times that Tindall didn't worry about the time. Too bad it wouldn't last, since he had to return back to work around 1:00 pm.

After finishing lunch, Kathleen mused, "Everyone in the county says that if you can't find a Swedish restaurant or bakery, you're not really looking for one."

"Agreed. And I've never been to Sweden. The taste and beer alone is enough for the two of us to make a visit there one day."

"The only thing about Sweden is that it has a bad rep for being one of the most atheistic and lefty places in the world."

"Det var synd."

Surprised, Kathleen asked, "What did you say?"

"Du kanna jag talar svensk."

"Et je parle seule francais a vous!"

"Okej, jag vill tala engelsk!"

"Merci beaucoup."

They both laughed loud and hard. Tindall and Kathleen also heard laughter in the kitchen. The caterers sounded like they heard every word and enjoyed it. Frowning, Kathleen realized that it was close to 1:00 pm. Time for Frank to get back to work, she thought. Kathleen as the adminstrator and boss lady could set her hours, but she didn't like to make it a habit since it set a bad example for the rest of the team. Frank couldn't do the same.

"Well, it's going to be a new life for us from today," noted Tindall, "and it's going to be exciting and challenging at the same time. Too bad we're going to have to part for a few hours. But it'll be the same time and same station."

"You bet! See you later, smarty pants!"

Tindall walked back to Headquarters and Kathleen

watched while the caterers cleaned up in the kitchen. "There's enough left for a day or two of leftovers," Kathleen said. "Would you and your team like to take some home, Flora?"

Flora, or more properly, Mrs. Degenhardt, replied, "No thanks, Mrs. Tindall. We're alright here. You and Mr. Tindall can keep the food."

"I just wanted to ask."

"Perfectly understandable. We're almost done with the cleanup."

"I'll be in the living room, Flora, if you need anything."

Mrs. Degenhardt nodded.

Kathleen walked back to the living room and sat down on the couch. It was an exciting day and she was so happy and relieved to give the delightful news to Frank. He was nervous and happy regarding it. Kathleen was nervous after hearing the news from Dr. Crouse and thought that it was a mistake. The good doctor advised that it was confirmed after three tests.

The University Inn caterers were the best in the county. They handled the food for all of the important occasions for the Meldrims along with the other prominent families in St. Marys County and Hamilton U. The catering business made big money for the Hedermans, along with the University Inn and their bakery, Hedermans Bageri. Neither Tindall nor Kathleen would use anyone else.

Kathleen knew Mrs. Degenhardt for quite some time and she had been one of the lead University Inn caterers for years. It was an important job since the food had to be fresh and properly warm no matter what time of the year it was. The preparers and servers had to be well trained and sociable, able to handle sticky situations as needed. Not for the faint of heart, as Mrs. Degenhardt liked to say. Kathleen knew that Mrs. Degenhardt was married but wasn't sure if she had any children. She was very wary about asking personal questions to people she didn't know well.

By 2:00 pm the caterers had left and Kathleen was alone in the house after cleaning up. Time to go back to work, she silently thought. The rest of the day wasn't going to be busy, just taking care of a few odds and ends, Kathleen mused as she went back to work.

"Did you enjoy lunch?" Parkins asked as Tindall returned back to his office.

"I did, and it was very interesting," Tindall responded. "There's something in the air and it's quite delightful to me and mine."

Frank's sounding odd, Parkins mutely noted. Something interesting must have happened to him. But he only said, "That's good to hear."

"And how did you and Mike's lunch go?"

"We enjoyed ourselves at Grissom's. It wasn't as crowded as usual around this time of the day."

"I need to go there with the two of you sometime. Is Mike back?"

"He's back. He just stepped out for a minute."

"Ok. I'll be in my office doing paperwork for the rest of the day unless something comes up regarding Davies."

"I'll tell Mike."

"Have a nice evening if I don't see the two of you later."

When Tindall arrived back at his office, he saw a voice mail message on his phone. It was from Steve Gould from Appleton stating that he received the information regarding Cecelia Killian and that they would be keeping track of her. Steve was good at that kind of thing, Tindall noted. He and his team would keep tabs on her without having to worry about a lawsuit. Killian's goose was soon to be cooked, Tindall somberly noted as resumed his paperwork.

30

Kathleen woke up at 8:00 am on a rainy Friday morning and flung the bed covers to one side. Frank had already left for Headquarters and didn't disturb her while she slept. She decided to play hooky from work and to do some things regarding her pregnancy. I don't want to do anything to hurt our baby, she thought as she went downstairs to eat breakfast.

After eating her muesli, Kathleen went back upstairs to shower and brush her teeth. Afterwards, she brushed her hair, applied petroleum jelly to her skin and lips, and put on a pair of blue jeans and a turtleneck sweater. Kathleen only liked to dress up for work, special occasions or church, an attitude similar to Frank's.

Aileen's Attic went off at 9:00 am and Kathleen was only able to listen to snatches of it while she was getting ready. Even when she was at work she was too busy to listen to it. When she was busy she had to have absolute peace and quiet. The only acceptable sounds were classical music or wordless elevator music. Frank also had the same requirement when he was mentally busy. It amazes me how similar the two us, Kathleen noted with a smile. I wonder if the baby will be like us or someone else in our family.

She also wondered if the baby would take after her, Frank or some other member of their families. Kathleen knew that the gene pool operated in odd ways sometimes. She knew of some people who looked nothing like their parents, others who looked like their father or mother and still others who looked like other family members. It would be funny if the baby was over six feet tall since the tallest family members on either side were 5'10.

Kathleen logged on to her laptop and then logged into Amazon and placed some orders for pregnancy books. She also loved the Amazon.fr site to purchase different books and DVDs, Harry Baur being one of her favorite French actors.

Dr. Crouse advised that she could continue to exercise during her pregnancy as long as she didn't overdo it. Kathleen loved to jog and hike along with some weekend bike riding. She also liked to work out at the gym. Frank was strictly a walking kind of guy and they often hiked together. Even though he didn't work out, Frank wouldn't have been a pushover in a fight.

She also needed to stop by D&H Pharmacy to get some prenatal vitamins. Kathleen also stopped drinking alcohol to avoid damaging the baby. Smoking wasn't an issue since she didn't smoke. It was a filthy habit that led to the smell of smoke getting into your clothes, house, or car, and it was very difficult to get the smell out once it set in.

Frank didn't smoke either and he told her that years ago he lived in an upstairs apartment and a smoker moved into the downstairs apartment. The person downstairs smoked so much that the fumes were coming into his apartment. It was so bad that Frank had to move out and had to throw out almost all of his clothes and other items. He told Kathleen that he wasn't angry over it since he had the money to replace everything.

After leaving D&H Pharmacy, Kathleen decided to take a look at some baby furniture. She saw some lovely items, but she needed to talk to Frank about it. He would probably defer to her judgment. Men normally did in cases such as this. Once she found out if the baby was a boy or girl she could then get the baby clothes.

Kathleen and Frank already decided on which room in their house would be the nursery. It was an airy and roomy room on the second floor. It was empty and only a few changes would need to be made. They also needed to decorate the room itself. There would be no need to repaint it since it was white, and it wouldn't take too much time to add a few decorations to it. And since it was empty, nothing would have to be moved out of it.

Glancing at her watch, Kathleen saw that it was close to noon. She decided to go to Winternitz's for lunch. After she was seated, she went through the menu for a few minutes as her waitress took care of other customers.

A few minutes later, the waitress came back and asked Kathleen, "What would you like to order?"

"What's the lunch special today?"

"Swedish meatballs with mashed potatoes and lingonberries."

"I'll order it and I'll also have some lemonade, please."

Beaming, the waitress replied, "I'll be back with your

lemonade first and then your order."

"Thanks."

Kathleen was hungry and hoped that she didn't have to wait too long. She didn't have to worry about it since the waitress came back about fifteen minutes later with her lunch—it only took about five minutes for her to receive her lemonade. She liked the Swedish meatballs at Winternitz's since they didn't use cream in the gravy, just drippings, flour, salt, pepper and spices. She, liked Frank, didn't like cream sauces or any of those things. Too rich for her.

Kathleen was surprised at how ravenous she was right now. She wasn't that hungry earlier in the day and seriously thought that the baby may have been hungrier than her. Once her pregnancy was advanced, she would have to change how she slept since she couldn't sleep on her stomach when she wanted. Kathleen dreaded the nausea, vomiting and food cravings that sometimes affected pregnant women such as her. Ce la vie, she ruefully noted as she ate.

The food was delicious as usual and after Kathleen cleaned her plate, she sighed with satisfaction. The waitress' "Do you want anything else?" broke Kathleen's food fueled reverie.

"I don't want anything else and thanks," Kathleen replied. "I'm all set."

"Let me clear all of this for you," the waitress replied, removing all of the table -and silverware. "I'll be back with your bill in a moment."

Five minutes later, the waitress came back with Kathleen's bill. The latter payed her bill and left a generous tip. Walking back home, Kathleen noted with joy that Frank proposed to her at Winternitz's. Since then, it had been their favorite restaurant. She felt like taking a nap and not doing anything else for the rest of the day. They still had leftovers from yesterday so neither of them needed to cook.

Once at home, Kathleen saw a message on the phone in the living room. Even though she and Frank had their own cellphone—they both wanted a land phone in case of emergency. Kathleen saw that it was from Frank and she called him back.

"Hello Katy! You're playing hooky today?"

"Yes I am, Frank! I just came back from lunch at Winternitz's after buying some prenatal vitamins and checking out some baby furniture."

"We can go this weekend to check out the furniture if nothing has come up regarding the Davies case. If necessary, you can purchase it yourself and have'em ship it."

"Ok and how is your day going?"

"I'm working on some paperwork and we're still waiting on further information regarding the Davies case."

"Too bad you can't tell me anything."

"I would love to, but I can't mess this case up."

"I understand, since there's times that there are things

going on with the company that I can't discuss outside of it."

"Well, I have to get back to work. I can't waste the taxpayers' money," Tindall said with a laugh. "Bye for now."

"Same here."

Kathleen hung up and decided to listen to classical music on the radio for a few minutes in the living room on the couch. Just the kind of music when you're half awake and half asleep. She didn't want to read anything since she was too tired to think about it. She was surprised to find out from her watch that she had nodded off for about a half hour. Shaking her head and yawning at the same time, she walked upstairs to the bedroom, changed into her nightclothes and drifted off to sleep.

Tindall returned to his paperwork after his chat with Kathleen. He knew that Kathleen was not going to work since she normally left around the same time as him and kept around the same hours. Usually she was at home by the time he arrived there. He would have to be more active around the house since she was pregnant to avoid her or the baby being hurt.

One of the things about children is that things changed in a different direction. Up until now, Tindall had to take Kathleen's thoughts and concerns into account if he had to make an important decision. He didn't mind since the two of them were partners. With the child, Tindall would have two special people to consider when making an important decision. Also, trips and expenses would have to change. He liked to travel in the fall but with a child it would have to be in the summer or on school holidays.

Tindall still hadn't received anything yet from the Crime Lab regarding Dr. Bruschetta's laptop and Smartphone. He already briefed Capt. Carter earlier regarding the status of the Davies case and advised that it could be anytime this week or even Sunday before the Crime Lab disclosed whatever information they had. Capt. Carter agreed.

As for Dowling and Rowlands, Tindall figured that Appleton and Detroit may call him back regarding the status of their investigations. The same would be true regarding the Blandick case. If he didn't hear from them he wouldn't be surprised since they would want to keep the information close until any charges would be filed.

Tindall left Headquarters at 5:00 pm after saying goodbye to Perez, Parkins and everyone else who was left. When he arrived home and opened the door, he noticed how quiet it was. Normally, Kathleen was up and about and either the radio or the TV was on. Her car was in the driveway.

Tindall figured that Kathleen stepped out for a minute, possibly for a walk or a jog. He went upstairs to change into sweats and blue jeans and saw that Kathleen was peacefully asleep. Tindall changed silently and quietly walked back downstairs. Turning the TV on, he was engrossed in watching some old show when Kathleen bounced down the stairs.

"Hello Katy! Did you enjoy your nap?"

"I did, Frank! Why didn't you wake me up?"

"Moi? It would've been rude to do so. You also looked like you were enjoying it."

"I did. And it was the first time in quite some time that I did so. You know that I don't take naps during the day."

"Agreed, but there's always a first time for everything."

"You bet. Anyhow, I'll probably be up a good chunk of the night while you're sleeping like a baby."

"Not necessarily, since some babies toss back and forth at night and others cry all the time."

"Well, as one of my bosses a long time ago used to say, 'We'll work it out.'"

"We will," Tindall concluded as he and Kathleen hugged each other.

31

"Time to get up, sleepyhead!"

"Mom! I gotta get up now? It's Saturday!"

"It is, but it's already 9:00 and you can't stay in bed all day."

"Ok." Shawna Stevenson slowly got out of bed and took a quick shower. Quickly dressing, she rushed downstairs for breakfast. The smell of bacon and maple syrup was in the air and her mouth watered. Shawna noted that her parents were waiting for her since they always had breakfast together on Saturdays and Sundays.

Tomorrow she and her father would be attending First Baptist Church in the village while her mother relaxed at home. Except for weddings and funerals, Shawna's mother rarely attended church and didn't talk about spiritual matters, preferring to leave those things to Shawna's father. Shawna herself was unaffected by all of this, since 10-year olds like her had other more pressing things to worry about.

"Eat you breakfast, Shawna," her mother replied lovingly while she and her parents ate their breakfast. "You know that there are too many starving children in the world. And don't forget you lunch."

"I won't, Mom."

Shawna's father replied wryly, "Well, we'll have one more free day tomorrow before all of us have to go back to work. Ironically, all three of us will be in a classroom."

"We know that," Shawna's mother replied, "and we also know that Shawna will be at the same high school with us in a few years."

"Which means that you'll have to be on your best behavior since we'll know about it."

"Oh! Dad and Mom! Can't I go to a different high school?"

"No, since it's the only high school in the area and you're not going to a private school in St. Marys."

"Arrgh!"

"Eat your breakfast. We have to get out of here by 10:00 so you won't be late for your Girl Scout troop meeting."

Silence reigned in the living room while everyone ate their breakfast. Crispy waffles with maple syrup and butter complimented the meaty beef bacon. For parental reasons, Shawna's household was pork free for the most part. She was delighted that her parents weren't crazies like some of her friends' parents who were complete vegans who didn't eat anything that came from an animal, which was shocking to her.

Shawna was old enough to know that she didn't want to lose her bacon, burgers, pastrami or corned beef. She also didn't want to lose her milk or cheese. Nor did she want to lose her leather shoes or belts. If, in adult words, the animals got the short end of the stick, then it was their problem, not hers.

After breakfasts, Shawna ran upstairs to brush her teeth and comb her hair. She wanted to use makeup but her parents nixed the idea, telling her she was too young for that kind of thing. Oh, parents! Why she couldn't put on some lipstick or lip gloss? And wear shorter skirts and dresses? After all, girls her age such as Dina Marshall already did so. Too bad she couldn't bring Dina to the house. From her mother's tone Shawna knew not to even bring it up. It was a bummer to have parents who were teachers, since they had friends who were also teachers in her school. Some of the other kids along with the teachers thought that Dina was bad news.

Sighing, Shawna finished brushing her teeth and ran downstairs, coming her hair as she did so. Surprised at seeing her back so soon, her mother asked, "Did you brush your teeth that quickly?"

"I did, Mom."

"Don't lie, 'cause if you do, the plaque monster will take all of your teeth and you'll have to wear dentures."

"Mom!"

"Let's go!"

Shawna's mother drove her to First Baptist Church, where Shawna's Girl Scout troop was located it. She noted that the other girls enviously looked at her mother's nice blue Subaru Forester when they drove there. Very rarely did her father drive her to Girl Scout meetings. It's a mother thing, she morosely thought, since most of the drivers were mothers.

It was 9:50 am when they arrived at First Baptist Church. Some of the girls in the Scout troop were members and others were members of the different Lutheran, Catholic and Evangelical churches in the county. Only a few were non-believers and neither they nor their parents wanted to discuss it. After dropping her off, Shawna noticed that her mother decided to talk to Mrs. Vasiledes, the Scout troop leader. The conversation was longer that it normally was and Shawna was curious regarding it. She closely watched the two of them while chatting with the other girls. After about five minutes, Shawna's mother drove off.

Shawna knew better than to ask Mrs. Vasiledes what happened. Kids didn't ask adults those kinds of questions and Mrs. Vasiledes would graciously but firmly say that it was none of her business. What a kid's life, Shawna silently complained. Adults get to make decisions regarding us kids without us being listened to. She would love to be a grownup to make her own decisions and to live her own life. On the other hand, Shawna knew that her parents loved and they would die for her. And she for them. Shrugging off those thoughts, she went inside the church with Mrs. Vasiledes and the other girls.

Cecelia Killian drove off from First Baptist Church with pride and satisfaction at how Shawna was growing up to be. Yes, she tended to be stricter with her than Jeff was, but she didn't want Shawna to end up being mixed up in drugs, crime or promiscuity. Like she did. Cecelia shuddered regarding that things that she was involved in prior to college. She and her BFFs were sisters in a lot of things, blood being one of them.

She sensed that her days of freedom were coming closely to an end. Cecelia heard nothing further from the policeman in St. Marys, Tinker or Tindale. She couldn't even remember his name. A man easy to forget. But he didn't forget her, since Cecelia suspected he said something to the Appleton police since she noticed them around her area more that she normally did. It wasn't paranoia on her part, just like it wasn't paranoia when she noticed someone in her house but she couldn't see anyone.

Confessing would be a joke, Cecelia would say. It would mean losing her career, family and freedom. Teachers were automatically stripped of their teacher's certificate if they were convicted of felonies, no matter how minor, and once paroled, they couldn't even apply to clean toilets in any school. She would also lose her freedom since she would never be let out of jail, even if she was eligible for parole. Finally, she would lose her family. Would Jeff stick around and be content to see his wife on weekends and perhaps a few holidays? Not for something like this. If he stayed it would be a form of martyrdom and what about Shawna? Cecelia knew how cruel children and teenagers could be to those who didn't fit in and the daughter of a notorious criminal certainly wouldn't fit in. Oh yes, the school and the administrators and the teachers would blather about sympathy but they couldn't be around all of the time.

Besides, I don't feel a shred of remorse about what happened, Cecelia thought. The first person humiliated me time and time again to the point that when I had the opportunity to destroy them, I did so. They learned first-hand not to trifle with my emotions. The second person had pangs of conscience and was going to expose me for the first incident. We had been intimates once. I had a grudging respect for both of them since when the final confrontations occurred, both of them were defiant and didn't beg for mercy.

Cecelia also thought about her parents. Since their talk, she felt peace with them. The anger and resentment she brooded over for years for how they treated her dissipated. Jeff urged her to come to peace with them for her own good but she angrily brushed it aside. She was ashamed afterwards and apologized. Jeff never did anything to hurt her. He had quiet strength, the kind of quiet strength that most people admired.

She also admitted that her parents did change their lives for the better. She heard it when she rarely called them in Ironwood. They stopped drinking, began going to church and were living peaceful lives. No more screaming at the top of their lungs and throwing things around the house while a little girl cowered in a corner, afraid that Mommy and Daddy would kill each other while drunk. They never put their hands on each other nor did they abuse her physically or sexually. Someone else did the latter. Cecelia's parents weren't monsters. Their abuse was neglect and indifference to their growing daughter's needs due to their drinking. She was close to sobbing.

When she arrived home, Cecelia asked Jeff after she opened the door, "Can I have a hug?"

Jeff wasn't surprised to hear Cecelia sound like a little girl. She only did that if she was extremely stressed.

Without a word, he hugged her. And as he did, she began to weep like a frightened child. Jeff carried up to their bedroom and laid Cecelia on the bed. He said nothing while she wept for about twenty minutes. Afterwards, she fell asleep.

Quietly, Jeff went downstairs to the living room. In a few hours, he would pick Shawna up and afterwards Cecelia would wake up and not recall a thing. This only happened a few times and he never discussed it with her. Jeff wasn't a social worker, but he worked with teenagers long enough to know if they came from abused backgrounds. You could smell it in the air.

When he first met Cecelia, he sensed that she was abused, most likely sexually. Jeff didn't know if it were her parents until he met them face to face. He didn't sense that they were the culprits, though he knew that their household wasn't healthy for a child to grow up in just through observing them. Cecelia never told him who abused her and he didn't ask. Some people didn't want to discuss it and others made a cottage industry out of it.

Jeff thanked God for Cecelia and Shawna. Other than God, the only other people close to him other than the two of them were his parents. His other relatives and friends were and important part of his life, but they weren't on the same level as God, his wife and kid. Jeff had serious concerns about getting involved with Cecelia due to age and religious concerns. She was barely out of college and he was already in his mid-thirties. He was also a Christian while she was agnostic on most days and atheistic on other days based on her mood. Everything worked out for the good. Checking his watch, he saw that it was time to pick

Shawna up. Before leaving, he left a note to Cecelia on the bedroom nightstand.

"I've never been to Diane's Baby Shop," Tindall said as he and Kathleen finished breakfast. "How was it?"

"I loved it," Kathleen replied. "The selection was great and the people were friendly."

"But what about the cost? Are the more expensive than, say, Value City?"

"They're probably slightly more expensive than Value City but honestly, do you want to be cheap regarding our baby?"

Tindall noted the tone in Kathleen's voice and the look on her face and didn't want to be in the doghouse for an extended period of time. He groaned, "We can go to Diane's and take a look. But I can't promise that I'll want to shell out a lot of money there."

"Done!" Kathleen replied gleefully. She always knew how to get what she wanted from Frank, but she considered it the nuclear option, something only to be done on very serious occasions. She was perfectly willing to do so since it had to do with their baby. Expense wasn't a worry for her as long as it was high quality. Frank had the same attitude, though he would go through a song and dance of objections before giving in.

The parking lot of Diane's Baby Shop was slowly filling up when Tindall and Kathleen drove in around 10:00 am. There were different groups of people going inside, some husbands and wives, others comprising families and still others single women. Everyone was looking for baby furniture and decorations for their nurseries. Some of the women coming in were more along in their pregnancy than Kathleen. For a moment, she wondered if she would have a weight problem after her pregnancy, but she shamed herself into silence. The weather was nice as it could be for a Saturday.

Both Tindall and Kathleen noticed how well stocked Diane's was with cribs, bassinets, decorations and other kinds of baby furniture. The former's eyes took in all of the items, impressed with the selection but wary about the cost. Kathleen was also impressed with the selection but she was determined to get the best for her baby. Frank would simply have to give in or else, she grimly noted.

Tindall noticed the look on Kathleen's face and knew that he would likely have to cough up some big money. Wives ultimately had the upper hand in relationships since if they were displeased, their husbands would face the possibility of a long stay in another room for an extended period of time. Most husbands didn't want to be in that position so they gave way sooner than later.

A ring from his cellphone ended Tindall's train of thoughts in this area. "Hello, this is Frank Tindall. What do you need?"

"Hello, Frank. This is Pat Sholes from the Crime Lab."

"Hi Pat. Do you have any news regarding Bruschetta's stuff?"

"I'll tell you when you get here."

"How long will you be there?"

"Until about 5:00."

"It's around 11:30, so I'll be there as soon as possible. I'm doing some furniture shopping right now."

"I'll see you then. Take care and say hello to Kathleen from me."

"Will do and the same to you and yours." Tindall hung up and faced Kathleen with a sheepish grin on his face. Her wrathful response: "You better not say that we're going to leave here early because of a case. And it better not be the Davies case."

Smiling, Tindall replied, "We'll leave once everything has been picked out, Katy."

Suspicious, Kathleen asked, "You promise?"

"Of course. I wouldn't dream of us leaving early. Nor would I leave you here while I take care of a few things."

Kathleen laughed. "You can go to Headquarters after we're done then. I really want you to be a part of this."

Tindall figured that Kathleen could pick out the stuff on her own without him being there and then Diane's would ship the items to their house. But he understood her feelings regarding this and he was willing to go with the program out of love and to keep a peaceful home. The two of them continued to look around, with Tindall advising Kathleen that he trusted her taste and judgment. Since Kathleen's pregnancy was early, the specific boy or girl decorations couldn't be picked out yet.

By noon, Tindall and Kathleen were done with what they wanted to purchase. After tallying up all of the items Kathleen said, "We're getting a high chair, a crib, a bassinet, blankets, baby clothes and a baby bed."

"Let's go up to the cash register and pay for everything," Tindall replied. They walked to the cash register where they were waited on by Gina, a pleasant middle-aged woman. Once everything was rung up and next Saturday's delivery date was confirmed, Tindall, shocked by the cost of everything, pulled Kathleen to the side and whispered, "Are you sure we can't look around in some other stores for a better price?"

"No!" she whispered back. "We're not going anywhere else, so suck it up."

Tindall just shook his head and said nothing further. Gina rang up their purchases and he paid with his credit card. I'm giving the banksters quite a bit of flesh, he silently grumbled as Gina handed him their receipt. As he and Kathleen walked out, she said, "Now was that bad? We have the finest things for our baby, so stop grumbling!"

"Me? Grumbling?"

"Yeah, you. I know that you weren't happy with spending so much but you didn't want me to make a scene. And I would have if I had to."

"I'm not grumbling since I want you to be happy."

"No, you don't want me to put you in the guest room."

"You don't think—but that's nasty! You don't do something like that."

"Not true. Dr. Crouse told me that it still could be done during a pregnancy as long as there are no complications."

Disgusted, Tindall said. "This time I'm the one who's saying no. It'll be different after the baby arrives, but for now I'm not doing it."

"Alright, but at least read some of the information that Dr. Crouse gave me. She's not a quack and she's one of the best ob-gyn's in the county."

"Look, I don't want to get into an argument about this. We have plenty of time to talk about it."

"Are you serious?"

"I'm serious. I'll go through the information."

Kathleen hugged Tindall and said, "Thank you!" He was leery about the entire thing but he didn't want to hurt her. Kathleen probably thought that with the pregnancy he wouldn't consider her desirable. Tindall still considered her attractive but anything else other than hand holding, hugs and kisses wasn't proper. Distasteful, to be precise. Well, he would do what he could to keep her at bay until after their baby was born.

As they drove home, Tindall asked Kathleen, "Shouldn't we think about moving our bedroom downstairs? Once you're full term, it may be difficult for you to navigate the stairs."

"We can do a test to see if I can navigate the stairs and if so, we can move some of our stuff into the downstairs bedroom."

"I don't want anything to happen to you or the baby."

"I know, and that's why I love you so much."

"Same here."

Once Tindall let Kathleen in the house and made sure she was okay, he said that "I have to go down to Headquarters. Pat Sholes has some information for me regarding the Davies case."

"I knew it when you got the call in Diane's. Go right ahead. I love you!"

"Yeah, yeah, that's what they all say," Tindall said with a laugh as he walked back to his car and drove off.

"Did you find anything interesting, Pat?" Tindall asked Pat Sholes in his office at the Crime Lab. With the exception of the desk sergeant on duty and some uniforms in the front, the place was practically deserted. Even a few ordinary policemen could keep the local criminals in their place, Tindall laughingly thought.

"We did, Frank, and you're not going to like it," replied Sholes slowly. "It turns out that someone used data erasure software to clean Dr. Bruschetta's laptop hard drive."

"Like BleachBit?"

"Or something similar. Whoever did it was very thorough regarding it to the point that any information on it was irretrievably erased. We checked the doctor's Smartphone and there wasn't anything on it regarding Davies or the other parties involves."

"I'm not surprised. Since she's not a stupid woman, she would use a disposable phone if needed."

"Sorry I couldn't give you better info."

"Nothing to apologize for, Pat. You've done all that you could."

"Thanks for your understanding. Some people around here think that we can perform miracles."

Lauging, Tindall concluded, "The last time you guys performed a miracle was when I was still in grade school."

"Take care too, Frank," Sholes said as Tindall walked out of the Crime Lab. Since he didn't want to disturb Mike and Jim, Tindall decided that he would wait until Monday. The same decision applied to Capt. Carter. They were scheduled to meet on Monday and he could give him the news then.

Tindall didn't even try to ask Sholes if anything further could be done regarding the laptop since the freeware hard drive cleaners and the corporate ones were very good if they were used properly. The rule of thumb regarding it was to let the cleaner run at least 8 hours and possibly up to 24 hours and if the computer was junk to send it to one of those companies that completely shredded the hard drive. Clever woman, Tindall mused as he returned home.

32

"Looks like I'm going to be a bearer of bad news," Tindall said to Capt. Carter on Monday morning in the latter's office, "since Pat in the Crime Lab stated that the hard drive on Dr. Bruschetta's laptop was wiped clean and there wasn't anything of interest on her Smartphone."

Frowning, Capt. Carter asked, "So that means we don't have a case?"

"That's right. We don't have enough evidence to get an arrest warrant from the Prosecutor's Office and we can't interrogate Dr. Bruschetta further without evidence. Neil Baron would howl and scream about police harassment."

"Looks like it's time to close the Davies case until there's further evidence."

"Agreed. I'll give the info to Mike and Jim and I'll also talk to Davies regarding this. Talk to you later, Captain."

"Same here, Frank." Capt. Carter sighed as Tindall left his office. The latter didn't know that the word came down from the police chief to call off the investigation if there wasn't enough evidence to get an arrest warrant from the Prosecutor's Office. It was causing a lot of grief and embarrassment for those higher up on the food chain. Tindall would have agreed since the department couldn't spend time and resources on dead end cases. Capt. Carter wondered what kind of settlement Davies' family would get from Rothmann.

Tindall walked out of Capt. Carter's office and down to Perez' and Parkins' cubicles. Parkins asked, "What happened in your meeting with Capt. Carter?"

"We both agreed that since we don't have enough evidence to get an arrest warrant from the Prosecutor's Office for Dr. Bruschetta, the Davies case is closed for now. It can always be reopened if there's additional evidence."

Perez agreed. "There's nothing more we can do at this point except to close it. Are there any other cases in the pipeline?"

"Nothing right now," replied Tindall. "Just the ordinary stuff. I'll also talk to Davies in person regarding this."

"We'll get back to work then," said Parkins.

Tindall began to walk to his office when he stopped and asked Perez, "Mike when's the next time you and Jim will be going to Grissom's?"

"We don't know, perhaps Wednesday."

"I'll love to go to lunch with you. I haven't been there in a while."

Parkins smiled. "That's fine with us."

"See you later then." Once Tindall was back in his office he reviewed the morning results. The Davies case was in storage, which would infuriate some people such as Ernest Davies and please others such as Rothmann, who wanted this matter to go away. He had no other serious cases so he could plan on visiting Uncle Matt shortly. Something like this had to be done in person, just like he had to speak to Davies regarding the closure of the case. If Tindall was a betting man, he would say that Rothmann and Davies were probably in negotiations right now.

Ernest Davies and his attorney, Joe Wieczorek, closely reviewed each page of the settlement offered by Rothmann Lutheran Hospital. On the other side of the conference table, Richard Balliett of the Balliett Law Offices and Dr. Dave Ankeney, Rothmann's interim CEO, quietly looked on. The negotiations were personal to Davies, professional to Wieczorek and business to Balliett and Ankeney. The meeting had reached its second hour and noon was arriving very quickly. It was as quiet as a church meeting in the Balliett Law Offices' conference room and all of the participants wanted the settlement to be reached as quickly as possible.

Because of the seriousness of the case, Rothmann's board insisted that Balliett directly handle the settlement as the head of the law firm who handled their legal affairs along with Ankeney. The Bal5ietts also handled the legal affairs of most of St. Marys' prominent families and companies such as St. Marys Bank and Trust and St. Marys Gas and Electric Co. They also had slices of shares in some of the largest companies, dating back to the Founder, Elias Balliett, who often took shares in companies when businessmen strapped for cash needed legal services.

Balliett's father always taught him and his sister that

patience was a virtue. He also always advised steering clear of "unsuitable" people. One such example was when Mr. Balliett was in Chicago in the thirties or forties and met a very nice man, a fellow attorney from a quite different background than his. The only thing about the nice man, whose name was Sidney Korshak, was that he was friendly with people who weren't so nice like Tony Accardo and Murray Humphreys. Fortunately, Mr. Balliett walked away from that situation in time.

At 11:30 am, Wieczorek announced, "We've reviewed the paperwork and my client accepts the offer."

Ankeney beamed. "We're delighted that Mr. Davies has decided to accept our settlement. It's quite generous and while we know that it won't change what happened, it will provide some relief."

What a slug, Davies contemptuously noted. He thinks I'm so brain dead that I believe his shit. Not even Balliett, the hospital's attorney, would say anything like that. Davies merely said, "I'm glad that this is over and done with."

"I want to advise you again, Mr. Davies," Balliett said dryly, "that if you accept our settlement, you're giving up your rights to pursue legal action against Rothmann and/or its agents and employees along with being able to publicly discuss the settlement and the circumstances regarding Mrs. Davies' passing."

"I understand perfectly," Davies replied as he signed the settlement. He wanted to get out of here and go home. Since that day with the cop in charge of Barbara's case, he hadn't touched a drop of liquor. Gwennie called him from time to time and they chatted sometimes for about an hour. Davies was interested in her but he wanted to wait for about six months or a year before he would consider it.

After a few minutes, Balliett's secretary Jenny returned with copies of the settlement and handed them over to Davies and Wieczorek. "Thank you," both men replied.

"Again, my sympathies to you and your family," Balliett said as he shook Davies' hand. "Good afternoon to you and Mr. Wieczorek. Jenny will show you out."

"My thoughts exactly," Davies replied as he and Wieczorek walked out of the conference room with Jenny.

"I'm glad this mess has been taken care of," Ankeney muttered once Davies and his attorney were safely outside of the conference room.

"It has and everyone wins," Balliett noted. Checking his watch, he said, "Since it's noon we can have lunch in the conference room if you wish."

"That'll be fine and then I'll get back to Rothmann posthaste."

"The food will be here in about ten minutes."

"That's great."

Balliett silently reviewed Ankeney. Not that bright and pompous. Not up to the speed of Judith Bruschetta, whom he considered a friend and whom he still kept in touch with. He heard that a few of her "friends" no longer bothered to keep in touch with her. One who did was Paul Peppiatt, whom he kept at a distance socially. He knew that Peppiatt wanted more than friendship with Dr. Bruschetta and she was clever enough to steer clear of it.

Wieczorek showed in his negotiations how a good attorney should operate and function. Balliett had a high regard for his toughness and flexibility. He preferred to deal with someone on his level and not hacks. Given the fact that the Ballietts came from the crème de la crème of St. Marys society and Wieczorek didn't, it would have been considered at best patronizing and at worst insulting, for Balliett to praise him in any kind of way. Another easy piece of cake, Balliett silently mused as he ate lunch.

"I'm sorry to disturb you, Mr. Davies," Tindall said as he sat down in the latter's living room, "but I wanted you to find out directly through me than through the news."

Concern flooded Davies' face as he asked, "Is this regarding Barbara?"

"Unfortunately, yes. For now, Mrs. Davies' case is closed indefinitely."

"Why?"

Tindall chose his words carefully. "There's not enough evidence to bring Mrs. Davies' case to trial. When we have enough evidence to do so, it will be brought to trial."

"So there's nothing further that can be done?"

"That's correct. It's not pleasant to tell you this, but I decided that you needed to know directly from me regarding this since I'm the chief investigator in the case."

Quietly, Davies asked, "You have someone whom you

believe killed Barbara?"

"Even though the case is closed, it could be reopened at any time. Because of that, I can't say anything else further regarding this case. If I could say anything more, I would."

"Please go, Lieutenant,"

"I will." Before Tindall left he said, "Mr. Davies, if you need to talk to someone, please do so. I don't want someone from downtown having to pick you up because you did something rash."

Davies merely waved him out. Tindall did all that he could do. Now it was in God's hands.

Cecelia Killian was finishing her lunch in the teachers' lounge when Jamie Bosson, Woodfin High's secretary, came in and said, "Principal Finkbeiner wants you in his office now!"

"What is it?"

"You'll find out when you get there! Hurry up!"

"I'm coming right now." Cecelia was surprised at how excited Jamie was. True, she could be excitable at times, but never in an annoying way. Well, I hope that it's nothing serious."

Within five minutes, Cecelia saw Finkbeiner and a uniformed police officer standing at the door. The man looked familiar, though since Appleton was so small, all of the police there were familiar in some kind of way. "I was advised, sir, that you needed to speak to me. What's going on, please?"

Finkbeiner cleared his throat before beginning. "Cecelia, Sgt. Gould from the Appleton Police Department needed to speak to your regarding a case. Unfortunately, he isn't at liberty to tell me what it is in regards to."

In response to Cecelia's glance, Gould merely replied, "We have some questions regarding a case or cases that have occurred outside of this village. It may take a while. Did you drive yourself here?"

"Yes, I did."

"Can you have someone pick up your car? The questions may take some time."

"My husband will take the car back home. We're both teachers here."

"Ok. Do you want to tell your husband you're leaving?"

Cecelia saw Jamie hovering around close to Finkbeiner. Concern shown in both of their eyes. "Jamie, can you please tell Jeff that I will be down at the police station asking a few questions."

"Will do, Cecelia."

"Thanks."

Cecelia tried to get Gould to say exactly why she needed to answer a few questions but the latter was tight lipped regarding it. They drove to the Appleton police station in silence.

After they arrived, Cecelia was escorted into an interrogation room. This doesn't look good, she glumly noted. Her wariness increased when Gould introduced her to Inspector Charlie Watkins of the Detroit Police Department, who stated that he had "questions regarding her relationship to a Ms. Heather Rowlands, who passed away in an incident that was now being classified as a homicide," and Sgt. Beth Graham from the Ironwood Public Safety Department who had questions regarding "an old high school classmate of yours named Lesley Blandick, who tragically passed away in a hit-and-run accident while jogging."

Cecelia requested her one phone call and it was granted.

You probably know by now that it was I who killed Barbara Davies and Edith Dowling. I'm neither proud of what I did nor do I have any guilt over it. I would have killed Cecelia Killian if I was able to do so. Since there is no statute of limitations regarding murder, if Tindall or anyone else who takes over Davies' case gets enough evidence, then I would probably spend the rest of my life in a prison cell. There's no way I would get away committing two murders, even under the circumstances in question.

The positive item about Cecelia is that she's going to be spending quite some time dealing with the legal system since both Ironwood and Detroit want pieces of her hide regarding the deaths of Little and Heather. Neither of them deserved to die and hopefully she will pay for it. If she's convicted for one charge but not the other, then I would be content since she will be rotting away in a prison cell for the rest of her life. If she manages to be acquitted, it would be in God's hands from that point on.

I need to tell my children about Little someday. They know her as the aunt they never got to know due to her condition but not that she was actually their much older half-sister. As for Little's father, I don't even know what happened to him. He could be dead by now and even if he was still living, I'm not going to ruin his life because of it.

In a few months, I will be leaving St. Marys, possibly permanently, to do work as a medical missionary for a Catholic charity. It will be in Latin America, where I can use my Spanish. I will miss St. Marys, since it's been my home for years, where I've loved my husband and raised my children, but I have to go. My children are grown and my career and position here are gone. There's nothing left for me here. I've said goodbye to my remaining friends and acquaintances and promised them that I would be back from time to time; I also promised my children that I would come running back if they needed me. I've even told Tindall where I'm going to in case he has to extradite me back to the States. He's not surprised since he probably knows me as well as I do. Sort of like a WASP Columbo. I really love that show. He wished me the best of luck as well. And I wish all of you the best of luck in your lives as well. Take care and God bless.

Epilogue:

A Few Weeks Later

"Welcome back, stranger! How did it go?"

"It went well, Katy. It was the first time I've ever been to Bloomington. Very nice place."

"Sounds like you don't want to say too much about it, Frank."

"Maybe later. By the way, we may have some guests coming up from there next year."

"Well, we'll have to be prepared like the Scouts when that happens. Let's eat, dinner's ready."

"I hear ya."

ABOUT THE AUTHOR

Raylond Gee lives in Royal Oak, Michigan and he looks forward to telling new tales of Lt. Tindall and his team along with the delightful and not so delightful people of St. Marys.

Made in the USA
Middletown, DE
16 April 2019